Blackberries Are Red When Green

Keith Frohreich

Blackberries Are Red When Green

In memory of my mother and brother.
And to my fellow Hoosiers,
wherever you may call home.

We shall not cease from exploration
And the end of all our exploring
Will be to arrive where we started
And know the place for the first time.

T.S. Eliot

One

I ran away from college late in my freshman year plagued with a plummeting GPA and an impairing question of, "Why am I here?" Mom, none-too-pleased, reminded me of Dad's wishes.

The draft in the late 1960s hung over young men like a scourge, rounding them up, especially if not in college. Vietnam raged. The Army sentenced draftees to one-way tickets to Nam. They "volunteered" the unlucky ones for their platoon's point, risking walking into Viet Cong ambushes or the crosshairs of a sharpshooter.

College dropouts climbed the draft charts faster than songs performed on Dick Clark's American Bandstand. I leapt to the head of the selective service class, 1A, besting any grade in college. They say government bureaucracies move slower than snails–not my county draft board. Uncle Sam's personal greetings and induction notice arrived in less than two months.

After eight weeks of basic training, I emerged sheared, immunized, buffed up, spit-shined, sergeant-drilled, sharpshooter-skilled, now a lean, mean, killing machine.

Uncle Sam dangled the trade-off enticement of specialized training following basic training if I gave them a third year of my life. I bit, rolled the dice, and chose medic school, knowing the risks of combat and the movie-depicted battlefield cries for "medic!" Lady Luck sent some love. After six months of training and six months of stateside postings, I spent two years in Frankfurt, Germany, assigned to a 1,000-bed Army hospital.

Military duty suspended life even if returning home alive and unscarred, physically or emotionally. Tick tock. Tick tock. Tick tock.

Movies depicted mail-calls as troops in formation while names rang out. A soldier ran up, collected his mail, and fell back into formation, letters not ripped open until the sergeant commanded, "Fall out."

No mail-call formations or mail slots existed at my battalion barracks next to the Frankfurt hospital. The battalion postal clerk delivered mail to my hospital ward. Mail interrupted the routine. Most days, none came. But each day, I longed to hear the nurse-in-charge call out, "Specialist Baumann."

Mom wrote once a month unless something newsworthy happened, I less often with my musings and grumblings. Drafted soldiers grumbled a lot, even those lucky enough to be stationed somewhere other than Nam. This letter arrived sooner than her monthly routine, yet she opened with droning news about Adams Creek, the weather, church functions, neighbors' illnesses, and garden or orchard harvests. News of older brother Kyle with the Peace Corps in India piqued my interest, as did an update on oldest brother, Ken, now finishing his PhD at the University of Wisconsin. Then this,

"I know you would want to know Dutch passed a few days back. I know how close you felt. We all did. The Twin Rivers Review never listed the cause of death, old age I guess. Maybe his chewing habit caught up with him. James found him at his favorite fishing hole. Took me back some having seen him fishing off Ole Steely a few days prior. No service, near as I

could tell. Would like to have paid my respects, but I was visiting your Aunt Mildred in Monroeville. They buried him in the Mount Calvary cemetery. I cut some snap dragons and placed them at his small grave marking. He often remarked on them."

I requested a break from the nurse-in-charge and headed for the latrine. Checking for empty stalls, I latched the door, sat down, and wept.

A request for emergency leave would be denied even had I been stationed stateside. Dutch and I were not kin, but bonded in ways deeper than most families.

Two

I turned ten the year I met Dutch, the summer of 1958. Most Indiana summer days passed shirtless. This day, I wore one. Like the summers in the Deep South, during the Indiana sultry spells, shirts stuck like another layer of skin, the humidity dense enough to fog glasses. I mopped my brow with my shirt, ignoring the red kerchief stuffed in my jeans.

Mom protested, "I can't understand how you get your shirts so dirty."

The Eel River, swifter, muddier, and up about a foot following a recent storm, made fishing challenging and banned swimming, Mom's orders. I spent a lot of time by my river putting off chores or lazing away the day.

My river bore many faces; often muddy, sometimes filled with tree trunks and limbs after a crackling, marauding thunderstorm, sometimes slick and smooth after a long, deep freeze, and sometimes jolting with bergs thumping on the center bridge abutment following a spring thaw. Its usual face flowed along like the listless pace of a steamy day, slower than a walker's gait. This face I remembered most. Years earlier, I learned its waters flowed into the Wabash in Twin Rivers. The Miami Indians' name for Wabash meant "the river that shines white." Downstate at the southwestern tip of Indiana, the Wabash joined the Ohio and finally merged into the mother of all rivers, the mighty Mississippi. Part Huck Finn, I fantasized crafting a raft and floating all the way down the Mississippi.

The storm turned the riverbank path banana-peel slick, not that it mattered. I knew the trail as well as the path to our outhouse at night. I could swim well enough to make it ashore if I slipped into the swollen current. Slipping or not, dirt found its way onto my clothes.

Early summer storms thickened the weeds and sprouted the thistles chest high. Thistles scratched my arms as if trapped in the midst of a stray catfight. The thistles and low-hanging limbs needed whacking. Kyle and I usually kept the path clear but had not done so in recent days.

Kyle fished more, though not often. Mom never counted on our catch for supper's main course. If we hooked a bass or catfish, she fried it up the next day or froze it. I never noticed Dad fishing while alive, his days too demanding for such idleness. Fishing required time and patience. I had the time but lacked the patience.

The path opened to a favorite fishing hole a football field length south of the bridge. I'm certain he heard me coming but did not turn as I neared. Kyle spoke of an old man named Dutch moving into the two-room shack behind Widow Kreider's house on the east side of the river.

Moving nearer, "Are you Dutch?"

"Shush now, don't scare the fish."

His raspy voice gave me pause. Something felt safe. I inched closer. If Kyle knew of him, he must be okay. Approaching from behind, I could not make out the look of him, hands hidden, cradling the fishing pole between his knees. Even in the summer's heat, a tattered jacket covered his arms. A red bandana hid his neck. A ratty hat sporting several fishhooks topped his head. Both the jacket and hat looked strange and not from around here.

He turned his face. Dutch was a Negro.

Negroes lived in Twin Rivers. We saw them on trips to Twin Rivers on weekends. They ventured out to fish off the bridge or on the bank across the river, "the public access part," Mom said. I remember her saying, "They seem like nice folks but keep to themselves." A Negro boy attended my grade school, though most lived clustered in a separate area of Twin Rivers, an area unfamiliar. If Kurt mentioned Dutch's color, I must have been out of earshot.

He had a pleasant face, though in need of a shave, his smile, friendly.

"You must be Kurt."

"How's come you know my name?"

"Kyle brings me the Sunday paper."

I plopped down on the bank. "Mind if I sit a spell?" Dutch sat on the log Kurt and I had rolled close to the water a couple weeks prior.

"Suit yourself, just don't talk too much."

"Catch anything?"

"Couple of cats, enough for supper. Hoping for a bass."

"Good luck trying to land a bass."

Catfish always bit more in muddier waters.

"What are you using for bait?"

"Nightcrawlers. Gave your brother four bits for them."

"Four bits! That's a lot of money!"

"Keep your voice down."

"Sorry."

Dad used to give me two quarters to buy Christmas presents for older brothers Ken and Kyle.

Dutch propped his pole on one of the twigs Kyle and I earlier pushed into the bank.

The current moved too swift for a bobber. "You must be using a pretty big sinker."

"Big enough."

Cats fed off the bottom, so a sinker kept the bait close to the riverbed, especially after a storm.

He spat some brown bile onto the bank.

"Yuck, what's that?"

Pulling out a pouch of Red Man from his jacket he teased, "Chewing tobacco. Want some?"

"No way." After Dad's death, any thought of tobacco turned my stomach.

He snatched the pole so fast it startled me; the pole bent more than from the weight of the sinker and current. He could move for an old guy.

"Dadnabbit," reeling it in, "another stinking sucker. Wasted a big, juicy worm, too." Nobody liked suckers, too bony.

Mom's voice drifted down the river, "Kurt, dinner." It must be noontime. She'd stand on our front porch and yell, if not within eyesight. Kyle hired out for the day with a nearby farmer.

"Gotta go Dutch. Mind if I come back?"

"Sure, long as you don't talk too much."

A thunderclap rolled in from the west. "Mom says there's a storm a-brewin' so you might want to head home."

"Storms don't fret me much. It's only water. But I'll keep an eye peeled for lightening. Lots of trees around here."

"Still sounds to be a fur piece."

Back home, I asked Mom about Dutch being a Negro. She remembered from Kyle's report. "Then I met him. A couple of weeks ago during school, he stopped by and asked if he could seine for minnows in our creek. He finds minnows better bass bait. Nice man, very courteous."

Then Mom laughed.

"What?"

"Widow Kreider is nearly blind. I wonder if she could tell Dutch is a Negro."

I'd never met anyone named Dutch. I remembered Mom saying if I didn't finish my chores, "You're gonna be in dutch with your dad."

"Was Dutch wearing a funny jacket and hat?"

"You must mean his railroad uniform. He wore it the day he stopped by. I thought it looked familiar. Dutch used to be a Pullman porter with the railroads. The runs he worked came through Twin Rivers all the time. He liked to fish and remembered our rivers. When he retired, he decided he wanted to live near a river. He also said a good friend retired in Twin Rivers ahead of him and twisted his arm to come this way. He found the place behind Widow Kreiders."

I knew nothing of porters. I had never been on a train.

"They take care of the passengers doing just about anything, turning down beds, changing beds, shining shoes, bringing food and water from the dining car, chores like that. Sometimes they even lit your dad's cigarette. Remind me to tell you about a train trip your father and I made to Nashville to visit a cousin of yours when you were too young to remember. Ken looked after you and Kyle. I told Dutch about my first trip on a Pullman. Let me think, would have been right after high school around 1929, before the market crash, on my way to a Baptist youth convention in Detroit. Don't remember much about the porters, I was having too much fun with my church friends. Right now, I have some laundry and mending to do." Mom took in laundry and mending to help ends meet. She worked part-time at the grain elevator in nearby Ten Mile.

"What's a market crash?"

"Oh dear. It's complicated, and I'm not sure I understand it to this day. Your father could have explained it much better. Let me try. They called the 1920s the Roaring Twenties. Life was pretty good for most Americans. Businesses did well. Your father and I were still in high school. Lots of folks invested money in the stock market.

That's on a street called Wall Street in New York City, not where your Dad used to go to buy Holsteins. One day, a whole bunch of investors decided to sell, fearing the prices of their stocks were going to drop. They did. Everyone panicked. In the massive selloff, the stock prices not only went down, they plunged. They called it Black Tuesday. People lost lots of money. They say some killed themselves. Can you imagine? Taking your life over money? The crash caused the Great Depression. You will study it one day. The Depression years were very tough for your father and me."

"Why did they call it Black Tuesday instead of Red Tuesday or Blue Tuesday?"

"Good question. Over the years black, became more associated with something bad more then any other color, like a black cat crossing your path." Mom laughed.

"What's funny?"

"Well actually, when it comes to earning more money than we spend in a year or a person does well on Wall Street, we say we are 'in the black.' If folks are losing on Wall Street or we spend more in a year than we make, we say we are 'in the red.' Lots of words have different meanings, hard to be mindful. 'In the black' means good times on Wall Street, but the day the stock market crashed is still called 'Black Tuesday.'"

"When I get older, remind me to never put my money in the stock market."

"Can't say I know anyone around here who puts money in the stock market. Folks I know don't make enough to risk such foolishness; too much like gambling to my way of knowing. Certainly your father and I never made enough to give it a second thought. Most years, we lived month to month. I still do."

Another thunderclap interrupted, this one closer.

"Almost forgot, listening to myself carry on. Go pick me three quarts of blackberries. Don't dally. There's still time, but the storm's sounding closer, maybe a few miles out. A hard rain might knock them to the ground and spoil them. Most of the thicket next to neighbor Mabel's fence looks ripened. I'm baking a blackberry pie for dinner tomorrow. Don't confuse them with the nearby raspberries like you did the last time. Remember, blackberries are red when green. Red blackberries won't pull off the plant, but the ripe ones will. Try not to scratch yourself or catch your shirt. I don't get paid to mend your clothes." Mom baked a pie for every Sunday dinner following church. I preferred peach or blueberry, but also liked blackberry and apple. I did not share her love for rhubarb, gooseberry, or mulberry. Yuck. Nor did Kyle.

Meeting Dutch recalled an encounter two years prior. Basketball is a second religion in Indiana. In 1954, Milan won out, the smallest high school ever to win the state championship. I remember sitting glued to our kitchen radio when Milan sank the winning bucket over Munson Central. The paper reported forty thousand well-wishers lined the road back to Milan, a town of only a thousand, way down at the southern end of the state. Munson, a city of over 60,000, and Twin Rivers, shared the same sports conference.

The next two years an all-Negro school from Indianapolis, Crispus Attucks, won the state title, led by Oscar Robertson. While playing with Tommy Webster at his nearby house the day after the 1956 title match, I overheard Mrs. Webster say, "Why don't they send those niggers back to Africa where they belong?" I zipped my lips. I never heard such talk. They moved away a year later. The previous year, Dad treated me to football and basketball games in Twin Rivers. A Negro starred in both sports. No one raised a ruckus.

I told Mom what I heard. She paused, wiped her hands, and said, "Sit down Kurt, and hear me good. You must never use that word in our house or anywhere, you hear me? It's a hateful word used by folks who hate Negroes and by folks who don't know any Negroes. Negroes are like the rest of us, only their skin is different. Jesus teaches us to love all the little children, 'red and yellow, black and white, they are precious in his sight.' Same for grown-ups." I knew the song by heart from Sunday school.

"I have never told you this story, but you remember your grandpa the preacher? Like now, we never had much money. When I was six, the Lord called your grandpa to this small Baptist congregation, maybe fifty members, about half the size of our Adams Creek church. Grandpa found odd jobs to make ends meet. A parsonage sat next to the church. In back of the church sat a small house, a shack really, lived in by a Negro family. The father took care of the property, the church, and the graveyard, and hired out for small jobs. The mother cooked for our church functions. Somehow, they got by. Your grandma often sent over food, shared our garden, and invited them to supper on occasion. There was a girl my age named Esther. We became the best of friends. We played together all of the time when not in school. Two years later, we moved to a farm and new church fifty miles away. I never saw her again. Now I hope you understand why I will never use that word. As long as you live under this roof, I will not countenance any such language. You hear me?"

"Yes Mom." Then I remembered. For years, I recited the lines, "Eeny meeny miny moe, catch a nigger by his toe." I never gave it a second thought.

Mom said, "That's a perfect example. White folks just adopt these sayings or words. You hear it somewhere and start using it, grownups and kids. I hope you will keep that in mind if you hear the word at school, and don't go along just to get along."

Mom's story surprised me, but not because of her friend Esther. Mom and Dad rarely spoke of their pasts, not around the supper table, not in the car going and coming, ever. I reckoned their lives forced them into the here and now, the past, past. Had Dad lived a story similar to Mom's? If not, would his reaction to Dutch support or counter Mom's banning of the word or her welcoming of Dutch into the neighborhood? I will never know.

Now, a not-from-around-these-parts person, and a Negro to boot, joined the neighborhood. With only the one Negro classmate in grade school, and seeing a few across the river and in town, my young life remained segregated in a colorless culture. Boys' names like John, Mike, Steve, Paul, Tim, Dan, Dave, Tom, Mark, Richard, David, and Don populated my elementary school. I knew nothing of Mexicans or anyone of Spanish heritage living within my remote, rural life. American Indians? Not to my knowledge. Asians? No. I sensed but knew little of a vast world beyond the boundaries of Adams Creek and Twin Rivers. A few books and our globe atlas teased of it.

Change colored the air.

Three

Indiana is a fly-over state, like most Midwestern states. Midwesterners, high-minded and high-panted, don't take kindly to the slight. I chuckle at folks who lump states like Kansas and Nebraska to the Midwest. Those are plains states and having traveled through them, they can be plain– and flat. Winds howl through with little to slow them. The song "Oklahoma" says it best,

"Where the winds come sweepin' down the plain."

I will not argue Indiana is less plain, though at least the term Hoosier arouses more curiosity than a label like Kansans or Nebraskans. As to the origin of Hoosier, there are multiple versions, none official, to my way of knowing.

Actually, Indiana's terrain is more interesting, considering the mosaic of the northern Indiana lakes and the rolling hills in the southern parts. I will leave it there. There is a northern and southern tongue in Indiana. If one drives south from Indianapolis to Louisville, a noticeable southern drawl emerges closer to the Kentucky state line. Many folks born and reared in Indiana no longer live there. I am one. I still harbor warm feelings, despite the events recorded here.

I called Adams Creek home, twenty-five houses spread out on both sides of the Eel River, miles from Nowheresville, and eight miles northeast of Twin Rivers. My family moved there from Fort Wayne after I turned two. If folks asked, "Where you from?" we wouldn't say Adams Creek unless visiting with a fellow Clay County resident. When talking with a fellow Hoosier, we said we lived outside Twin Rivers. Hoosiers knew Twin Rivers.

Adams Creek dwellers painted their houses white, though most needed painting. No large house sat on a hill where highfalutin types lorded over; no house haunted us. But the Mount Calvary Cemetery spooked me, eerie enough to pedal past fast, especially after dark, its headstones chiseled with lots of the same last names.

"Why are you so out of breath?"

"Mom, I pedal faster downhill past the cemetery when it's getting dark especially with the wind blowing spooky sounds in those trees."

"Well that's silly."

A few shacks and mobile homes propped on concrete blocks dropped the village's average economic status into lower middle-class. This label befitted my family. As a boy, I knew little to distinguish one class from another, other than to notice a house nicer than ours and with indoor plumbing. Most were.

No stories about a missing body or one found under mysterious circumstances kept the party lines buzzing. Nothing too special or too mischievous called attention to Adams Creek. The weather, the number one conversation starter, prompted a frequent exchange.

"Think it'll rain tomorrow?"

"I would bet on it; my rheumatism is acting up."

"I hope to finish plowing the back forty before it gets here."

"Let me know if you need some help. My Farmall and I have the afternoon free. But I need to be home by six. The missus has a pot roast planned, and a cousin is coming by for supper. Don't care much for him, but you know, kin. Gets dark then anyways."

"I installed lights on my Deere so I can plow later. I'll let you know. Much obliged for the offer."

In the warmer months, thunderstorms rolled through so frequently they never gave anyone pause. Storms disrupted plowing, planting, and harvesting schedules. Regardless, rain provided the mother's milk for bountiful harvests. Lightening unnerved us, as did the threat of tornados. Dad taught, "Count the seconds from seeing the bolt. Five seconds equals one mile." Taller trees, as if magnetic, attracted the lightening's lasers, cleaved down the middle like a giant Paul Bunyan wielding the world's largest axe. Farmers' skills included weather prognosticating, their agrarian guru, the *Farmers Almanac*. The pattern played out predictably, rarely varying. Fluffy clouds conjoined, turning gray, then smoky, then bluish black on the western horizon. Lighting veined the skyline like a leg's capillaries. The baby breeze gave way to mother wind, first billowing the willow tree's skirt, and then blustering through. Leaves rustled and then whooshed. Taller timber swayed and groaned, as if fearing Paul Bunyan's axe. The first drops tickled windows and windshields, and minutes later splatted like water beetles. Thirty minutes later, the marauding menace moved on to the next county.

The county posted no speed signs since the narrowness and condition of county back roads, some potholed, some dirt, controlled the speed. Still, every couple of years a lead-footer tested the curve next to our house, barreled across the bridge, rolled the car, and took out pasture fencing. Hearing a speeding car, Kyle would look up, "Not sure he's going to make it." Rounding a bend or cresting a blind incline too fast might lead to a blunt encounter with a loose cow, pig, or the plodding-pace of a tractor or harvester. Two-laned Highway 24, the widest road around and three

miles south of Adam's Creek, split northern Indiana east to
west. With just enough curves and rolling terrain, especially
in northeastern Indiana, lead-footers fidgeted waiting to
pass slow-moving vehicles. Worse yet, getting trapped
behind a truck hauling pigs stunk up the day. Nothing fouled
the air worse than pig poop.

Neighboring farms grew corn, wheat, alfalfa, and
soybeans, the acreages and farmhouses modest in size.
Corn, like in the *Oklahoma* soundtrack, grew as high as an
elephant's eye. Corn planting signaled spring's onset, and
corn harvests heralded the advent of fall.

The village included the Adams Creek Baptist Church, a
schoolhouse from a bygone era, boarded up and windows
shot out, and Carrolls Country Store. Folks idled on a bench
outside the front door chewing straw or working a chaw of
tobacco while chatting the day. Next to Carroll's, railroad
tracks wound through the village's west end ferrying
passengers and freight between Detroit and St. Louis, the
village too small to be called a whistle stop. The whistles
teased of wonderment far away.

My river bordered the east side of our farm. Our six-
room, two-story house, adjoined six acres of unfertile land
the day we moved in, much of it exposed limestone. Over the
years, we layered on enough topsoil to grow alfalfa, a
garden, and an orchard. Our garden and orchard sprouted
abundance akin to a farmers' market. We could have
operated a fresh fruit and vegetable roadside stand, but so
few cars passed our house daily even turtles crossed the
road without fear. The short strawberry season produced
too many quarts to consume, although during June,
strawberries became a food group. Strawberries tasted best
picked off the vine. Mom cautioned, "Wash them in the creek
first." Kyle and I never did. What's a little dirt? Root
vegetables like carrots were not the same. We washed those
in the creek. Whatever fruits and vegetables we didn't eat or

share with church and neighbors, Mom froze or jarred for the winter.

Dad said much of Indiana, especially the southern part was embedded with limestone, which builders considered the mother lode for structures, and used to craft icons like the Empire State Building, the Pentagon, and National Cathedral. He said the state motto should be, "Land of Limestone." Limestone framed several Twin Rivers' buildings, and two quarries bookended the city, one west and one east.

A creek trickled through, feeding the river. I never knew whether Adams Creek earned its name this way or not. Neither did Mom or Dad. Toads, minnows, crawdads, small turtles, and snakes populated the creek. I hated snakes, freaked me out.

Dad took me to task over my vendetta against snakes, smashing them with large stones. "Why do you keep killing them? They're not poisonous. They help keep the rats under control."

This never made a lick of sense. No snake I ever saw could have bested our barn rats. The rats scampered around as if navigating a hidden maze, and only they knew the way. We set traps but only caught mice. Cats patrolled the barn and controlled the mice population. Funny thing about cats, they never ate their prey, but killed and pawed it like a toy or a trophy to admire. "Look what I brought you. Now can I have a scratch behind my ears?" Maybe we should have tried snakes and turned them loose on the rats. But I'd rather combat barn rats than fret about slithering snakes with more places to hide.

The Miami Indians named the Eel River, "river of the snakefish," based on its once-upon-a-time, large population of eels. I never encountered or caught a snakefish in Adams Creek, tougher to kill than slithering snakes. Snakefish don't lollygag and sunbathe on the rocks.

21

Our red barn, also needing painting, included Dad's workshop, feed bin, two milking stalls, hayloft, firewood, tractor, farm implements, and the welcome mat for swallows, owls, bats, rats, and mice. The bats, just to pester, dive-bombed us. Have you ever tried whacking a bat with a bat? Don't. Dad erected a basketball hoop, an Indiana icon, on one side. Along state highways, the barn side facing a highway often doubled as a billboard, usually for cigarettes. Chesterfield celebrity endorsers included Bing Crosby, "Buy my Cigarette, Milder," and Bob Hope, "Much Milder." Midwestern farmers wouldn't be caught dead painting their houses red, but barns opened the door to go hog wild, red the fancied color.

Our Ford tractor, small by comparison to neighboring farmers' John Deeres, Farmalls, or International Harvesters, served us in all manner of tasks, whether pulling a hay wagon, plough, scoop, or tugging a massive boulder half-buried in the ground. A favorite book as a youngster, *The Little Engine that Could,* inspired me to dub our little Ford, "The Little Tractor that Could." Dad taught me to drive it at age eight.

A chicken coop sat next to the barn. A grape arbor abutted Mom's clotheslines. Even in winter when the temperature barely topped thirty-two degrees, our laundry adorned the front yard.

"Mom, do we have to hang my underwear in the front yard?"

"Yes, if you want them dried before you run out."

"I'd rather wear them wet."

Mom cultivated a flower garden on our home's west side: bachelor buttons, cosmos, geraniums, marigolds, nasturtiums, snap dragons, sweet peas, and her pride and joy, roses, followed by snap dragons. They lightened the burden she carried, her life tougher and lonelier after losing Dad.

Dad strung up a swing in our front yard sycamore. At age four, I fell headfirst onto a small rock. Rushed to the emergency room, the gash required several stitches. I climbed back on the swing the next day. Years later, Kyle teased, "That swing accident explains a lot about how you turned out."

Half of a football field from the house, a steel bridge spanned the river, the year 1898 etched on its frame. Its single lane slowed cars approaching from either side. Large trucks rarely ventured this far from Twin Rivers, but when they did and crossed the bridge, she'd shake and tremble. To the locals, and to Twin Rivers' folk, the bridge was known as the Adams Creek Bridge. Folks reflecting on their childhood might christen any manner of iconic images, a home, a car, a landscape, a church steeple, or a schoolhouse. For the Baumann boys, the bridge centered our lives, so much so we named it Ole Steely. Kyle and I climbed on it, spooked cars, dropped a fishing line over the railing, or just watched the water's wandering journey. If waters could talk, the stories they could tell and the places they have seen. I never scaled to Ole Steely's top and walked across. I doubt I could have, born with a fear of heights. Kyle claimed he did on a dare. Ole Steely, not only our playground, substituted for a rifle range, aiming at whatever caught our fancy. Ole Steely and the river grounded us. Years later, Mom would say, "Whenever I saw one of you boys up at Ole Steely leaning on the railing and staring at the water, I knew you were thinking things through. It seemed like you boys and Ole Steely were having a chat." Flowing waters cast spells.

A pump supplied our water, the river too far to source. It was hard to imagine drinking river water even if it were boiled. Who knew what folks up river dumped in it? Even during deep freezes, the water pump never froze, its source too deep. Pumping water for cooking, dish duty, and bathing headed my chore list. I accused Kyle of lots of trickery, but for the record he never tried coaxing me into sticking my tongue on the pump in the dead of winter.

We used a galvanized, steel tub for laundry, bathing, plucking chickens, and making lye soap. How lye, abrasive and burning to the skin, when combined with tallow, chemically turns into bathing soap baffled me. Mom stirred, wearing gloves, hovering over the concoction like a mad scientist or a witch over a cauldron, "Double, double, toil and trouble." I remained chemically-challenged, earning a D in my senior chemistry class, my worst grade in high school.

The Saturday night routine began with baths on the back porch. As the youngest, I bathed last, sharing Kyle's water. Kyle, just to get at me now and then, said, "Hey Kurt, I pissed in the water."

"Mom, Kyle says he pissed in the bath water!"

Mom intervened and assured me he had not. I could have tossed out the water, toted in more from the pump, and heated it on the stove. During winter nights, toting more water from the pump did not appeal. Doing so would have made me late for a favorite Saturday night supper and radio program. Years later, Kyle admitted he never pissed in the bath water.

On school days, we sponged off in the kitchen sink. In warmer months we jumped in the creek or river depending on which looked the clearest. In summertime, after a day of toil, a quick dip in the river soothed tired muscles.

Saturdays, following our supper tradition of bacon and syrup-sopped pancakes, found us hovered over the National Barn Dance broadcast out of WLS in Chicago, a blend of country humor plus country and folk music. The broadcast featured regulars like Captain Stubby, and Homer and Jethro. Gene Autry and George Gobel began their careers there. What's not to like about musical groups called the Hoosier Sod Busters or the Four Hired Hands? *Grab your partners, folks, it's the National Barn Dance!"*

From Captain Stubby,

"My uncle taught me to swim. Every Sunday afternoon, he used to take me out in the center of the lake, throw me off the boat, and make me swim to shore. It wasn't so bad once I got out of that sack."

And this,

"My neighbor lady left a note for the milk man saying she wanted 72 quarts of milk. The milkman thought this was unusual, so he knocked on the door to check. He said, 'What do you want with 72 quarts of milk?' She told him she was going to do like they do in Hollywood and take a milk bath. He said, 'Do you want it pasteurized?' She said, 'No, just up to my waist.'"

Launched in the mid-1920s, the broadcast inspired the Grand Ole Opry.

Each Memorial Day weekend, we hovered again listening to an Indianapolis station airing the annual running of the Indy 500, "The Greatest Spectacle in Racing." Two years before Dad died, he treated Kyle and me to a day of time trials, the backstretch the only tickets he could afford. Why would so many folks pay good money to pack the grandstands and watch a lone roadster speed around a racetrack?

We shared our phone line with five other homes. Mom warned us, "Be mindful; chances are folks are eavesdropping." A noticeable click meant a buttinski monitored the line. I sneaked a listen now and then.

"I'm feeling poorly today, and my corns are acting up."

"I'm a bit under the weather myself, but I still have loads of laundry to do. It's a good drying day, nice breeze."

"Did you see the Clems got a new pickup?"

"How can they afford that? I have no clue how they earn a living."

"Hard to figure. What are you bringing to the church social Sunday night?"

"Haven't decided yet. Probably a casserole."
"I'll do something with potatoes, maybe scalloped."
"I love your scalloped potatoes."
"Kurt Baumann, are you on the line again?"
Click.

Ken, twelve years older, left for college shortly after I turned six, my memory of him fuzzy from those earlier years. He did not come home often due to his weekend job to pay his tuition and living expenses. Mom and Dad could not afford much support.

Kyle, six years older, was okay, except when he wasn't. Besides teasing and taunting, he targeted my head with corncobs, rotten eggs, and snowballs. His BB gun aimed lower, stinging my butt and thighs. BB guns lacked enough power to break the skin. I gave as good as I could, for my age, all outside the range of Mom's ears or eyes. I knew better than to tattle. Neither BB gun nor my aim threatened Kyle or the blackbirds feasting in our cherry tree. They seemed the size of crows. I'm positive they mocked me. "Caw, Caw, Caw. You can't hit the broadside of a barn. Caw, Caw, Caw." It could have been worse, blackbirds dive-bombing and splatting me. I hated blackbirds. BB guns could take down a sparrow, but not a blackbird.

Kyle never punched me, though I'm certain it crossed his mind, especially when I caught him filching Dad's cigarettes. "I'm telling Dad." Kyle glared at me, "I'll knock your butt to the moon if you tattletale." I believed him. He liked baiting me, once challenging me to a pissing contest to see who could hit the electrical fencing, the one time I wish I had lost. The worst, he called me Kurtsy. I could put up with the taunts and projectiles, but Kurtsy grated my craw.

We never bought a hay mower or baler because our "back forty" was only three acres planted with alfalfa. We harvested hay with two-handled scythes, raked it into stacks, loaded it onto our flatbed, and pitched it into our haymow. Kyle and I inhaled a lot of chaff.

Clearing the garden and strawberry patches of rocks every spring became an annual grind. Our soil grew rocks. I'd swear to it. When plowing the garden each year prior to spring planting, I followed the fresh furrows harvesting bucket after bucket of sprouting rocks and lugging them to the rock pile. The task brought to mind the hymn, "Rock of Ages," sung frequently at our church,

"Rock of Ages, cleft for me, let me hid myself in thee."

As I often did with hymn lyrics, I asked Mom to explain, she my go-to-person for all things churchy. In this case, what is a cleft, and how did it find its way into a hymn?

"Well a cleft is like a hiding place. Think of Jesus as the rock of ages, and if you walk with Jesus, he will be a protective place for you."

"Okay, I think I get it. But you'd think they could have found a better word than cleft."

Years later, during a college geology class I realized I harvested rocks of the ages. This did not change my attitude about the chore.

Turning eight, I began rising with Kyle at 5:30 to milk the cows before washing up and catching the school bus. Dad said this is why they had us; he didn't have to get up early. We milked by hand. Locked in stanchions, the cows munched on grain and hay while we washed their teats. Contentedly chewing their cud after chowing down, the milking usually flowed smoothly. It took a few milk sessions for the cows to adjust to my new hands. Cows needed milking twice each day even when early morning temperatures dipped below zero. Those days, Kyle and I huddled closer to the cows, their heat warming us.

For the record, just like owners of cats and dogs talk with them all of the time, farmers talk to cows, pigs, sheep, and chickens. Chickens rarely stop clucking, so I cannot claim any discernable response. I never got a moo out of any cow or steer I engaged in conversation, but I did get blank looks. We did not raise pigs or sheep.

Each morning Mom fired up the kitchen's pot-bellied stove before yelling up the stairwell, "Kyle, Kurt, rise and shine."

"No one should be so cheerful this early. It's still dark," Kyle yelled down.

The heat took a month of Sundays to spiral up the stairwell.

We delayed as long as we could. "Kurtsy, tap your shoe on the floor a couple of times, so she'll think we're up." In winter, the floor felt frozen in mornings, so we slept with our socks on, then dressed quickly.

Shortly after joining the milking regimen, Kyle initiated me. "Hey Kurtsy," calling from behind. I turned, catching a direct hit, not the most efficient way for a growing boy to drink his daily milk quota. Milk fights became routine. Kyle perfected the arc shot over a cow's back and onto my head. If Dad noticed a declining milk output, he never said. What we didn't drink, we sold to a local creamery.

Not all milkings flowed smoothly. Barbed or electrical wiring apportioned our acreage plus the pastures we rented from our neighbor, Mabel. Dad believed electrical wiring a better deterrent than barbed wire, though in total our fencing split fifty-fifty. The slightest thunderstorm with gusting winds snapped off branches, crashing them onto the barbed wire. Even smaller branches shorted the entire electrical fencing circuit. Curious cows, nearing a fence, tested it with their noses much like I tiptoed gingerly onto the frozen river. Usually, a barbed wire prick or an electrical jolt kept them in line. Watching a cow recoil from an electrical jolt tickled my funny bone for a week. If spooked or jostled, their 1,000-pound bodies mangled our fencing, and barbed wires slash teats. Slashed teats turn contented cows into bucking broncos. I never knew cows could kick so high. We ankle-shackled the ones with the slashed teats during milking. The milk had to come out. They bucked anyway. "Come on Betsy, settle down." Betsy, in no mood to settle, once escaped the shackles and nailed Kyle in the head, causing headaches for days. I would later retort to Kyle's swing accident put down, "Getting nailed by Betsy explains a lot about how you turned out."

Even for cows, the grass always looks greener on the other side, especially if alfalfa or our garden lured. They often broke loose. In the distance, Mom or Dad yelled, "Kyle, Kurt, the cows are out!" We dashed around like trained herd-dogs until we corralled them back into the pasture.

Cows love sweet corn, but they covet fresh alfalfa. Cows do not graze on alfalfa; they gorge. Alfalfa, wet from storms, bloated their bellies. We summoned the veterinarian. As the cow lay on its side gasping for air, the veterinarian plunged a sword-length spike with an airshaft into the belly, creating an escape for the gas. After a few minutes, the cow scrambled to its feet and moseyed away, just got up and walked away, after a one-inch-width shaft pierced its belly. Since cows have four stomachs, I asked Dad, "How does the veterinarian know which stomach to puncture?" He said he didn't know but it always worked. Dad bought his own piercer. Veterinarians cost too much.

Too much alfalfa caused diarrhea. Never stand near the backside of a cow with diarrhea. The manure drips all over the tail. Cows swat flies with their tails. Swarming flies amassed in our barn and used cows' backs for landing zones. Too often, a tail nailed me right across the kisser, not a pleasant way to start my day. Those times, I wished we docked the cows, cutting off their tails like sheep farmers. I milked with my mouth closed and washed up before school. Neither Kyle nor I ever recalled anyone at school refusing to sit next to us.

Cow waste never went to waste. More than any other chore, Kyle and I loathed scooping the manure from the milk stall trenches. We hated cows pooping during milkings, more like splatting, another unpleasant way to start a day. Along with the decomposed food scraps from our compost, we spread the manure over the garden and strawberry patches and let it leach into the soil, just as rain leeched cow manure in the grazing pastures, a self-fertilizing system. During dry spells, the dried manure became the cow pie toss, akin to a track and field discus competition.

"Next up for the United States in the cow pie discus toss, Kurt Baumann. He spins twice and lets it fly. Oh no, it disintegrates in mid-air. Must have used a cow pie with too much moisture in it."

Only in farming country does a word like pie have two opposite meanings, one, fresh or dried manure, the second, one of the best desserts ever.

We weren't poor; we just never had any money. Our garden, orchard, henhouse, and a steer or cow butchered every year blessed us with most of our daily bread.

I wore hand-me-downs from Ken and Kyle. When those became threadbare, Mom ordered jeans from the Montgomery Ward's catalog. They stretched three sizes too long, meant to last several years. I rolled up the cuffs two turns. Mom teased, "I could add a layer to my flower garden with the dirt you collect in those cuffs."

Our food groups consisted of meat, vegetables, fruits, casseroles, Wonder Bread, and Miracle Whip. All worthy Midwestern moms mastered the casserole. Even with our compost next to the barn, Mom begrudgingly tossed out food. She baked this concoction Kyle and I called Everything-in-the-Refrigerator-Because-I-Refuse-to-Throw-Anything-Out Casserole. Mom called it her Hotchpotch Casserole. Mom never made a Wonder Bread sandwich without Miracle Whip, cheaper than mayonnaise. I never told her how much I disliked Miracle Whip. I never told her that I hated baloney either.

"What do you want for your school lunch sandwich today?"

"Peanut butter and jelly."

"Are you sure? I just bought more baloney."

"I'm sure."

As an adult, I researched baloney. Mom could have been charged with child endangerment. Some days, she surprised me with bacon and tomato on Wonder Bread, a favorite, even with Miracle Whip.

An early ritual mandated beheading a chicken. The How-to-Raise-Farm-Boys Rule Book states, "By age eight, learn boys how to behead chickens." We gobbled fried chicken. Mom's fried chicken reputation extended to at least the end of our driveway. Chicken and Dumplings placed a close second. We rigged a wire hook to snare them around the neck. We hammered two closely placed large nails into a chopping block, and stretched the neck between the nails. Usually one swift chop from an axe did the trick. Grasping the legs, the bird bled a few minutes. Mom stood by with a scalding tub of water; yes, that tub. She dunked the bird several minutes before the plucking ritual. Plucked clean, she gutted it, saved the neck, gizzard, heart and liver, fed the guts to the stray cats, portioned it, and began the coating and frying process. Lard could have been another food group.

Mom needed two chickens. After watching Kyle, I took my apprentice turn. Three important tips: the axe must be razor sharp, the aim true, and the legs grasped firmly. My first try, I scored two out of three. A headless chicken mutates into the strength of Samson.

"Hold tight Kurt!" Mom pleaded.

"Trying Mom, but it's a strong one!"

My grip held fast until the gyrating headless chicken spurted a stream of blood into my eyes. I let go, and the bird flopped around in the dirt. Mom, not amused, made me wash off the chicken in the creek.

"I'd like to see you hold onto the legs if blood spurted in your face." I never dropped another chicken.

A separate boy-meets-reality did not end well. One day, a cattle truck loaded up one of our steers. I overheard Mom say, "Karl, why don't you take Kurt along with you to the slaughterhouse?"

"Don't you think he's a bit young?"

The slaughterhouse, a one-room, small building, chilled me, even in summertime. I watched them herd our steer into a narrow pen. Sometimes, we named our cattle, but not this one. I taught it to wean and slurp out of a bucket, one of my first efforts. Its head locked in a stanchion like the way we locked in the milking herd; a man picked up a rifle, aimed point blank between the steer's eyes, and fired. BLAM! The steer crashed to the floor. I shuddered, turning away. We drove home in silence until I said, "Dad, if it's okay with you, I'd just as soon not go there again." Dad said nothing. He fell ill shortly after.

Our back porch housed two stand-alone large freezers. Following each slaughterhouse trip, they trucked back the quartered carcass. Mom and Dad bought a how-to meat-carving book. We spread each quarter on our kitchen table, cut it into portions, packaged and froze them for the winter. Mom used the bones for broth and the fat for lye soap. Kyle and I would have donated the liver to charity, even fed it to the cats. Mom served liver and onions once a month. Yuck. Along with the steer, the harvest from our garden and orchard filled both freezers.

Ken, Kyle, and I slept in one of two upstairs bedrooms. Storage filled the second room. I shared a double bed with Ken until he left for college. The summer after I turned twelve, Kyle joined the Navy. Always ajar, the door to the second room didn't have a latch, its darkness haunting me to the extent of my imagination. I have no clue from where this fear came. I did not read mystery books, go to spooky movies, or like Kyle, listen to *The Shadow*. Neither Mom nor Dad ever threatened me with the boogieman, but I remained certain he hid in the other room. During daylight hours, I walked in and out of the room without trepidation. At night, no way Dad would allow a lit lamp, too costly. I would have hammered two-by-fours over the doorway and a built a limestone wall. Kyle, not bound by Mom and Dad's rules, teased me, "Kurtsy, Kurtsy, scaredy-cat Kurtsy." The fear plagued me through junior high school.

Kyle and I felt much closer to Mom. She rose before us and retired after, averaging five hours a night. She stayed busier than a cat in a roomful of rocking chairs. Her internal motor never stopped unless sitting for something like snapping beans, hulling peas, shucking corn, plucking chickens, or attending church. Playing Canasta, we nudged her, "Mom, your turn." She played, and dozed off. I frequently caught her nodding off in church, not as a review of the sermon, just tired. Her fortitude and humor sustained us, her affection warmed. She gave all credit to her best friend, Jesus. If crossed, her glare could crack a statue.

Kyle and I dreamed up our own entertainment, we didn't own a television. Mom and Dad treated me to a movie a few times a year at the Twin Rivers' State Theatre, *Bambi* and *Dumbo* early favorites, and later, westerns. I carried a transistor radio while hoeing the garden or picking strawberries. At night, I tucked it under my pillow, listening to WLS out of Chicago and the new Rock N' Roll sounds of Buddy Holly, Chuck Berry, and Jerry Lee Lewis. Chicago seemed a country away. The silly lyrics of songs like *Flying Purple People Eater* and *The Witch Doctor* cluttered my brain. Memorizing them, I drove Mom batty.

Now an adult, I marvel and feel some shame for the mischief Kyle and I dreamt up. Rats and mice call barns luxury living. Rats grew to nearly a foot, not counting the tail. They gorged in our grain bin. Since we never put snakes in the barn to thin the pack, we volunteered one of the latest stray cats passing through. Folks from Twin Rivers drove into the countryside and dumped dogs and cats no longer wanted, or sick, or dying. Stray dogs stayed a spell, savoring Mom's scraps. Ken kept a dog, which Kyle adopted after Ken left. Cats wandered through, often dying from some disease, maggots, or from a critter, most likely a raccoon. We carried the largest, orneriest cat to the top of the bin, and while a rat pigged out, dropped in the cat. The cat usually won. If not, we jumped in and whacked the rats with two-by-fours, or used a pitchfork.

We never figured out how to rid the barn loft of bats. The owls hooted and ogled, amused.

We stuffed a dying, maggot-infested cat into a burlap sack, tied it, and tossed it into the river, just the nature of farm life. Kyle shot at it as it floated away. We practiced on the turtles perched on the rocks down river from the bridge during low currents. A perfect ten flipped the turtle in the air. I always missed. My gun skills never improved until Army basic training in Kentucky.

My favorite time was dusk, in the summer, after supper. I sat on the creek bridge, dangling my feet in the stream, the croaking frogs and crickets chimed in, a master chorale, frogs on bass and crickets on tenor. The whip-poor-wills' calls favored dusk but preferred going solo, waiting for the frogs and crickets to take a breather. Country singer Hank Williams found the whip-poor-will call one of loneliness.

"Hear that lonesome whippoorwill,
He sounds too blue to fly.
That means he lost the will to live,
I'm so lonesome I could cry."

There's too much sadness in country music to suit me, but whip-poor-wills calls do sound lonely.

At times, skeeters spoiled the setting, savoring my presence, all plumped up from supper. During peak sweet corn season, between lulls in the chorus, I swear I heard the sweet corn growing. The creeping darkness began flickering with hundreds of lightening bugs. It was magical, twinkling stars above, twinkling lightening bugs all around, and the frogs, crickets, and whip-poor-wills in full voice.

Mom knew where to find me. After Dad died, she joined me now and then, putting her arm around me.

Four

Emma Baumann, born Emma Steinke in 1911 in Missouri, grew up in eastern Illinois. Kyle and I teased her about her maiden name, calling her Emma Stinky. She said, "You're not the first." Mom never took herself too seriously.

Emma claimed two family firsts: being delivered by a doctor and graduating from high school. The fourth of five children, three brothers and a sister, she abided the most teasing. Rural pastors earned a pittance; the family lived frugally. If one looked up frugal in the dictionary, the first definition might read: Steinke Family.

At age one, the family parsonage burned to the ground, all escaped safely.

Attending a one-room school, thirty students spread over eight grades, meant a two-mile trek for Mom, weather permitting. The closest neighbors lived a quarter mile in each direction. Aunts, uncles, and cousins lived within buggy-ride range. The family entertained themselves, Grandpa on the accordion, one brother on the harmonica, and another played the spoons. Neighbors would listen in to the Steinke amateur hour on the party line. They spent other evenings playing checkers, flinch, and dominoes. Grandma and Grandpa forbade card games, those joining the sins of dancing and pool. She cut pictures out of the Sears catalogue and crafted paper dolls, the catalogue the source for most of the family's shopping. Each year, two weeks prior to Christmas, a large box arrived from Sears. Tucked away in her mom and dad's bedroom, the anticipation began to build.

At age nine, she joined her mom for the milking chore, milking twelve cows twice daily.

World War I, one of the two calamities affecting the world in 1918, did not directly impact the family. The Army drafted Mom's oldest brother, but the combatants reached an armistice before he shipped out. Her other draft-age brother mangled his hand in a feed grinder and could not serve. Grandpa read the Chicago Tribune unfailingly each day for war news. News of the armistice traveled by telephone. Whenever the community needed to receive a message, the operator would ring several long rings on the party line, and everyone picked up the receiver.

The other 1918 calamity, the Spanish Flu Pandemic, spread from the trenches of war-torn Europe, jumped the ocean, and devastated the Midwest, afflicting Emma and two brothers. The death juggernaut pounced on pregnant women, killing thousands. Emma and her two brothers survived, as did her pregnant sister-in-law, beating the odds. Worldwide, the plague claimed more victims than World War II or the Black Death Bubonic Plague of the 1300s.

If the Amish are known for barn-raisings, then Midwestern farmers were known for threshings. Threshing separated grain from the straw. One nearby farmer owned a coal-powered steam engine. It pulled and operated the threshing machine. The machine moved from farm to farm until they harvested all fields. Threshing noontime feasts fed twenty and more.

Age ten marked a year to remember. Emma's mom and older sister began her home schooling in the kitchen, starting with pies. The family bought its first car, a Tin Lizzie, expanding the circumference of her world. She broke her leg falling off a pony. Though a doctor served the area, and the Tin Lizzie at hand, grandpa insisted on mending it. He pulled out the medical book and set the leg. The healing took six weeks, but no more pony rides. Emma feared horses ever after.

The Missouri relatives visited the farm each year. Emma remembered little about her grandma other than she sat puffing on a pipe. Steinke family train trips to her grandparents in Missouri required a change in St. Louis, which were like a fantasy world to a young farm girl.

The farm subsidized Grandpa's meager preacher salary. Besides cows, chickens, and vegetables, the family butchered hogs each year. Emma's older brothers, took on more responsibilities around the farm, allowing her dad to tend to his other flock. Her younger brother, at age eight, began driving the Tin Lizzie to help out. In Emma's early teens, Grandpa assigned her the chicken coop. She raised five hundred chicks one spring.

The modest farm abutted a stretch of railroad tracks, and train whistles interrupted the daily routine. Emma recalled seeing hobos using the tracks, both walking and hopping rides, often coming to the front door asking for a handout. Emma's mom always handed them a sandwich. The men graciously said, "Thank you, ma'am," or "God bless you, ma'am."

Emma's proudest moment growing up was scoring 100 on both the math and grammar township-wide exams. Feeling too prideful, pride being one of the seven deadly sins, Emma later admitted to only thirty taking the test.

Graduating from high school, she thought about college, but the Depression narrowed her options. The idea faded. Her first job paid twenty cents an hour. Emma joined a new church following high school pastored by an ordained woman minister in her late twenties. She, after Emma's parents, became the most influential person in her life. Grandpa left the ministry two years earlier. Her church activities grew, and two years later, she attended a national Baptist Youth Convention in Detroit, her first time ever in a Pullman.

When she and Dad began courting, wanting to impress, she shyly told of her testing feat. Dad, not so shyly, bragged he scored the highest in his county.

On an early date, Dad told the tragic story of losing his mother at a young age.

For their honeymoon, they drove to Chicago for one night to attend a live performance of the National Barn Dance.

They survived the latter part of the Depression, barely scratching out a living, and moving many times. Ken lost track of the schools he attended until the family settled next to the Eel River. Many families tried their hand there. If northern Indiana folks gambled, they would have wagered Karl and Emma would fail next. They did not know Karl and Emma Baumann.

Five

If Midwestern rural towns and villages scripted their own Ten Commandments, one commandment would decree, "Thou shalt attend church regularly." Mom decreed my attendance. No one kept a log; folks left other folks alone, at least to their faces. But with gossipy party lines, little escaped notice, the heathens, sinners, and backsliders known; no tribunals, only whisperings. The Adams Creek Baptist Church charted the village's moral compass, but served a broader purpose, a social calendar, something to do. Church socials, fish frys, and Baptist Youth Fellowship cultivated community. The BYF sponsored hayrides, weenie roasts, and sing-alongs, even non-churchy songs.

Mom and I, if healthy, never missed a Sunday. Dad, a backslider, rarely attended, same for Kyle once he entered high school. Mrs. Williams taught my class. She liked me. I paid attention to her stories about Jesus. Jesus seemed like a fine fellow doing some pretty righteous things like feeding a whole bunch of folks with a few loaves of bread and some fish. Mom often fed lots of folks but nothing like this Jesus fellow. I liked what he preached in the Sermon on the Mount, "Blessed are they who mourn for they shall be comforted. Blessed are the meek for they shall inherit the earth," and "Blessed are the peacemakers for they shall be called children of God." He said a bunch of other "blessed are," but those three stuck. Mrs. Williams called these The Beatitudes. I'm fuzzy about what meek meant, but it sounded like my family. I'd rather be a peacemaker than troublemaker. Mrs. Williams told New Testament stories. First, she'd put on her glasses and read from the Bible, Bibles having small print. She removed her glasses and carried on and on about something Jesus said or did. She went back and forth that way during the entire class, putting on and taking off those glasses.

I didn't care a whit for the Sunday morning sermonizing. The pastor preached stern lectures, his message a far cry from the Jesus lessons Mrs. Williams taught, leastways, the ones I remembered. He cited Old Testament scriptures for his scolds. Don't upset God. If you did, hell awaited. "As the Bible says, if you do not atone for your sins, you will be damned to hell." I fidgeted in the hard pews, especially in the stifling summer heat, cooling myself with a fan with Jesus depicted on one side and a Twin Rivers funeral parlor on the other. I was not certain what atone meant or if my tomfooleries rose to the level of sins. I wondered how Jesus felt about killing snakes or blackbirds. I let Kyle worry about his target practicing on maggot-infested cats.

One Sunday after services, we drove half a mile up river to baptize folks. Mom said they accepted Jesus as their savior and being baptized would wash away their sins. This didn't make a lick of sense. Everyone knew the Eel flowed muddy much of the time, especially that day. The congregation sang, "Shall We Gather at the River."
"Yes, we'll gather at the river,
The beautiful, the beautiful river,
Gather with the saints at the river
That flows by the throne of God."
Whoever wrote this song did not have the Eel River in mind.

The preacher waded in anyway, about waist deep, read something out of the Bible, and before dunking three people one by one said, "I baptize thee in the name of the Father, the Son, and the Holy Ghost." I didn't much care for one of those sinners, so it would have been fine by me if the preacher held him down longer. There was nothing saintly about him.

Driving home, I asked Mom what Holy Ghost meant.

"It's part of the holy Trinity, God the father, God the son, and God the Holy Spirit."

"Why did the preacher say 'Holy Ghost? "

"Just the way we Baptists have always preached it. Other denominations use Holy Spirit."

"So God is a ghost and a spirit?"

"I understand your confusion. It might be better if we Baptists used Holy Spirit. Hard to think of God and ghost in the same manner."

Equating God to a ghost befuddled me. Being a spirit didn't help much either. What's a spirit? How can the father, and the son, and now a spirit be the same person, assuming a spirit can be a person? The hymn "Holy, Holy, Holy," a song our church sang regularly, included the line, "God in three persons, blessed Trinity." Everyone knows about the birth of Jesus and the three wise men. Is there something about the number three and Christianity?

I did not believe in ghosts, or spirits, despite my urge to board up the second upstairs room. Why risk it?

Communion Sundays never made a lick of sense either, grown-ups eating a single breadcrumb and drinking an amount of grape juice no bigger than Mom's stitching thimble. Mom said the bread represented the body of Jesus, and the grape juice, his blood. That's weird. Why would anyone want to drink someone's blood, even Jesus's? The thought freaked me out. Mom said only those who had accepted Jesus as their savior and been baptized, like in the river, could partake in Communion Sundays. So when the trays came down the rows, I passed them along. I still resisted that dunking thing. But truthfully, I often felt a mite hungry by late Sunday morning, and dinner still at least an hour away.

Every summer, the church hosted Revival Week, like Sunday sermons all week, except at night. For some reason, our pastor never felt up to preaching during Revival Week, so another preacher substituted. Midwest Baptist revivalists recruited stem-winders from the Deep South. The stem-winders' quivering, southern drawl sounded like another person took over his body. If this was God, I wanted no part of it. It gave me the heebie jeebies. He made our preacher seem like regular folk. Mom said he represented the Southern Baptists.

"Are we Northern Baptists?"

"No, we are American Baptists."

"Aren't Southern Baptists Americans?"

"Of course they are. They just worship a little differently."

"How so?"

"Well you got me there. There are so many Baptist denominations, hundreds actually, most without much difference. I do know Baptists believe in immersion when baptized, like down at the river. Your grandpa was an American Baptist minister. This is how they raised me. I've always felt comfortable."

After listening to a Southern Baptist preacher all week, I felt better about being an American Baptist even if it meant being dunked one day.

I devoted another week of summer mornings to Vacation Bible School, or I should say Mom devoted me. All week long, I sat through a much longer version of Sunday school hearing more Jesus stories. Luckily, Mrs. Williams taught the class. Adults can be cruel, asking kids to sit quietly for three hours for five days in a row in the summertime. I might have concocted a mysterious illness if they held Vacation Bible School and Revival Week the same week.

Mom extracted my Vacation Bible School and Revival Week attendance with the promise of church camp at Lake Tippecanoe, an hour north of Adams Creek. At the end of my first summer week there, I didn't want to leave, even though my cabin counselor embarrassed me. At home, I never slept in pajamas; didn't own any. Why would anyone take off clothes and then put on other clothes to sleep in? You might as well sleep in the clothes you wore that day. Mom thought it proper I sleep more like city folk and bought me pajamas. "Don't you embarrass me, wear these pajamas." I never wore them. All the campers in my cabin did. I didn't know what worried Mom so much. I knew no one in my cabin. How could she be embarrassed? Our party line would never find out. One morning on the way to breakfast, some campers pointed to the flagpole, giggling. Instead of a flag, my pajamas waved in the morning breeze, courtesy of my cabin counselor. I still refused to wear them, stubborn that way. My cabin counselor never figured out who kept putting frogs in his bed. He was lucky I hated snakes.

If we wanted to play and dive off the pontoon furthest from the shore, they required us to pass a swimming test. I passed, but I set a record for slowest ever, swimming not my best athletic skill. The week, like a dream, sped by; kids my age, swimming, and games like volleyball, basketball, and tetherball everyday. We sang lots of camp songs, church songs, both at services each morning, and vespers each night following supper. We sang "Kumbaya" twice a day. It took a month to get the tune out of my head.

Six

Several days passed before I saw Dutch again, though I returned to the fishing hole each day hoping to find him. The river's rapids slowed to gurgling speed. Kyle and I whacked back the thistles. The path dried. Dry or slippery, walking the path required vigilance, even if I knew it well. Otherwise, animal scat, usually from a deer, would foul your shoes. More than once, I stepped on scat, slipped, landed on my butt, and soiled my jeans. Mom had to separate them from the other laundry and wash by hand.

This time, Dutch looked up. Today, he used a red bobber. I plopped down on the bank and whittled the time away. I teased Dutch with made up lyrics to a song.

"When the red, red bobber comes bob-bob-bobbing along
When the red, red bobber comes bob-bob-bobbing along,
along."

The popular song made no sense either. Robins aren't red. Cardinals are red. I tossed a few twigs downstream from Dutch's line wondering where they would end up. Dutch didn't seem bothered by my singing. But I had something on my mind. The question gnawed on me for days. I feared asking. How would he react? I decided to go for it. What could he fear from a 10-year-old? Then there was this sense of a kind person.

"Can I ask you a question?"

"Sure."

"Do folks call you nigger?"

Dutch put his pole down, removed his cap, spat, and scratched his head. "Where did you hear that word?"

I told him about what a neighbor said after Crispus Attucks won the championship and what my Mom said later.

"Your Mom is a fine Christian lady, and I appreciate what she said. I have been called many hurtful things, but nigger is the worst. Someday I'll tell you the story about being called Nigger George. Like your Mom, I hope you never use the word the rest of your life, even if part of a joke. Lots of white folks say they won't use the word, but they will still howl over a nigger joke. I don't think I have any comparison you would understand. The closest I can think would probably be hick. You don't like being called a hick or a clodhopper, do you?"

"I guess not. Clodhopper, that's a new one."

"Of course you know where you live. You live in the sticks. Makes you feel looked down on, doesn't it? That's how nigger makes me feel, only worse. Think how hick makes you feel and triple it."

I did not feel looked down on in my grade school. Sure, lots of playground taunts, including from me. The one time I did hear "hick" directed at me, I threw the boy to the ground and pounced on him. The playground patrol teacher broke it up. I never heard the word again, leastways not to my face. Physically, I could hold my own, usually picked first when choosing sides for playground games. No one ever broke through me in Red Rover.

"Does Widow Kreider know you're a Negro?"

Dutch smiled. "Hard to say. I pay the rent like clockwork, in cash. All those years on the railroad serving white folks, you pick up lots of sayings and mannerisms. If someone was blind, I bet I could pass for a white man. If she knows or one of her neighbors told her, she hasn't remarked on it. The widow is also a bit hard of hearing. "

"Mom says she seems like a fine Christian, attends church regularly. She said we never know what's in peoples' hearts, what they learned from their parents or if never having known a Negro before."

"Do you know who Crispus Attucks was?"

"Nope."

"A runaway slave, they say he was the first person killed by the British in the Boston Massacre in the late 1700s prior to the start of the Revolutionary War. His father was a slave and his mother an Indian. I bet no one called him a nigger. You may not hear his name when your schooling gets around to teaching you about that war."

Dutch spat, put his cap back on, and picked up his pole. The day flowed by, and not even a nibble.

I knew nothing of runaway slaves or the Revolutionary War, but Crispus Attucks seemed like an important person. When I first heard about Crispus Attucks High School, I had no idea they named it after a person. What an odd name, Crispus Attucks. Maybe Negroes have more interesting names.

"Do you fish, Kurt?"

"Some." Fishing poles cost money so I made my own. Willow branches make the best ones, bendable yet hard to snap. A large willow tree grew next to the bridge. Actually, I found fishing boring, but I didn't say so. "I always stick myself baiting a hook."

"I did the same at your age. Let me show you. Pick out a crawler." Handing me an old Hills Brothers coffee tin, I buried my hand and found a fat one.

"You hold the crawler between your thumb and forefinger close to the fattest end, like this. Stick the hook there first."

The hooked crawler squirmed like a snake when grabbing it behind its head. Kyle could do it, but I feared trying.

"Move your fingers down a bit and pierce it again until you get to the end. Stick it at least three times depending on how long it is. Never leave too much dangling because the fish could bite off just that part without swallowing the hook. You bait the next one."

The baited hook looked like an S. For the first time, I didn't stick my finger. Handing it back to Dutch, I wiped the slime on my jeans. "Tell you what. How about catching me a can of worms? Kyle won't do it no more for four bits. I'll give you two quarters for a dozen worms."

"Sure, but I don't know how."

"Ah it's easy. The best time is after a good soaking from a thunderstorm. Otherwise, you take a big washtub, the kind you take your bath in, and fill it up with water. Put in a couple of cups of bleach; pour it over a patch of grass near the big light pole in your yard so you can see them when they slide out. Don't use a flashlight–makes them crawl back in their hole. When they look like they are almost out, grab them between your thumb and forefinger just like you did baiting the last hook. Pull slowly otherwise they will break in two. Crawlers break easy. I don't want half worms. If the ground is moist enough, they should slide out easy. Make sure you get them before the woodcocks do. Woodcocks feed on crawlers."

"I'll try tonight."

Dutch and I spent a lot of time together the next couple of weeks. My new skill, nabbing night crawlers, kept his Hills Brothers can stocked. One day, the fish must have been napping. We stared silently at our lines. Dutch dozed now and then. My willow pole worked fine. So far, not many words passed between us.

Needing to take a leak I walked back to the bushes. Unzipping, Dutch warned, "Careful back there I saw a snake earlier." Jumping back, I wet my jeans. Backing off to clearer ground, I finished my business and sat down.

"What happened to your britches?"

"Dutch, there's no snake back there."

Dutch chuckled, "Maybe there was, maybe there wasn't. You can't be sure about snakes in these parts."

Water snakes filled the waterways of northern Indiana, though not poisonous, like Dad said, which is good considering my close call at Ole Steely the previous summer. Crawling on the rails beneath Ole Steely, I slipped and fell about fifteen feet into the slow, moving current. The river ran low, measuring a mite less than four feet under Ole Steely. Several large boulders protected the center abutment. My head missed one by a couple of feet. The fall took me under. Finding my footing, I spotted a snake swimming away. Later, I discovered a bite on my right ankle. The snake must have been sunbathing on a nearby rock, and my fall frightened it. It scared Mom–scared me too. The encounter fed my hatred for snakes. Mom knew her lecture about climbing on Ole Steely's rails would fall on deaf ears, like her lecture about walking on the frozen river.

I knew little about Dutch other than his comment about being called Nigger George. "You ever been married, Dutch?"

"Nope, never was. Those years kept me on the rails so much, it never took. I enjoyed my share of lady friends. Both of my folks have passed; also an older brother and sister, one from sickle cell and the other from a car accident. I have a younger sister in Alabama. I see her every year. She drives up and brings me to stay with her a few weeks. That's about all I can handle down there. I like living alone and inside my head. I see my friend James regularly. He lives in Twin Rivers. You'll soon meet him."

"What's sickle cell?"

"It's a blood disease. For some reason, Negroes come down with it more than white folk. For my brother to come down with it meant at least one of my parents likely carried the gene, and so do I. Gave me pause when I thought about marrying and having children. Didn't want to pass it on."

"What's a gene?" I wore the only jeans I knew about.

"Our genes are what determines how we are put together, tall, short, skin color, hair and eye color, and the way we act. Good or bad, genes get passed on. That's why you have brown hair, brown eyes, and how tall you will become. That's why my skin color isn't as dark as most Negroes."

"You scared you might come down with sickle cell?"

"So far, so good. If my chewing habit doesn't kill me, I'll probably slip on a wet bank someday, fall in, and drown. I can't swim."

"Dutch, you can't drown in this part of the Eel River unless you bash your head falling off the bridge or it rises up over your head after a storm. Not deep enough."

"Could be. I'd probably panic and scare myself to death. You got a girlfriend?"

"Course not, I'm only ten." Based on what I knew or thought I knew about girls and sex, I knew less than more. Until recently, the girls in class kept to themselves on the playground, same on the school bus. This past school year, they began whispering and giggling, hanging nearer the boys and asking to join in our playground games. A neighbor, Cindy McBrady, three grades older with hair the color of field corn silk ripe for the fall harvest, and much taller, rode around the neighborhood on her horse, Calico. Twice, she offered me rides, my arms circled around her waist. I knew enough to carefully place my hands. I liked her smell. I liked her cowgirl hat and boots. No cooties on her.

Dad died shortly after I turned nine. No reason for him to have mentioned sex this soon. Kyle told jokes I didn't understand. The strangest sexual thing I ever saw happened when the veterinarian came out to impregnate one of our cows. We castrated the steers so no bull lorded over the pasture. The vet put on an arm-length glove and shoved his arm into the cow almost up to his shoulder. With his other arm, he inserted a long syringe with a bulb on the end and pumped this fluid into her. I'll never forget the first time Dad let me watch, a pretty crude initiation into sex. I shared this with Dutch. He smiled.

A racket arose from a tree above us. A bird sounded upset, jabbering away.

"Sounds like a jay," Dutch said, looking up. "See, there it is."

Up above, a blue jay fluttered around from limb to limb. "Wonder what it's jumpy about."

"Probably spotted a hawk. Hawks scare jays. Makes them raise a ruckus. Jays are my favorite."

"Why's that?" I hadn't given much thought to a favorite bird, although cardinals struck my fancy. Dad fancied robins. Jays were okay except when all flustered. They acted like they owned the place and scolded the other birds like Mom scolds me. I want to cover my ears. I liked blue, and those feathers stuck up on the back of their neck made them look important, like the roosters strutting near our chicken coop.

"They remind me of me, independent and ornery. When I die, I'd like to come back as a jay."

"Don't talk like that. I don't like dying talk," remembering my two grandpas, a grandma, and Dad lying in open caskets. For some reason, Midwest folk liked looking at dead people in open caskets.

"Kyle told me about your dad. Sorry to hear of it. I know how it feels to lose a father. We all go sometime. Your dad was too young. Your mom says those cigarettes killed him. You got a long life ahead of you, but I'm getting up there in years. I'm an old coot, wrinkled and grizzled. I chew too much. I don't know what happens to us when we die, maybe nothing. But if I could return, I always thought I'd like to fly free like a bird and be dandy as a jay."

My mind wandered to my first funeral, Dad's dad. We didn't visit much, but when we did, he took to me, slipping me candy when Mom and Dad weren't looking. He passed late one fall. The hour-long trip seemed fitting for a funeral, a gray, sunless landscape colored only by red barns, fields in hibernation waiting to spring forth months later, the trees barren and naked without their green clothes.

Lots of folks I didn't recognize attended, probably town folk. I remembered some from family reunions. Mom made me wear a clip-on tie. I felt like I couldn't breathe. The open casket sat at one end of his living room. Grandpa lived alone, losing Dad's mom nearly forty years earlier. He looked asleep. Everyone murmured and whispered, as if fearing grandpa could still hear. Later, we drove to the cemetery without talking and walked to the burial site. A light snow coated the ground. Passing near a gravestone, I touched the top, jerking my hand back, cold as ice. The preacher spoke some fine words, and the grownups sang a song I didn't know. I looked up at Dad. Why didn't he cry? His dad died. Mom cried. Grandpa wasn't her dad. Maybe men don't cry. Mom and Dad drove home in silence. I kept thinking about Grandpa in the cold ground.

"I bet you miss your dad."

"Sometimes. He was pretty smart and good at explaining things. I don't think on it much." I felt it best to not say much about my dad, no need for Dutch to know.

"I know what you mean. Course, I was much older when my pappy died. But after a while, you get on with your life."

"You think nothing happens to us when we die? They just put us in a casket in the ground? Mom says if we're good, follow Jesus, and love God, we go to heaven. Where's heaven? Sometimes, on a clear night I go outside, search the sky, and wonder about heaven." I tried not to think about hell, despite what the preacher preaches.

Dutch spat and didn't answer right away. "I had similar questions at your age. I also wondered about the color of God's skin."

Dutch's question confounded me. Does a spirit have color? The Jesus paintings hanging at church showed a bearded, longhaired white man, though his face looked like he spent a lot of time in the sun. I never saw a picture of God. Mom said the part of the area where Jesus came from, Bethlehem and Jerusalem, all of the people had darker skin or at least darker than ours.

"As dark as Dutch's skin?" I wondered.

"I have never been there, but I from what I hear tell I would guess it's pretty close."

Long hair must have been normal when Jesus lived after seeing paintings of his disciples. Times change. In the late '50s, if you saw a man with Jesus-length hair, a beard, and darker skin around Adams Creek, someone would ring up the sheriff. Dutch had darker skin, and maybe someone already rang up the sheriff.

"My family attended a Negro church in Alabama. Once we moved north, I drifted away. My folks got after me more about my school attendance than church. The long porter runs kept my pappy away from home most Sundays. Mom attended on occasion. Then I became a porter. It's hard to belong to a church being a porter, though plenty of my fellow porters kept up attendance when home. Some held prayer sessions on runs. You are a bit young to figure this out, but belief in God and heaven is about faith. You have to have faith they exist. Right now, you're hearing Bible stories in Sunday school, but it may take a while for you to just go on faith. There is no proof of heaven or God. I bet even your mom would say so."

"Not sure I understand faith."

"This is not a great example, but it comes to mind. When you go to bed tonight you have faith you will wake up in the morning, as well as your Mom and Kyle. It'd never cross your mind to think any other way. They're not sick like your pappy was. Jesus, now he is a different matter. By all accounts, he walked on this here earth. How much of the Bible actually happened is open to question as is with much of history. Around eight hundred years ago, I hear tell a whole bunch of Bible scholars got together and wrote most of the Bible most folks read today. I have trouble remembering stuff I did twenty-five years ago, and I sure as shootin' don't remember exact conversations, just bits and pieces."

"Eight hundred years ago! That would be even before grandma and grandpa. You think they had snakes then?"

"Yes, even a bit earlier than that, and I am sure they had snakes."

"All I know is I like this Jesus fellow. Even if God is kind of fuzzy, Jesus is a person I'd like to be friends with. According to my Sunday school teacher, Mrs. Williams, he did some pretty neat stuff."

"I'm with you. Christians claim him to be the Son of God so if you're fine with Jesus and you want to become a Christian and be baptized, you have to accept God as your creator as well, them being father and son and all, according to the Christian faith."

"Mom tried to explain the Holy Ghost part after we watched baptisms in the Eel River. She said ghost meant spirit. Still not sure I understand either one. Is there more than one God? I sure like Mom's and Mrs. Williams' God better than the one our pastor carries on and on about. Maybe God has an angry side like my Dad did. Like a nice God, mad God."

"Just keep asking questions. No one can figure this out at such a young age. Don't fret on it much. If you did nothing else but model yourself after your mom and the Jesus your

Sunday School teacher teaches you about, you will turn out fine. I'm also pretty partial to the Golden Rule, 'Do unto others as you would have them do unto you.' Words to live by. I tried keeping that in mind while working the rails all those years. White folk made it very hard."

"I like that one, too. Twin Rivers has a clothing store called The Golden Rule. Not sure I get the connection. I asked Mom to explain it. She couldn't."

Thinking of Twin Rivers reminded me of our frequent trips to town. Weekly trips to the A & P stocked bread, bacon, coffee, flour, seasonings, and Dad's Chesterfields. Friday or Saturday night trips to downtown Twin Rivers highlighted our week, folks everywhere, meandering up and down Broadway, the main shopping area. Twin Rivers seemed a metropolis. We window- shopped and gawked, rarely buying. I dallied longer in front of Bickels, the bicycles shop. Our family lingered longer in stores selling televisions, now sold in color. Imagine that, color. In the warmer months, the trip ended with a five-cent frosty mug of root beer at the B & K Drive-In on the town's east side. Each summer month, Dad treated us to frozen custard at the Sycamore Drive-In. This was the Twin Rivers of the 1950s, pure Midwestern Americana.

Seven

Karl Baumann was born on, and grew up on a small farm in the flatlands of northwestern Indiana about fifty miles northwest of Indianapolis. Beginning with one square mile (640 acres), farms were subdivided into 320, 160, 80, and 40-acre spreads. The meandering Iroquois and Tippecanoe Rivers interrupted the straight-line sectioning of farms, often resembling a symmetrical quilt from the air. Small towns, populated by shops, churches, a school, a gas station, and small offices, sprung up eight to nine miles apart. A grain elevator and silo, symbols of the area's agrarian culture, marked a town from miles away. The silo spiked the terrain, loftier than any of a town's church steeples. A small town's layout looked like a fish bone, one long main street with side streets branching out. Dad's family, tenant farmers, did not own the farm but shared the harvest with the landowner, keeping enough to sell and survive. An annual profit of $1,200 marked a good year. Gardens and chickens helped nourish them.

Karl's grandparents and close relatives, suffering under serfdom, immigrated from Prussia in 1875, partly lured by America's bold adventure, but mostly fearing conscription of their sons into Prussia's militaristic system, or abduction of their daughters by military or landed gentry. They weathered the journey, camping on the exposed top deck of a transport and processing through Baltimore. The hard crossing claimed lives, but the Baumanns survived. Early in their marriage, Dad taught Mom how to make potato peel soup, passed on from his grandmother. On the crossing, the family often ate scraps.

Customs cleared, the family split, half settling in northern Minnesota, and the rest in Indiana. Finally free of servitude, the Baumanns faced new hurdles as foreigners in a strange land. Early on they encountered prejudices felt by other non-Anglo-Saxon immigrants whether from Ireland, Italy, or Germany. New immigrants initially spoke only their native language, taking decades to completely assimilate. This eased by the time Karl entered public school, English now his first language, and German rarely spoken in the home.

The Flu Pandemic of 1918 claimed his mother and unborn brother, Karl just nine. This devastated him. His mother was the strong, disciplinarian force in his life. His father, more compliant, struggled raising Karl and his two younger sisters. Restless and confident, Karl began rebelling and quarreling with his father over any little issue. I recall Dad arguing with his father during times we gathered, never clear on what set Dad off. In high school, Dad began smoking, it being the grown-up thing to do. He stayed focused on his studies, driven by his mother's memory.

He joined the Army Air Corps during the deepest of the Depression years and spent much of his service at Chanute Field, a small air base in eastern Illinois. But for this posting, he never would have met Emma Steinke at a local church youth group outing.

After exchanging bragging rights with Emma over high school exams, he liked to tease her about her family descending from Missouri hillbillies. After hearing her story about the pipe-smoking grandmother, he felt certain of it.

Eight

Unlike Mom, Dad never hugged us. Money-wise, our farm couldn't support the family. The milk sales to the creamery generated our only steady source of farm income. Dad never worked long at each job. He drove a school bus, mopped floors as a janitor at a Twin Rivers school, was a parts manager at a Mercury dealership, and sold life insurance door-to-door. When I reflected back on this, some insurance company talked Dad into going door-to-door in a community with twenty-five homes. I remember seeing two men one day in white shirts and ties, talking with Dad in our driveway, Dad dressed in his overalls. If he sold a single policy, he did not speak of it. He earned a few bucks each month recording river level readings at the gage hut next to Ole Steely. To save money, Dad cut my hair. He never used a bowl, but sometimes my haircut looked like it. He excelled as a jack-of-all-trades, competent at everything, except cutting hair. He kept our old Packard and Ford tractor humming, patched electrical shorts, designed and built the new barn, repaired doors, windows and roofs, and re-routed the creek. But he was more. He consumed books and subscribed to Scientific American. I tried reading an issue once. Its language might as well have been Greek. On Sunday afternoons after dinner, he dozed listening to the Texaco symphony hour on our Philco. He seemed at peace during those hours. I shared the hours with him, reading. I relied on Dad for homework help, especially with math. He dreamed of Ken, Kyle, and me graduating from college.

One year while serving in the Army Air Corps in the 1930s, Dad read over one hundred books, writing a review of each. I found his review booklet one day, rummaging through Mom's box of memorabilia. She said, "If you'd like it, it's yours." Dad longed to attend college, but it remained a dream too far. One picture in Mom's collection showed Dad standing with a friend in front of what looked to be a college building. Dad wore a tie, puffed on a pipe, and a suit jacket draped his arm, a real college man pose. The Depression shackled him into eking out a living, day-to-day, week-to-week, month-to-month. Each year an eternity, Mom said. Ken arrived shortly after marriage, sealing his future. Before my birth, he suffered a breakdown, diagnosis not known, becoming bedridden for several weeks. Mom later said, "He just did not want to get out of bed." In the mid-1940s, the idea of professional counseling was unheard of even if affordable. High-minded and high-panted Midwestern-types did not seek counseling.

I shared his love for reading. One favorite, *The Adventures of Huckleberry Finn,* fed my wanderlust. I think I read every western biography in the Twin Rivers Library: Kit Carson, Wild Bill Hickok, Davey Crockett, Daniel Boone, and other adventure heroes. The Chip Hilton series fed my sports fantasies. Each Christmas, I found two new books under the tree. Chip Hilton earned all-state honors in every sport, at least the more popular ones: football, basketball, and baseball. I dreamt about being like Chip, especially Chip Hilton the quarterback.

"Hello again football fans this is Vince Shepherd with the play-by-play of this crucial conference game between the Beavers and the Munson Central Bearcats. Coming into this

game, both teams are undefeated and ranked in the top ten statewide. Senior all-conference quarterback, Kurt Baumann, leads the Beavers. Representatives from several Big Ten schools, as well as Indiana Tech and Indiana are here tonight. Baumann already owns all of the passing and total yardage records for Twin Rivers. Now it's all about championships, both the conference, and maybe even the state. Munson Central owns the best pass defense in the conference. The Beavers can expect double-coverage on Baumann's favorite target, Butch Logan.

"It's late in the fourth quarter in this hard-fought game. Munson clings to a 24-21 lead, but it's the Beavers' ball, first and ten on their own 36 with less than two minutes left in the game. Can Baumann do it again like he has so many times?

"This could be the ballgame, fans. Baumann faces third and eight on the Twin Rivers 48 with just 25 seconds left, and he's out of timeouts. Baumann takes the snap and drops back, looking for Logan who's covered like swarming hornets. Baumann eludes a hard rush and rolls to his left, looking downfield. He spots an opening down the sidelines. He's going to run! No wait, he plants his foot right at the line of scrimmage. The run fake drew in the linebackers. He spots his tailback Flory streaking over the middle. It's complete at the 20-yard line. Flory splits two defenders, and it's a race to the end zone, 15-10-5, touchdown Twin Rivers! Baumann did it again! The fans go wild, and Bucky Beaver and the Beaverettes are jumping all over the place!"

"Kurt, what are you daydreaming about?"

"Nothing Mom, thinking about stuff."

"Well, think about stuff while you spread more mulch under the orchard trees, then finish weeding the garden." Dad once said, "Weeds are just plants in the wrong place."

Dad and Kyle built up the garden topsoil. Dad could be clever. He first built a dam to collect eroding dirt washing down the creek from the farms west of us.

I asked Dad, "Why don't we have to pay someone upstream for their dirt?"

"That's just the way nature and flowing waters work. How could I possibly figure out how much mud came from which farm? I am not causing their erosion. The storms erode our creek banks and end up in the river. Who do I go see about that?"

Dad had a way of making sense of things.

After a storm, both the creek's level and flow surged. Dad capped most of the culvert, and the dirt settled into the size of a small pond. Removing it became known as "slipping dirt." Every time Dad announced, "Time to slip some dirt," Kyle groaned. Any sizeable rainstorm soured his mood.

Being Dad had its privileges; he drove the Ford. Dad and Kyle hooked up a slip scoop to the chain and the tractor and dragged the dirt onto a pile. Kyle wore only jean cut-offs and old sneakers. We never knew what the upstream mud brought with it. Going barefoot risked scrapes and lacerations. Kyle dragged the scoop over the quicksand-like mud. Sinking to his hips, he sank the scoop tip deep into the mud "Not yet, not yet, ready, go!" As Dad gunned the motor, the chain tightened. Kyle stood on the handles to tilt the scoop at the proper angle. If Kyle buried the scoop too deep and the chain snapped, Dad turned red-in-the-face sputtering, spitting out his cigarette. Dad taught me lots of new words. Kyle peeled off leeches while washing off after each dredging. "Hey Kurtsy, catch." After the dirt pile dried, we layered it over the garden and bare patches, year after year.

If a marketable crop, selling our rocks could have afforded us indoor plumbing. Dad used those rocks to plug leaks in the dam. The rocks bubbled up every year no matter how much topsoil we layered on, tempting me to spew Dad's new words. Mom admonished, "Never take the Lord's name in vain." I did not know what "in vain" meant, but I'm pretty sure it meant never saying in frustration or anger words like "Jesus Christ" or "God damn it." I cussed quietly, thinking neither Mom nor God could hear. She gave a cussing pass to Dad. Like I said, being Dad had its privileges. "You must be dumber than a bucket of rocks" topped my taunting list.

Dad used dynamite to bust up the boulders too heavy to wrap a chain around and drag out. We learned the hard way. Dad and Kyle wrangled a chain around a partially buried boulder. Gunning the motor, the Little-Ford- that-Could could not, tilted vertically, though did not topple, more new words from Dad. This called for drastic measures, time for TNT. Kyle joined the trip to town. Driving home, he cradled the sticks in his lap. Later, I heard Kyle tell Mom, "I never felt more scared in my life. My hands shook and sweated." Back home, Dad lit the fuse, yelled "Cover," and dashed for the nearest tree. I cowered behind him. He never expressed confusion over the exact amount of TNT needed.

"Dad, how do you know how much TNT to use?"

"Trial and error, and the folks who sell TNT give advice, but over the years, I figured it out."

Once, while re-routing the creek, a blast somersaulted a boulder fifty feet in the air, arcing down ten feet from the kitchen window, more new words from Dad. Mom never noticed. Dad could have used a little more figuring.

Dad carried a darkness, like a boll weevil gnawing on his innards. The slightest setback lit him up. Usually, the cussing warned us. Kyle and I fled. But it could come outta the calm of the day. Smarter than most, he dreamed dreams too far-fetched, and in falling short, it tied him up in knots. I rarely saw him drink, a beer on occasion, though he kept a small bottle of Old Grand Dad on their bedroom dresser, "for sore throats" he said. They gave me a tablespoon whenever a sore throat threatened. It tasted something awful. Whenever frustrated, or Kyle and I messed up–or he suspected such–

his darkness turned outward and mean, cuffing us around, enough to undo any affection I might have felt. He once threw a pitchfork at Kyle. He dodged it.

We never knew day to day which Dad showed up, good Dad or bad Dad, and sometimes both in the same day.

The Baumann clan congregated for a family reunion once a year at a small town park an hour's drive west. The potluck dinner consumed, the oldsters lounged on picnic chairs reminiscing and updating kin on their health, the weather, crop harvests, and their children's lives. I found such talk boring and joined my cousins in softball games or horseshoes. Once, between games, I sneaked another cookie and overheard Dad bragging, "Kurt earned all A's this past semester." Indiana folk kept their bragging to small doses. Dad never praised me to face the way he boasted to our kin that day. I never heard him praise Kyle.

Dad first went off on Mom a night our report cards came home. Ken began his second year of college. I had entered the third grade and Kyle the eighth.

Report card days put Kyle in a foul mood. After the bus dropped us off, I tossed my report card on the kitchen table, but Kyle did not. Later at dinner, Dad asked to see his report card.

"It's somewhere in my notebook," Kyle muttered.

"Speak up, I can't hear you," Dad's voice rising.

"I think it's in my notebook."

"Well find it and let me see it!"

Kyle pushed back from the table and disappeared into the dining room.

"Emma, have you seen it?"

"No Karl, I haven't, but it's probably not much better than the last one considering how little time he spends doing homework."

Kyle returned, gingerly laid the report card on the table, and turned to leave.

"Wait a minute, stay right here."

Dad's eyes darted over the card, his face slowly turning to a scowl. Come to think on it, his face lately seemed to be a permanent scowl. Mom looked down at her plate and chased some peas around with her fork.

Turning to Kyle, "You disgust me. No one in our family ever got all Cs and Ds. Not your mother, not me, not Ken, and not Kurt. What do you have to say for yourself?"

Kyle kept his eyes downward and shuffled his feet side to side. "I don't know, I just don't like my teachers, and I missed a whole week with the flu."

"Hold on, Kurt missed a week, too, and I don't see any bad grades on his report card."

Uh oh, Kyle's gonna get me good for that comment. I could feel the sting of the corncob. "Go into the dining room and get to work on your homework. If you don't get this report card up to at least a B average by the end of the year, there will be hell to pay."

I wondered what Dad could do. We didn't own a television to ban Kyle from watching. Kyle couldn't drive. Dad couldn't yank him out of sports. The rest of the dinner passed in silence. I even passed on dessert, a favorite pie, wanting out of there. Mom's look said it was okay.

Later that night after bedtime, Kyle and I awoke to loud talking in the kitchen. Then we heard the sound of a fist hitting flesh, mom's arm.

Mom cried out, "Karl don't, you're hurting me."

Dad lashed back, "You hurt me by defending Kyle's bad grades, and Kurt's laziness, and blaming me for not keeping a job. I can't help it if my bosses don't know what they are doing. And then there was the time I had to grovel as a janitor. You try doing that someday."

"If that's what it took to bring in some money, I would."

Whack!

"Karl, Kyle is still just a boy, only in the eighth grade. He's a good boy. He'll be all right. I wasn't much better at his age myself."

"Well, look how you turned out, working as a secretary at a grain elevator."

"That's enough, Karl. Go to bed."

"Don't talk back to me, I'm still the man around here."

Several slaps and thumps could be heard. Mom began sobbing.

"Kyle, do something."

"What the sam hell am I supposed to do, you goody-two-shoes? I'm half Dad's size. Remember, he threw a pitchfork at me."

Dad must have left the kitchen because all we heard next was Mom's quiet sobs. I don't know how long Kyle stayed awake, but I could not sleep for some time.

This scene and sounds became routine over the next year. Kyle and I never said anything to Mom or she to us. The mornings would come and go as if nothing happened. Mom would be up at the usual time and cheerfully roust us. I now knew a family secret that would never reach outside our farm. Dad's abuse of Kyle and me was one thing. Hitting Mom was another. Between then and the time Dad died, I felt nothing for him. Truth was, I felt hatred. Mom's bruises on her upper arms kept her from wearing sleeveless dresses, even in the heat of a summer. Family secrets must be covered up.

Abuse colored the air.

Dad smoked two packs a day, even with our scraping-by income. At first, he coughed off and on, then sat to catch his breath. He declined quickly, most days bedridden while Mom fed and bathed him. The wheezing sounds grew louder and more persistent. A doctor visited a few times. Dad's dying conflicted Kyle and me. Mom pleaded with us to spend time with him. I closed my eyes and thought real hard about the good Dad; his trying to teach me the basics of fending for myself, the homework help, his boasting at the family picnic, his love of reading and music, and his explaining things. I promised myself one day I'd read one of his favorite books, Emerson's *Self Reliance*, one he read while serving in the Army Air Corps. He could quote from it. He would not live to see any of his sons graduate from college, yet I felt certain we all would, Ken soon being the first. I think he loved me in his own way, but I could never sort out the two persons going toe to toe inside him. I could never forgive him for hitting Mom. When I went in, I just sat. I felt no words. He knew I was there. Kyle never went in. Mom did not blame him. Nor did I. Dad never bought one of those life insurance policies he once sold.

Not many attended Dad's funeral, mostly family and Mom's church friends. He had not made many friends. Though not a regular churchgoer, Mom said he loved the hymn, "In the Garden." Someone from the congregation sang it.

"I come to the garden alone,
While the dew is still on the roses,
Blackberries Are Red When Green
And the voice I hear falling on my ear
The Son of God discloses.
And he walks with me and he talks with me,
And he tells me I am His own,
And the joy we share as we tarry there,
None other has ever known."

I will never hear or sing the song without thinking of Dad. I wish he tried humming it before he went off on Mom or Kyle and me.

Kyle and I did not speak of it, a burden we shared. Kyle bore the brunt, being older. He took the blame once, protecting me. I forgave him for all of the BB gun, corncob, snowball, rotten egg projectiles, and Kurtsy.

A week after Dad died, Mom asked me if I wanted to meet with the pastor. I said no. Asking why, I told her I felt uncomfortable around him. Again, she asked why.

"Mom, the God he preaches about seems threatening, especially if you sin or do something I don't even know if it is a sin or not. When I fidget during the sermon, he glares at me. I like your God and Mrs. Williams' God better than his." Mom didn't ask again.

We noted little visible grief from Mom after losing Dad, except at the funeral. Mom kept her sadness to herself, though early on we heard her weeping softly through her bedroom door. The pastor stopped by a few times. They talked quietly in the kitchen. She ratcheted up her workday, dealing with her grief, too busy to feel sorry for herself. One of her favorite sayings went something like this: "It is not what happens to us in life that matters, it is what we do with what happens to us that matters." I don't know if she read this somewhere or just thought it through, but it stuck.

I am certain they loved each other, being married over twenty years. I never saw them hug or kiss except the time we put Dad on a TP & W train to somewhere in Illinois. Before the beatings began, Kyle and I could hear them quietly talking things through in the kitchen late at night, their sentences undistinguishable.

I thought about Ken, away at college. I wondered what he knew. While home and sharing a bed with him, I don't recall hearing a fight in the kitchen. Maybe someday he will shed some light on the father he knew growing up. Did he know good Dad or bad Dad?

The weeks following Dad's death, Mom sold the dairy herd but kept the chickens and one of the freezers. There would be no more trips to the slaughterhouse and no more rising at 5:30 to milk the cows. We stopped growing alfalfa on the back acres and planted walnut trees and blueberries on the acre closest to the bend in the river. The other alfalfa acres went to seed.

I learned later that Dad's death hit Mom harder in other ways. Mom and Dad had no health insurance, let alone life insurance. But other than my swing accident, our family remained pretty healthy, with no serious illnesses or broken bones. Though the hospital never admitted Dad, there were medical and drug bills to lessen Dad's pain. The family doctor let Mom pay his charges over time and even accepted fruits and vegetables as partial payment. I remember Mom saying at the time, "I sure hope I can stay healthy and on my feet. I do not want to be a burden to you boys."

Nine

A few days after Dutch schooled me about faith religion, I sat next to him working on a new slingshot. The previous one snapped after using too large of a stone. The river again flowed slower than a walker's pace. The fish played possum. A train whistle echoed down the river.

"Must be the Wabash Cannonball. I worked that run a couple times a year. She's a real hotshot."

"Hotshot?"

"A railroad term for a fast train."

"I didn't know the Wabash Cannonball came through here. I remember the song. I hear it a lot on the National Barn Dance."

Dutch began humming and then sang out,

"Listen to the jingle, the rumble and the roar
As she glides along the woodland, o'er hills and by the shore
Hear the mighty rush of the engine hear those lonesome hobos call
Traveling through the jungle on the Wabash Cannonball."

The whistle and the song teased my core. Did wanderlust pulse my veins or just a sense of the "other" out there; a train whistle, a starry night canopy, reading about Huck Finn, fly-over planes with trailing vapors, or dropping Ken off at the bus depot and reading the bus destinations:

Chicago, St. Louis, Detroit and Indianapolis. They spoke of a world beyond.

"It may surprise you that I listen to the National Barn Dance. Those folks tickle my funny bone. Captain Stubby is from around these parts, the next county south of Twin Rivers."

What I liked most about those folks, they made Dad laugh. He rarely laughed. I liked the music less.

I could sing like a bird, a boy soprano. Mom entered Kyle and me in contests around our county. A neighboring lady played the piano for us. Kyle played his violin in an older competition. I have no idea how Kyle took to the violin. Mom says it must have been when an older cousin fiddled at a family reunion. Mom found a used violin on sale in the paper. I entered and won my first contest at the Ten Mile Fair, not as big as the Clay County Fair, but the biggest whoop-dee-doo in Ten Mile each year. Kyle won, too. Kyle demonstrated another skill, winning the greased pig contest. Imagine that, winning both his musical talent class and the greased pig contest. I sang songs like "Lazy Bones" and "The Little Red Schoolhouse." "When I sing 'Lazy Bones' I go onstage barefoot wearing a straw hat and shouldering a fishing pole. Mom rolls my jeans up just below my knees. I feel odd. I never wear a straw hat around here, but the audiences seem to like it."

"You ever hear of Louie Armstrong?"

"No."

"He's one of our greatest living Americans–and a Negro. He wrote 'Lazy Bones.' Man can he blow that trumpet. Best chops I ever heard. Sings too, if you could call it singing. Has a raspy, gravelly voice, even more than mine. Saw him perform once in Chicago."

> *'Up in the mornin'*
> *Out on the job*
> *Work like the devil for my pay*

> *But that lucky old sun, got nothin' to do*
> *But roll around heaven all day.'"*

"What are chops?"

"It's a Negro term for a person's musical ability. Like asking 'Does Louie Armstrong have the chops to play the trumpet?' Speaking of chops, maybe someday you will learn about Billie Holiday. Then there is Ella Fitzgerald. She can sure sing some serious scat."

"Dutch, that's not nice, using a word for wild animal poop to talk about a lady singer."

Dutch chuckled. "I get your confusion. Scat is also a jazz term for singers who just make it up as they go, never following sheet music. If there's no singer, jazz combos call it jamming or riffing, which really means improvising. Ella is the best scat singer, and yes, she is quite a lady. Also saw her perform. Made me wish I were a younger man."

"Some words are weird."

"The English language can be funny that way."

"Okay, what is jazz?"

"Negroes created it down New Orleans way back around the time I was born in the late 1800s, along with Blues and Ragtime. Don't know much about those last two, other than a Negro pianist name of Scott Joplin popularized Ragtime. A pianist name of Fats Waller wrote this famous blues song, at least among my kind, name of 'Black and Blue.'"

> *"Cold empty bed, springs hard as lead*
> *Feels like ol' Ned wished I was dead*
> *What did I do to be so black and blue."*

"Dutch, you're not black. Brown, I would say."

"And you're not white."

"I'm confused. You folks are Negroes, aren't you?"

"Yes, but that's mostly the current white folk label for my kind. Trouble is, Negro is too closely associated with the word nigger. So amongst ourselves we are beginning to refer to ourselves as black. But even saying black and white, I call the lazy way of folks looking at things. To many, white represents pureness, and Negro, or black, represents something bad."

"My mom talked about that."

"If a person just thinks of us as black and all alike, then they don't have to spend any thought or effort to get to know the person under the skin. Anyways, Fats died too young."

"Funny name, Fats."

"He was a mite on the chubby side. As for jazz, Louis Armstrong is probably the best-known jazz musician. I miss listening to jazz. I had a record player and some jazz albums, but the player broke down. Couldn't see the sense in buying a new one. There is a radio station in Chicago that plays jazz, but its signal doesn't reach this far south."

We didn't own a record player, and the only two Chicago stations we could pick up on fair-weather days aired the Cubs and National Barn Dance. I knew little of the music world beyond The National Barn Dance, what WLS played, and hymns.

"I also sang 'Davey Crockett.' Mom made me wear a 'coon hat, and I carried a BB gun on my shoulder."

"Don't use that word."

"Why not?"

"It's another bad term for Negroes, like nigger. Raccoons can be pests, stealing food from garbage cans and gardens. Many Southerners considered Negroes lower than thieves so they began calling us 'coons.'"

I knew about raccoons, always causing a ruckus in our henhouse. "Sorry, from now on, I will call it a raccoon hat. But hearing this, I am not sure I want to sing that song anymore."

Kyle and I entered the contests as soloists and as a duet, our favorite duet, "This Ole House."

Blackberries Are Red When Green

"This ole house is a-gettin' shaky
This ole house is a-gettin' old
This ole house lets in the rain
This ole house lets in the cold."

Our house could have doubled for the house in "This Ole House." In the dead of winter, freezing temperatures frosted the rooms, especially upstairs. You could see your breath. Each fall, Dad replaced the downstairs with storm windows but left the screens on upstairs. When I needed to take a leak after bedtime, rather than go downstairs and go off the front porch, or sleep-walk the path to the outhouse in the dead of a freezing night, I sprayed through the upstairs screen. Dad never figured out how the screen rusted. Once, in a fog of sleepiness, I left the window ajar. In the morning, I stepped out of bed and onto snow.

The phrase "four rooms and a path" fittingly depicted our plumbing. The path, embedded by railroad ties, led to a two-seater outhouse, a short walk from the back porch, and a slippery slog in winter. It could be freezing in wintertime, cold enough to stick to the seat. In winter, Kyle and I took turns pelting the door with snowballs whenever one of us needed to sit a spell. I learned to do my business efficiently without ever sitting. Dad kept an out-of-date Sears catalog handy in case we ran out of toilet paper. In milder months when nature called while working the back acres, a few large leaves did the trick. Kyle once tricked me into using poison oak leaves. It took two weeks to clear up.

Our home used a wood-burning, pot-bellied stove in the kitchen, and an oil burning stove in the family room. The living room housed a floor-model Philco and a never-in-tune piano. Mom pecked at it now and then. Since I was so musical, she wanted to give me piano lessons, but money was too short. Most other furnishings could be labeled Early-American garage sale, plus family hand-me-downs. An apt adjective would be "old." After school, I huddled close to the Philco listening to *The Adventures of the Lone Ranger*.

"A fiery horse with the speed of light, a cloud of dust and a hearty Hi-Yo Silver! The Lone Ranger! With his faithful Indian companion, Tonto, the daring and resourceful masked rider of the plains led the fight for law and order. Return with us now to those thrilling days of yesteryear! From out of the past come the thundering hoofbeats of the great horse Silver! The Lone Ranger rides again! 'Come on Silver! Let's go big fellow! Hi-yo Silver! Away!"

"Kurt, are you working on your homework?"

"Aw Mom, let me finish *The Lone Ranger* first." Mom had no use for shoot'em up Westerns.

Mom admonished me about bragging, but maybe just a wee one. Kyle and I usually took home the top prizes in our talent show age group, at least in Clay County. Then God must have figured we were getting too big for our britches. One year, we competed at the Indiana State Fair in Indianapolis, a league too far, and no blue ribbons. But the rest of the fair made up for our red ribbon performances. The midway stretched forever and likened our Clay County Fair to a school playground merry-go-round and a swing set. I had never seen so many people in one place.

"Mighty fine voice you got there, Kurt, but you sound like a girl."

"Yeah I know. Kyle says the same thing, one of the reasons he used to call me Kurtsy. He said when I finish singing, I should curtsy."

I could tell Dutch struggled hard to fight off laughing.

"I get teased at school. It makes me want to quit singing. Been in a couple of fights over it. Mom says my voice will change in a few years. Sure hope so."

Just then, a big old bullfrog jumped into the river.

"Speaking of songs, you know this one?
'The Froggy he am a queer bird

He ain't got no tail almost hardly
He runs and he jumps and he lands on the place
Where he ain't got no tail almost hardly.'"

Dutch chuckled, "Can't say I do. But we porters passed the time out on the runs while shining shoes singing lots of Negro spirituals or about this froggy who went a courtin' after Miss Mouse. We'd make up our own lyrics. There's a really long version I've mostly forgotten. But it ends up something like this,

'Where shall the wedding supper be?
Ahum, ahum.
Where shall the wedding supper be?
Ahum, ahum.
Where shall the wedding supper be?
Way down yonder in an old holler tree,
Ahum, ahum. ahum,
What shall the wedding supper be?
Ahum, ahum.
O what shall the wedding supper be?
Sweet potato and a roasted flea,
Ahum, ahum, ahum.'"

"Old froggy and I share a love for sweet potato. Not so much roasted flea."

"Frogs are neat, unless they croak."

Dutch smiled. "Good one."

"I call mice baby rats. Our stray cats keep them under control." I shared what Kyle and I did to control the rats in our barn.

"Jazz, blues, ragtime, and now Negro spirituals?"

"The spirituals were like food for the soul. Helped my ancestors get through trying times, especially back on those plantations. I suspect you even know some.

'I looked over Jordan, and what did I see
Coming for to carry me home.

A band of angels coming after me,
Coming for to carry me home.
Swing low, sweet chariot,
Coming for to carry me home,
Swing low, sweet chariot,
Coming for to carry me home.'"

"I know that one."

"How about this?

'Not my father, not my mother
It's a me O Lord
Standin' in the need of prayer.
Not my brother, not my sister
It's a me O Lord
Standin' in the need of prayer
It's a me, it's a me O Lord standin' in the need of prayer.
It's a me, it's a me O Lord standin' in the need of prayer.'"

"Those songs came from Negroes?"

"Sure enough. Let me think on it, what else comes to mind? Oh yes, 'Nobody Knows the Trouble I've Seen,' 'Steal Away,' 'We Are Climbing Jacob's Ladder,' and 'Go Down, Moses.' Spirituals and Negroes go together like bacon, eggs, and grits.

"We sing most of those in church. If you don't attend church, how's come you know so much about Negro spirituals?"

"I recall some from my youth in Alabama. Then out on the rails, lots of porters sang songs in what was called the smoking car, especially on Sundays."

"What are grits?"

"Made from corn, then ground up. Kind of looks and tastes like oatmeal or Cream of Wheat. Southerners eat lots of grits. Can't find any around here."

I didn't much care for oatmeal. Looked too much like goop. If grits taste and look similar, I'll pass.

Dutch got up to stretch and then began searching the riverbank. Finding a small stone, he stooped as low to the ground as an old man could without falling, then side-armed the stone into the slow-moving current. It reminded me of a side-armed pitcher I once saw at a game in Twin Rivers. The stone skipped several times before sinking.

"Can I try one?"

"It takes the right kind of stone. Best size for a river is a tad smaller than a Campbell's soup lid and about as thick as your little pinky, the rounder the better. Don't toss it upstream; go a bit downstream with the current. Help me find some. You been to a lake yet?"

"Not yet. Later this summer, I go to church camp on Lake Tippecanoe."

"Lakes are smoother, almost like glass when the winds are calm. Smaller stones work fine."

We found a few stones, though none were perfect. Limestone was like that. My first try was a clunker, the second not much better.

"What am I doing wrong?"

"You need to get lower to the ground and then flick your wrist like tossing a baseball."

My next two improved. Then one skipped five times. I felt like I'd thrown the winning touchdown pass. Collecting stones and skipping them became a new pastime. I kept a dozen stashed under Ole Steely. If elected Chief Whoop-Dee-Do of the Clay County Fair, I would mandate a skipping stone, slingshot, and greased pig contest.

Later that summer at church camp, I tried out my newfound skipping stone skills on Lake Tippecanoe. They banned slingshots. Around the campfire, we sang two Negro spirituals, "Swing Low, Sweet Chariot," and "It's a Me O Lord Standin' in the Need of Prayer."

Ten

The next time down the riverbank, an old Studebaker sat next to Ole Steely. Someone new fishing down the bank? I only knew one good fishing hole close by, and Dutch claimed squatters' rights. Dutch had a visitor.

"Kurt, meet James." James looked to be about Dutch's age. James lived in town. Dutch didn't own a car or a phone. If he needed something in town, he gave Mom some money and a list. Or he walked to Carroll's Store. I learned James drove out and took Dutch to town for monthly provisions and to share suppers with other Twin Rivers' Negroes.

They knew each other from the railroad days. They were having a high old time laughing and telling tales.

I chipped in with a couple of cow jokes I heard from Captain Stubby on the National Barn Dance. "Why did the cow cross the road? It was the chicken's day off. Wait wait, one more. Why don't cows have more money? Because the farmers milk them dry." They chuckled some.

"Okay here's a true story. Dad rented the pasture James parked his car next to. A lightning storm took out a big limb, and it squashed the fence. One of the calves got through the opening and decided the middle of the road was just the place for lolly-gagging. A neighbor's pick-up truck came 'round the bend too fast. Hearing the crunch and the calf's bawl. Kyle and I ran to the road and saw it lying in the ditch. Thought for sure it was dead. Old man Gingrich cussed a blue streak and threatened to sue. All of a sudden, the calf leaps to his feet and dashes back to the pasture. We think the collision must have scrambled its brain because it kept running up behind urinating cows, shaking its head back and forth under the stream. After watching a few times, we named it Stupid. Two years later, we butchered Stupid."

Dutch and James thought the story hilarious.

"I felt kind of partial to Stupid since I weaned him."

"Weaned?"

"Right after birth, we separated calves from their mother and weaned them from the mother's milk. We needed the milk for our cream sales. The weaning job fell on my shoulders. I mixed this solution of dry milk formula and water, then poured half a gallon into a bucket. I soaked my index finger in the formula and put it in the calf's mouth. The calf began sucking on the finger, chewed on it pretty good, too. Fortunately their teeth had not come in yet. I pushed the head down into the bucket with my left hand but kept my finger in the mouth. The calf continued sucking on my finger in the bucket. After several trial runs, I began removing my finger and the calf slurped out of the bucket."

"So you've seen calves being born?"

"Oh sure. Most births came off without a hitch, the mom laying down and pushing the calf out. But if there's a breech, the calf could die. We pulled on whatever came first, the tail or the hind legs. We yelled 'Push,' as if she understood. We were partial to female calves over males because of the milk and cream. A male like Stupid ended up on our supper table years earlier than a cow. I felt sorry for male calves. We cut off their horns and castrated them. Dad learned to do both. We cauterized young males when they began growing horns. A fully-grown horn could rupture an udder."

"Learn something everyday. James, you'll remember this one. Hey George, how many porters does it take to change a light bulb?"

"I don't know, George. How many?"

"101. One to hold the bulb and 100 to spin the car."

They slapped their knees and belly-laughed. "Kurt, white folks riding our trains always tried to get us to tell nigger jokes. They loved that one."

"How come you called each other George? I thought your names were Dutch and James."

My Pullman porter schooling began.

"It's like this. In the beginning, all of the Pullman porters were Negroes. The Pullman railroad cars are named after their founder, George Pullman. Way back in the slave days, white folk called slaves by the first name of their owner. They couldn't be bothered having to remember so many slave names, especially since they considered slaves beneath them, same with porters. White folk called us George rather than showing any feelings for porters and asking our names. George, come here. George, do this. George, do that. Most anything they wanted fit our job description. That part we didn't mind so much. If they really wanted to put us down, they called us Nigger George."

I knew nothing of slaves. "That don't seem right. How could you work like that?" I remember Dad complaining to Mom about his bosses, especially during his janitorial job.

"A Pullman porter earned a decent living for a Negro. The tips made the difference."

"What's a tip?"

"Sort of like a pat on the back or an 'atta boy' for a job well done, usually no more than two bits. But they can add up."

"So in addition to your wages, folks tipped? Kyle hires out for a dollar an hour. He never said anything about tips."

"Lots of porters earned enough to buy a home. Being called Nigger and George hurt the most. They also called us 'Boy' and 'Uncle Tom' and 'Coon.' After a time, I stopped minding it much. Okay, that's not true. I minded it, but if every time I heard a put-down and it set me off, I'd have gone plum loco like a rabid dog a long time ago. And I would have been fired. So I put on my Pullman smiley face and looked forward to my days off. Once home, I spent time off with my own kind."

"I never did get used to it, but I know what you mean. Dutch worked the lines more than me; I was a student most of my Pullman years. I had my ways of getting even. The drunks were the worst. One time this fella said, 'No Nigger George is putting me to bed,' and then promptly fell down. I finally got him into his bunk and asleep. Then the snoring started, almost as bad as a train whistle. I looked around to see if anyone was watching, then I punched his face several times, and bloodied his lip. I put a glove on so there wouldn't be any bruises or cuts on my hand. In the morning, he didn't know what hit him. 'What happened?' I said 'You were so drunk you fell and hit your face.' I laughed about it for weeks. That story traveled up and down the tracks for a while."

Chuckling, Dutch put his hand on James' shoulder. "Still tickles my funny bone every time you tell it."

"Kurt, James here is a lawyer, so be careful what you say around him."

The only lawyer I knew stopped by with some papers for Mom to sign when Dad died, the deed to the farm now owned by Mom. Mom and Dad borrowed part of the purchase price from Mom's folks, the frugal ones. When they died, the loan was forgiven.

"Lots of porters earned college degrees. Some became doctors. A few, like me, earned a law degree, including one Thurgood Marshall. He represented the NAACP before the

Supreme Court of these here United States in Brown versus Board of Education."

"NAACP?"

"That stands for National Association for the Advancement of Colored People."

"I thought you folks were Negroes?"

"We are. When they formed the NAACP, several years before I signed up with Pullman in 1913, the nicest label folks had for us was colored. I figure the organization decided to stick with the original name. We think of it as the NAACP. Too bad people need to use labels. Color shouldn't matter."

Lawyer James added, "Brown versus Board of Education desegregated the schools, at least by law."

"Desegregated?"

"I'm sorry, you might be a mite young for this history lesson. It means that Negroes could attend the same schools as you. They couldn't before, least not in the South."

"There's been a Negro boy, Thomas, in my class since the first grade. Everyone treats him okay. He's pretty quiet. He can outrun me."

"That would have never happened in the South before this Supreme Court decision. Things progressed faster in the North. There are a few hundred of us in Twin Rivers, most of us attached to the railroads in some way, not so much now but in years past. Twin Rivers is not the South, but we have a long ways to go. As a student, Thurgood Marshall worked as a porter during the summers. Met him once. Smart man. Have you heard of Reverend Martin Luther King?"

"Nope."

"He and Rosa Parks caused a big dustup down in Alabama."

"What for?"

"Segregation. In the South, all Negros had to sit in the back of the bus and even give up a seat to a white person. It was against the law for a white person to stand if there was a Negro on the bus. A few years back, Rosa Parks refused to give up her seat and was arrested. Reverend King joined her in doing some righteous work. I doubt you will learn much about this until maybe late in high school. You following this?"

"I think so." Actually, I preferred sitting in the back of the bus but I sure as shootin' wouldn't have given up my seat to another boy unless he could physically take it from me. Cindy McBrady could have my seat anytime.

"If we owned a TV, I might have known some of this. Dad said he wanted Ken, Kyle and me to go to college. How about you Dutch?"

"No college for me. But I earned my master's degree serving white folk." Dutch chuckled. "Yes, words are funny sometimes, like the two meanings of scat. I said I earned my master's degree serving white folks. I did this while serving white masters."

"Ken graduated from college in June and up and enlisted in the Army."

"Now why did he go and do a fool thing like that with a college education?" James wondered.

"Mom said he needed some time to think about whether to go on to graduate school. She said she was relieved since she couldn't help him with education expenses. Ken promised her he would save as much as he could in the Army. He says he most likely will end up in Korea for nearly two years. Not much to spend money on over there, he says."

"We wish him luck with that. Pretty sure the Army pays worse than we porters were paid, at least during my later years," Dutch said.

Ken seemed more like an uncle than a big brother. He will become even more distant if he ships out to Korea in a few months. I admired him for achieving a college degree.

"Dutch, why do you keep wearing that ratty old porter hat and jacket if Pullman treated you so poorly? I'd think you'd want to burn them."

"I paid for this out of my own pocket. I'll wear them until they're rags. Already patched up the elbows. We porters were handy with needle and thread. I suspect your Mom keeps lots of your clothes darned."

"She does at that."

James asked if I liked baseball.

"Not as much as football and basketball, but in the summer no other sports are on, so I listen to the Cubs on my transistor. Don't know why, they always come in last. Something to do."

"Then you know about Ernie Banks?"

"You bet, my favorite Cub."

"Do you know Ernie is a Negro?"

"No." Since there wasn't a television at our house, how would I know? If the Twin Rivers Review printed his picture, I did not recall seeing it.

"Do you know who Jackie Robinson is?"

"No."

"He was the first Negro to play in the big leagues, started playing in 1947, played for the Brooklyn Dodgers."

I hated the Dodgers, always trounced my Cubs.

"Your favorite Cub would not be playing today if not for Jackie Robinson. Now there are lots of Negroes in the big leagues."

I lowered my hatred level for the Dodgers to dislike.

"Who's your favorite football player?"

"Jim Brown."

"Another Negro."

Wow, Crispus Attucks, Thurgood Marshall, Louie Armstrong, Billie Holiday, Ella Fitzgerald, Scott Joplin, Rosa Parks, Martin Luther King, Jim Brown, and now Jackie

Robinson; I wondered if the library stocked any books about these folks.

James went on, "Speaking of sports, my grandson, Danny, thinks he will make the varsity basketball team next season in Twin Rivers, maybe even start. He will be a sophomore."

"That would make him a year behind Kyle's class. I'll ask if he knows him." Kyle never talked much about school.

"Almost forgot, Dutch. Mom asked me if you'd like to come by for supper tonight. She's baking some kind of casserole. Could be leftovers, but she's a pretty good cook, usually pretty good fixin's. She appreciates the help you've been giving us."

"Mighty kind of her. Can I bring a mess of fish?"

"I guess so. If we don't fry it up tonight, there's always tomorrow. James you're welcome too, there's always plenty." I liked company now and then with only the three of us.

"Thanks, young fella, but I need to get back. My wife is expecting me for supper. Maybe next time if I'm welcome."

James said something I didn't understand, "Careful Dutch, you don't want folks getting riled up. You took on a risk moving out here alone. You might think about going in the back door."

"I hear you. So far, they keep their distance and actually nod now and then. I suspect some of them have ridden the rails before and recognized my uniform. I hoped they might and not fear me. Kyle and Kurt will be there. It should be okay. No way I am ever going in the back door again."

Mom noted a sheriff's car driving by more since Dutch moved into the neighborhood. A deputy sheriff came up to the porch a couple of times since Dad died, checking in on us.

Back home, Mom asked me to gather eggs and pick more blackberries. Our chicken coop housed ten to twelve hens and four to five roosters. Mom knew how to hatch fertile eggs, so our chicken brood repopulated itself. Dad built her a makeshift incubator. Mom said she liked incubating, reminded her of her childhood. Nesting chickens don't take kindly to giving up their eggs, but none ever pecked me when I reached under, just clucked a lot. Since roosters fertilized the eggs, they strutted around the chicken yard like they owned the place, taunting me as if knowing they'd be the last to face the chopping block; "I'm the king of the roost, and you can't touch me." Mom said, "Only one can be king." Even the roosters vying for kingly status strutted like one, like kings-in-waiting. It must be in their genes.

"Your time will come," I taunted back. The chicken yard entertained us. A rooster's daily routine counted pecking, pooping, strutting, mounting hens, cockfights, and crowing before sunrise. Kyle and I liked cockfights. We bet pennies on them. Once one rooster dominated, we separated them.

Mom, our in-house egg expert, sorted out the rotten eggs, like a sixth sense, either detecting an off odor or hearing a sloshy sound when shaken. I never learned the skill. Nor did I understand why she handed off the rotten ones to Kyle for disposal. I later learned the legal term for this is aiding and abetting.

Kyle returned from his paper route. Mom complained about the blackbirds in our cherry tree. Kyle craved cherry pie. Blackbirds earned public enemy number one status. Kyle, now the orchard guardian after Dad's death, usually patrolled the trees with his single-shot rifle, BB guns proven ineffective long ago. This time, after repeated misses, he ran to the back porch and returned with Dad's shotgun. Kyle could bag a rabbit with his rifle. I couldn't understand how he kept missing. Rabbits dart around, never running in a straight line. Birds sit on limbs passively unless spooked. The elusive blackbird escaped to a nearby apple tree. Kyle inched closer and squeezed the trigger. The recoil nearly knocked him on his butt. Bye bye blackbird. But the spray from the buckshot took out six apple pies. The next month, Mom sold the shotgun. She loved apple pie.

Apple trees populated most of our orchard, more than enough for Mom's apple pies. Before Dad died, he bought a used cider press. Each fall we pressed the harvested apples into cider. The cleaning task fell to me, almost souring me on apple cider. We fed the pomace to the chickens. Mom gave away gallons at church; what we couldn't drink, she froze for year-round use. Fresh apple cider is nectar of the gods.

Eleven

James Boyette grew up in Chicago and became a porter in 1914, a year after Dutch, also working the lines out of Chicago. Boyette is French, his early ancestry probably a French trader and a Negro mother. James' grandpa and grandma slaved in Kentucky and fled to their freedom via the Underground Railroad in the 1850s, up through Indiana and ended up in Chicago. James' father worked as a porter.

Like Dutch, James lived through a porter's life long before signing on; listening to tales told by their porter fathers, home after lengthy and bone-weary runs. They trudged on, hoping conditions and compensation would improve. Porter's sons, now growing up in northern cities, stirred the pot and dreamed bigger dreams than the southern Negroes still enslaved by Jim Crow laws.

After one year on the lines, James entered college, no porter's plight for him. He remained living with his folks to save money and worked the lines in the summer. Twice he delayed his schooling and worked full-time, taking seven years to finish. He saw the law as his ticket out of poverty, a way to the middle class, and a way to help his kind. He entered law school facing the same hurdles, not earning enough money and working the lines in the summer. He persisted, earning a degree in labor law in 1928 after six years. The Brotherhood of the Sleeping Car Porters union movement struggled in the early stages of their 12-year fight for legal stature and recognition. He joined the fight, no longer working as a porter but still carrying the emotional scars from those years. The movement welcomed him, employing his labor law skills. James drafted several of the documents forcing Pullman to the table, and the documents later signed. He semi-retired in 1954, settled in Twin Rivers, and litigated the occasional case there. James recruited Dutch to the Twin Rivers area, promising to look after him, brothers in every sense but blood. His only son died in a knife fight in Chicago, so James and his wife raised their grandson, Daniel, in Twin Rivers. Two married daughters remained with their families in Chicago.

James expected Dutch to live in Twin Rivers. Dutch, tired of city living, wanted no part of it, recalling his early rural raising in Alabama. He even balked at putting in a phone, though he could afford one. Dutch said after forty-two years of feeling second-class, he wanted to be alone. His new neighbors might try to make him feel second-class, but at least there would be fewer of them, unlike the trainloads of whites throughout his porter years.

James vowed to visit Dutch regularly, thinking one day he might discover Dutch dead, and no one would have known. Both neared seventy, James burdened by high blood pressure and Dutch with his chewing habit.

Twelve

Dutch showed up for supper toting a stringer of catfish. He kept his bass catch. Supper planned and on the stove, Mom would clean the catfish the next day. I staked them upstream from the creek bridge. Mom said, "The larger turtles don't come up the creek that far, so they should be safe overnight."

Dutch washed off at the pump, as did Kyle and I. We supped in the kitchen. We rarely ate at the dining room table after Dad died, unless enough kin visited.

Mom said grace. Usually Mom, Kyle and I held hands. Mom began the tradition after Dad died, but not this night. We never held hands when guests came for supper. Mom taught, "It's not good manners to ask folks to participate in family traditions. Might make them feel uneasy." When she said this at an earlier time, I wondered, "But we say grace." Mom said, "Everyone says grace." We passed the platters around and everyone dug in. After a few bites, Mom asked Dutch about James. I had earlier shared the conversation.

"Well, ma'am."

"Please, Dutch, call me Emma. Calling me ma'am makes me feel mighty old; I'm not even fifty. And by the way, your friend James is welcome any time."

I had not heard Mom refer to her age, but fifty seemed old. She could still hook up the plow to furrow the garden, run the cider press, cultivate the strawberry patch, spray the orchard, get after Kyle and me, and go on five hours sleep a night. She acted ageless. Dutch looked to be at least twenty-five years older, but who was I to judge, never having been around an older Negro before.

"Thank you, Emma. Old porter habits die slowly. James and I worked a lot of the lines together out of Chicago my first ten years on the job, mostly with the Pennsylvania Railroad. Let me see, through Twin Rivers, besides the Pennsylvania, there were the Wabash, Baltimore and Ohio, Illinois Central, Vandalia, and the Toledo, Peoria and Western, which folks called the TP & W. Not sure how it got the nickname Tobacco, Peanuts and Whisky."

"Karl once took that train to Illinois."

"We tried to avoid the ones going into the South after hearing stories from our brothers working those routes. Sorry to say the South hasn't changed much since I was a lad; Jim Crow laws in full force, public places still segregated, schools, bathrooms, drinking fountains, restaurants, soda fountains, and libraries."

I loved my Twin Rivers library. "Excuse me, you could not use the library?"

"No son, in most towns only white folk could use the libraries. Those laws began right at the Kentucky line. Still do. Indiana enacted an anti-miscegenation law in the early 1900s and didn't repeal it until a few years ago, the last Midwestern state to do so."

"What's miscegenation?" Kyle wondered, struggling with pronouncing it correctly.

"It means that people of different races can't marry. Its true purpose was to prevent Negros from marrying whites. And a person was deemed a Negro even if only twelve percent of their blood was Negro."

91

"How could they measure that?"

"Blood testing, I guess. I can see how being more than half Negro might be easy to measure. But, beats me how they measure twelve percent. Anyway, my sister still lives in Alabama. Not sure why. Some say it's better to live with the devil you know. James and I told Kurt about the Supreme Court desegregation case, the NAACP, and Reverend King and Rosa Parks. Negroes know a lot about the history of our kind."

Mom nodded as if in the know. "I remember reading about Rosa Parks. Kyle, they must be covering that in your modern history classes."

Kyle, a junior in the fall, said, "Not yet."

"Why do they call them Jim Crow Laws and not segregation laws?' I wondered.

"As the story goes, there was a song and dance number called 'Jump Jim Crow' making the rounds in the early 1800s, performed by a white entertainer in blackface by the name of Thomas 'Daddy' Rice. The song became so widely known and popular that Jim Crow came to mean another term for Negro."

Kyle did not know about blackface, nor did I.

"White men folk would paint their faces black and then mimic Negroes, both singing and talking. Whether singing or talking, their mimicking was meant to mock, not compliment. Their intent was for white folk to laugh at us."

Hearing about Jim Crow, I said, "White folks sure used lots of names to put down Negroes."

"Still do. Some you don't need to hear. What started the conversation was James bragged on Thurgood Marshall who argued the case on behalf of the NAACP. He used to work as a porter in the summers while in college and law school. We weren't able to avoid all runs into the South. We worked the run to Nashville through Twin Rivers, Indianapolis, and Cincinnati. Once a year, I worked the Pennsylvania

'South Wind' Chicago to Miami. She's a fast one, that one. They call her speed 'balling the jack.'"

"Wasn't that the train that derailed a few years back, a bit north of here near Winnemucca?"

"No, it was the Pennsylvania Southland. Worked it from time to time, but I wasn't on the run that day. Thankfully, no one was seriously hurt."

"I wish Karl and I had seen some of the places you've been; never enough money. Even if there was, it's hard to get away from crops, and cows always needing tending. You read about places and know you will never get there."

"I've been to more than my share, but if you're on duty you don't see much."

"Karl and I took the Nashville route once to visit my niece. We couldn't afford the sleeper car, so we napped in our seats. I made sandwiches and brought along fruit. I remember the porters always trying to make us comfortable. Real friendly. They fetched us water and offered pillows. The trip was a lifetime highlight for us, getting away for a few days; no cooking, and letting my niece look after us. I've been meaning to ask about your name. Don't hear the name Dutch much around here."

"My given name is Joshua Clemons. My folks were the children of slaves. But it gets kind of interesting. My Dad carried some Dutch blood. Must have been some hanky-panky happening on those plantations way back when. I was explaining genes to Kurt a few days back."

Mom blushed. I didn't know what hanky-panky meant, but it sounded sexual. Kyle kicked me under the table and glared, as if saying, "Don't ask."

"My mammy also carried some Cherokee blood. As early as I can remember, my folks called me Dutch. I took a shine to it since no one around carried the name. I later learned of the term Black Dutch."

"That explains your lighter skin color. Does it make you feel separate from darker Negros? I'm sorry, is that question out of line? Other than my friend Esther when I was very young, you are the first Negro I have gotten to know. I may ask silly questions."

"No ma'am. Sorry, Emma. That's fine. I trust your meaning. My family history wasn't unusual; though we lighter Negroes get teased some by our darker brothers. There's a High Yeller label. That's a Negro with mostly European blood, though I think it gets used even if a Negro is less than half European. In Louisiana, it's Redbone because of the Indian blood mixed in. James and I get at each other, all in fun. He calls me Red Dutch. James has some French blood in him, so maybe he's High Yeller. Boyette is French. Most folks from around here don't know that French fur traders down from Canada might have been part of the first white settlers in Indiana. There's a town called French Lick down in the southern parts. I call James Frenchy Yeller. I won't mention the other names we have for each other, Negro talk. Mostly we just call each other an old coot."

Mom squirmed, "Yes, please keep the other names to yourselves, thank you. So, you grew up in the south. How did you end up in Chicago?"

"George Pullman. His company recruited southern Negroes to work as porters. He figured former slaves or children of slaves would be the easiest to boss around on his new Pullman cars. They recruited my pappy, and we moved to Chicago. I was the first in my family to graduate from high school. I don't think I would have done so staying in the South. I cast about a few years after high school before figuring out the porter job might be my best option. For Negroes, being a porter or working for the post office were the best jobs. The Pullman Company also favored hiring the sons of porters, so I had that going for me. I started in 1913 when I was twenty-three. I retired in '55 after forty-two years."

Mom shared the story about the high school test scores she and Dad earned.

"That's a mighty fine achievement. Wish I could claim it. I was a fair to middling student."

"You called your fellow porters, brothers. I've never heard that term used for co-workers."

"I don't know how you feel about unions, but we porters formed the Brotherhood of Sleeping Car Porters in 1925. Then the struggle for better conditions with the Pullman Company seemed a lifetime, stretching over twelve years. It was looking like it might never happen, membership dropped, and Pullman Company had spies everywhere, even among the porters. We had to be on our guard or Pullman would fire us. They hired a bunch of roughnecks to intimidate us. One time, they fired a bunch of us and hired Filipinos as replacements."

"Karl and I never were in a union, but we were always sympathetic. I still am."

I knew nothing of Filipinos and certain I had never met one. "Who are Filipinos?"

"They're from the Philippines, a large island country in Asia. Anyway, President Roosevelt finally took some helpful steps like changing the Railway Labor Act to cover porters. Two years later, we signed the first collective bargaining agreement with Pullman."

"I remember voting for Roosevelt in 1932, my first ever, twelve years after women got the right to vote. Can you imagine, women couldn't vote until 1920? Gets my dander up every time I think on it. I have to ask the good Lord for forgiveness for the anger I feel. I know Roosevelt came from money, but he had a manner about him, as if he understood the struggles of folks like us."

"I understand, Emma, but you may not know that in some southern states, Negro women still can't vote. The Suffrage Movement was all about white women voting. And even male Negro voting in rural areas is almost non-existent."

"I had no idea."

"James and I were very active in forming the union, but I had to be invisible, never sure who to trust. James earned his law degree soon after our campaign began and was out of the company. We pro-union porters had our own way of communicating, not unlike how the Underground Railroad worked. We had a signal, one arm fully extended downward and fist clenched."

"What's an underground railroad?" Kyle asked.

"Well, of course it wasn't underground. It just means it was hidden, especially from slave owners and the law. There were the slave states and free states before the Civil War. The railroad connected escape routes and safe houses set up to help slaves escape to a free state or Canada. At first, slaves felt safe in northern states. Then, Congress up and passed a law allowing the return of escaped slaves back to their owners. It had an official name, but it became known as the 'Bloodhound Law.' Bounty hunting became a new business, capturing escaped slaves and returning them, so the routes then extended all the way into Canada until the Civil War."

Kyle interrupted, "Excuse me, but a bounty hunter could capture escaped slaves and return them to the South for money? They could just round up any Negro and sell them back to the South? How would they know who escaped and who had lived in the North all their lives?"

"They didn't. They snatched up free Negroes as well. But branding helped separate slaves from non-slaves. Some could be identified by the scars from whippings."

"Branding?"

"Son, slaves were treated like cattle. If you think of the ranches out west, it is like a steer that gets out of the pasture and wanders free. The only way an owner knows the steer belongs to him is the branding; same with slaves. Slaves carried no identification. The owner carried the only identification, usually a bill of sale, or a record of birth if born on the plantation. Most slaves didn't even know their birthday. When I think on it, the ending of slavery finally allowed my kind to create a family history. You have a family tree. I bet your Mom could fill it in going back over a hundred years. The early slaves carried African names with them across the ocean. Those are long gone. Birthdays were lost. Families were torn apart, relatives never to be found. An entire culture disappeared, kind of like that movie, *Gone with the Wind.* Except nobody equated it to Negro folk, only the white plantation way of life."

"Cattle are animals, Negroes are humans," Kyle protested.

"Not then, and for far too many, not today."

Mom said, "You know, I could fill out my family tree going back over a hundred years. And with some digging, probably further. I never thought about the Negro plight that way before, to have lost all family history."

Kyle still wanted to talk about branding. "So they branded them like cattle?"

"Yes, they did."

"I cannot imagine anything more humiliating, let alone painful."

"The preferred branding spots were the back, shoulder, or abdomen. For extreme punishment, they branded the face."

"Seriously, the face?"

"Yes. I doubt you will learn this in history class."

"But back to the underground railroad. Ohio probably had the most routes bordering on both Virginia and

Kentucky. West Virginia didn't become a state until the start of the Civil War. Indiana had several routes; one followed the Wabash & Erie Canal up through this neck of the woods. If Negroes could elect a saint, Harriet Tubman would head the list. She personally led several hundred slaves to their freedom. Served as a scout and a spy for the Union Army in the Civil War. Fountain City, some seventy-five miles east of Indianapolis, became known as the 'Grand Central Station of the Underground Railroad.' Mighty fine, righteous white man, a Quaker, name of Levi Coffin, headed that effort. They say that by 1850, as many as 100,000 slaves found freedom using the Underground Railroad.

"Fortunately, Pullman never found me out, and in 1937 when we finally sat down with the company, I didn't need to remain underground anymore. I was one of eight porter representatives the day a Pullman bigshot walked into the room ready to sign. James was there, too, as one of our union lawyers. The union became his biggest client. Over the later years, James came aboard from time to time just to check up on Pullman, even worked on occasion. Said he missed the travel. The rails do get inside your bones. I then became part of the union's governing board at the Chicago terminal, it being the largest. Stayed on it until I retired."

"Dutch, I did not realize you and James were such bigshots yourselves."

Dutch smiled, "No, Emma, we just did what needed to be done. Those were some hard years. Because of my position, I did come across some pretty important folks, bigshots if you will, from groups like the NAACP. They would attend our annual union conventions. It might surprise you to know back in the mid-30s, the Brotherhood of the Railroad Trainmen held their annual convention in Twin Rivers. Imagine that, a nationwide union convention right here. Twin Rivers was a busy railroad town. In the early 1900s, they say over two hundred trains passed through each day."

Good at math, I did the calculation. Over two hundred a day meant nearly ten each hour. Since there would have been fewer at night there might have been twenty an hour during daytime. Then I remembered Dutch said 'passed through,' so not all stopped.

"I learned from some of my older porter brothers that in the early 1900s Twin Rivers had electric-powered streetcars all over town. It was as if they had their roaring twenties twenty years early. The population doubled in a span of about thirty years."

"What happened that made it slow down?" Kyle wondered.

"I rightly don't know the whole story, but there was a really bad flood around the time I became a porter in 1913. Then there was a nationwide railroad worker strike in the early '20s. The Pennsylvania Railroad took offense to Twin Rivers' folks supporting the strikers. The story up and down the lines was that its president actually said, 'I will see grass grow on Broadway before I give in.' Then the railroad punished Twin Rivers by shutting down their repair and manufacturing shops and moved those jobs elsewhere. Of course, no town escaped the flu plague, the Depression, and two world wars.

"I had no idea. We moved here in 1950. Were the railroad trainmen Negroes, too?"

"Oh no. Ours was the only Negro railroad union. But the brotherhood term gets used a lot with unions. Our fellow workers are like brothers."

Kyle wondered, "Did you get any extra pay from the union serving on that governing board?"

"No, but I only attended a meeting once a month or so. The staff did most of the work. I think they wanted to thank me for doing so much to get the union started. They did pay my expenses when I attended a convention. Those were real eye openers for me, the people I met fighting for Negro rights, and the stories I heard. I learned a lot of Negro history at those conventions."

Mom looked thoughtful, and then said, "I wonder if those women marching for voting rights were called a sisterhood? I would have marched with them. Karl and I used to talk about that, the women's vote, and how important it was, both of us offended that it took so long. I don't know if that meant we were Democrats or not. It's one of the reasons I fell in love with him. He was so smart. He also supported Roosevelt."

"I'm rather partial to Roosevelt myself, but I have mixed feelings about democrats. When it comes to civil rights and racism, the democrats in power in the south seem like a separate party from the rest of the country. Jim Crow is still the law of the land, and the KKK is still very active."

"Next time you come back bring James and tell us more about those railroad years."

Throughout the supper, Mom kept glancing my way. Not sure if it was a look of approval, hoping I soaked it all in, or a look of concern. She never said anything, so I figured she approved.

After dessert, Dutch left. I found our World Atlas and located the Philippines. I added Harriet Tubman to my list to look up at the library.

Mom finished the dishes; I dried. Then she set to work on some mending. She'd be up until midnight.

"Mom, do you think folks around here might accept Dutch more because he's not so dark?"

"I really don't know. I'd like to think that you, Kyle and I wouldn't act any differently. My friend Esther was quite dark. There are all shades in the Negro community in Twin Rivers. If Dutch were really dark would that matter to you?"

"Nope. I met a nice man early this summer on the riverbank. He could be red like green blackberries for all I care. He is learning me a lot."

Mom smiled.

Kyle had gone outside to take a leak. I joined him. I asked him about what we just heard.

"I sure as hell haven't heard any of this in school. Dutch tells me stuff when I deliver the paper on Sunday morning but only if I ask. I think he shares stories with us because he feels safe. One thing I am sure of, Mom, you, and I need to look out for him here in Adams Creek. I saw his shotgun next to his door but I don't think much scares him. Whatever you hear, tell Mom. So far, none of my paper customers have said anything, not within earshot anyway."

Kyle tussled my hair. "I wish I had known a Dutch at your age. He likes you."

"Jump Jim Crow"

"Come, listen all you gals and boys, Ise just from Tuckyhoe;
I'm goin to sing a little song, my name's Jim Crow.
I went down to the river, I didn't mean to stay;
But dere I see so many gals, I couldn't get away.
And arter I been dere awhile, I tought I push my boat;
But I tumbled in de river, and I find myself afloat.
I git upon a flat boat, I cotch de Uncle Sam;
Den I went to see de place where dey kill'd d Pakenham.
And den I go to Orleans, an feel so full of flight;
Dey put me in de caboose, an keep me dere all night.
When I got out I hit a man, his name I now forgot;
But dere was noting left of him 'cept a little grease spot.
And oder day I hit a man, de man was might fat;
I hit him so hard I nockt him in to an old cockt hat.
I whipt my weight in wildcats, I eat an alligator;
I drunk de Mississippy up! O! I de very creature.
I sit upon a hornet's nest, I dance upon my bead;
I tie a wiper round my neck, an den I go to bed.
I kneel to de buzzard, an I bow to the crow;

An eb'ry time I weel about I jump jis so.
Chorus (after every verse)
Weel about and turn about and do jis so,
Eb'ry time I weel about I jump Jim Crow."

Thirteen

George Pullman incorporated the Pullman Palace Car Company in the late 1860s. He marketed this hotel-on-wheels, upper-class experience primarily to the middle class, featuring finer furnishings and a new level of service. George Pullman did not invent the sleeping car but outsmarted and outmaneuvered his competitors. Early on, he built more cars, standardized them, and made favorable deals with the railroad companies to lease his cars and crews. Adding "Palace" to the company projected class and royalty, often inviting European royalty to travel in his private car. Andrew Carnegie, a one-time competitor, became one of Pullman's most ardent advocates–and the largest stockholder.

Perhaps Pullman's biggest break came after the assassination of President Lincoln, though its account is disputed. Pullman crafted the Taj Mahal of the sleeper car he called Pioneer, personally supervising its construction down to the last detail. Those responsible for Lincoln's funeral train decided the Pioneer befitted the president's final journey from Chicago to Springfield, Illinois. Regardless of varying accounts, Pullman reaped widespread publicity for his budding company.

He created the job of the Pullman porter, finding his new porters in the South from the four million freed slaves, recently legalized by the Thirteenth Amendment. The first porter began work on a sleeper car in 1867, and by 1870, hundreds hired on. The children of slaves followed their parents to Pullman jobs and even later the children of porters. His reasoning: freed slaves understood servitude and would work grueling hours and long stretches for very little pay. Tipping, a new labor custom born in Europe, made its way to the United States following the Civil War. Pullman porters made their way because of tipping.

It can be argued the porter position institutionalized slavery Post-Civil War and Reconstruction by paying low wages for a job of kowtowing and servitude. Nevertheless, a job on a Pullman meant trading overalls and slave clothing for a starched cotton uniform, a chance to escape the cotton fields, segregation laws, and the Klan. Early on, most were grateful.

Each porter carried in his back pocket a compact version of the Pullman Car Porter Handbook, its original version totaling nearly two hundred pages. Pullman expected his porters to memorize these pages.

Initially, Pullman set certain physical and age standards such as a minimum height of five-foot-seven to reach the upper bunks, under six-foot-one to clear the car door, and slim enough to walk through narrow corridors. At first, Pullman only hired younger Negroes with at least a grade school education, new hires tested by a six-month probation. More high school graduates filled the ranks beginning in the 1920s.

Judging the character of a potential porter proved a challenge, but George Pullman left nothing to chance. Once a porter passed his six-month probation, Pullman began interviewing brothers, cousins, uncles, fathers, and close friends, looking for more hires. Pullman often rejected the lightest-skinned Negroes for fear of fraternization with female travelers.

Pullman's focus on the South uprooted families or separated them. Many porters left their families behind for cold-clime hubs like Boston, Chicago, and New York, not knowing when they might return.

Through the late 1800s, Pullman demanded of his porters 400 hours a month, sometimes 20 hours at a stretch, or 11,000 miles. During those stretches, porters worked shifts of thirteen hours while limited to three hours sleep a night. The company docked their pay or fired them over any minor infraction.

The infamous rulebook dictated exact standards for dress, grooming, passenger interaction, and a detailed how-to of every porter responsibility. If seeking other employment, porters could list "Bed Making" on their resumes.

Negroes branded with the common name George so offended white men named George that they founded the Society for the Prevention of Calling Sleeping Car Porters George, claiming over thirty thousand members, including George Herman "Babe" Ruth. Pullman hired more Negroes than any business in the United States and unwittingly created their opportunity to enter the middle class.

In the mid-1920s, the company changed its name to the Pullman Car & Manufacturing Company, reflecting the car manufacturing division. Ten years later, the company merged with the Standard Steel Car Company and operated as the Pullman-Standard Car Manufacturing Company. In the mid-1940s, the Department of Justice filed anti-trust complaints and broke the company up. Pullman-Standard manufactured its last sleeping car in the mid-1950s.

During the 1920s, Pullman's best years, the fleet grew to nearly 10,000 cars, employing twelve thousand porters, while ferrying forty million passengers during its best year.

Its sleeper cars bedded 100,000 per night. By the mid-1950s, Pullman passengers dropped to eleven million annually.

When George Pullman died in 1897, the company's chief counsel, Robert Todd Lincoln, son of President Lincoln, succeeded him. Lincoln served Pullman until his death in 1926, his last position as chairman of the board. Lincoln led Pullman during what could arguably be called the company's most repressive years, the years the company most feared unionization.

With the formation of the Brotherhood of Sleeping Car Porters in 1937, monthly hours topped out at 240, and overtime paid for any hours over 240, same as conductors. Sleep time increased, though still not remunerated.

In 1969, the same year a man landed on the moon, the Pullman Car Company formally dissolved.

Fourteen

Two weeks later, James accepted our supper invitation. He and Dutch showed up with more tales of the trains. Mom dished up fried chicken, mashed potatoes, green beans, corn on the cob, and rhubarb pie. A Midwestern homemaker wouldn't live up to her food bible, *The Good Housekeeping Cookbook,* if she didn't serve up at least five fixins for supper, and a potato dish would be front and center. Kyle and I grumbled, not wanting to share the fried chicken. Kyle grumbled more. With Dad gone, he claimed dibs on the first choice piece of chicken, pork, or beef. Guests always went to the head of the pecking order. Dutch and James could have our serving of pie. Mom gave us the look. Then I remembered; I took the heads off two chickens, more than enough to go around.

I fought my way through the rhubarb pie knowing Mom's rules. Mom countenanced no food left on our plates, illness being the only good excuse. We ate what she put before us whether brussel sprouts–yuck–or lima beans–double yuck. She served her yuck-pies too often for Kyle and me to claim upset stomachs each time. Kyle and I schemed to sabotage the sprouts and lima beans while tending the garden claiming some bug destroyed the plants, but Mom hovered near enough to stop the ruse.

During supper, James and Dutch asked Kyle and I about school. Kyle, a so-so student, or like Dutch said, fair to middling, talked about his hopes of joining the Navy after graduation. I, a better student, only cared about making the football team.

After dessert, James began by telling a bit of himself.

Mom asked Dutch and James how much porters made and then apologized for being too nosy.

"Oh, that's okay. Let me see, when I began in 1913, I made $35.00 a month. The hours Pullman demanded each month had come down some from the earlier years, but still totaled over 350. So that's about ten cents an hour."

"Are you serious?" Kyle said. "I hire out at a dollar an hour every summer."

"It did get better, but slowly. Once the union formed in '37, the monthly average jumped to around $175.00, and the hours dropped to 240. That took it up to a bit less than seventy-five cents an hour. Tipping made the difference early on. Tips averaged a dime when I hired on, then rose to twenty-five cents in the '30s. Pullman knew tips got us by. They also knew since we needed the tips, we would tow the company line and bend over backward to provide even more service. We were not paid for sleeping hours on a run, vacation, or the hours we had to be up and hard at it, preparing the train for the passengers. That always took several hours. We had to sign a waiver holding Pullman harmless for any injury suffered during a crash or derailment."

Mom's eyes widened. "Surely they paid any medical expenses caused by an accident?"

"Oh no. In the larger station cities, some porters became doctors. They treated us. That helped keep medical costs down. Fortunately, I was never injured. If a porter lived in smaller community and was badly injured, they lost their job."

"As long as the good Lord lets me breathe, I will never understand such treatment."

"I did better than most earning tips, averaging about a thousand dollars a year with tips and salary my first fifteen years or so. I made more in tips. Don't know how I would have made it without them even if I did have to grovel to get them.

Now my eyes widened, "Wow! A thousand dollars is a lot of money."

Mom schooled me. "It is if you were still living at home and had no living expenses. It's not if you had your own home, had a family, bought groceries, and needed a car. You're good at math. Thirty-five dollars a month is what, a little over $400 a year? Dutch is saying he earned more in tips. Try living on that."

"I lived alone. I don't know how my brothers with families made ends meet. But we had a lot more expenses than those basics you mentioned, Emma, what with buying our own uniforms, cleaning our uniforms, and shoe polish and brushes. Meals were half price. The shoe polish and brushes were our meal ticket to tips. Pullman knew this. The worst was making us pay for thieving passengers. They'd filch about anything. Pullman's motto was 'the passenger is always right' at least when it came to the porters. If a porter caught a passenger and tried reporting it, the passenger would claim the porter planted it in their suitcase. The conductor sided with the passenger. The Porter Rule book contained hundreds of pages. Making a proper bed ran over ten pages, also where we could sleep and how long. We used to joke 'the only instruction missing was how to use the toilet, tie our shoes, brush our teeth, and breathe.' It seemed like any possible activity was scripted. We slept in the smoking room unless deadheading. Let's see, no-nos on duty: chewing tobacco or gum, drinking hooch, a toothpick in your mouth, discussing politics with passengers, or frowning. Can't recall how I picked up my chewing habit, but I found it relaxing once home after a long trip of kowtowing and putting up with abusive passengers."

Kyle asked, "What's deadheading?"

"That's an empty train heading back to a station because it is scheduled to head out on a new run later that day or the next day. On those runs, the company allowed a porter to sleep in an upper bunk. On regular runs, we considered the smoking room our room though it rarely was. We shined shoes, pressed pants and jackets, and shared news and stories from up and down the lines. It was also the men's toilet and lavatory. But the good old rule book told us we could never ask a passenger to leave if we wanted to sleep, even if off duty. We had a way of getting them out if they wouldn't go quietly when asked. We mopped the floor with a smelly mixture. We could be fired for the smallest infraction. The Rule Book didn't say this, but we could be fired for not answering to 'George.'"

"Listening to you and remembering what Kurt passed on from your visits down at the river, how is it you know so much? I barely find the time to listen to the radio or read the Twin Rivers Review."

Dutch smiled, "Like I said a couple weeks ago, I picked up a lot from those conventions. But we do pay attention to news about our kind, and we read books written by Negroes. None of those authors would be required reading in the Twin Rivers High School, but maybe the boys will come across them if they end up in college. Check out W.E.B Du Bois. Also Richard Wright, author of *Native Son.* You boys should wait until college to chew on that one. It'll curl your hair, and then you might look more like James and me. Makes sense that we would know more about ourselves than white folk. We picked up lots of news overhearing passengers. Many left magazines, rotogravures, and newspapers behind. We had our own underground news system. Trains moved east and west and north and south all day long. If something happened in one place, or to one of us, the whole porter family knew about it within a couple of days. Most stations had Porter Houses close by. Porters could rest, sleep, clean up, or just have time amongst ourselves between routes. During the union-forming years, we usually knew the company spies. If none showed up, we could speak freely. This is why anything that had to do with organizing the union spread so quickly."

"You were probably more informed than Karl and me."

"Might have been."

"Coming back to your first question about how much we earned, it got even better. I averaged $5,000 a year, salary plus tips, my last five years. That came out to almost $1.75 per hour. I lived alone in a one-bedroom apartment. I actually saved money. Now I live on Social Security and a small union pension. I get by."

Mom never shared money woes but no way she made as much as $5,000 a year since Dad died. Good thing she owned the farm.

"James here did a whole lot better while I was slaving away on the rails."

"I did at that. I would have made more had I been a white lawyer, just saying. I lived at home part of my college years, but I had education expenses, and I gave money to my folks. Speaking of tips, porters would do just about anything for a tip: buff on an extra shine, mail a letter, run a bath, find a card table, remember a name or a favorite brand of hooch, finding someone a lower berth, darning pants split right down the back. White men can get broad of beam. I kept a bottle of hooch at hand, ready to spike any man's drink if asked. If his wife traveled with him, we had it figured out; he asked for a cola so she couldn't see the hooch. It got mean sometimes. I once saw an older porter barking like a dog for a tip. Another story my dad told from an earlier time, passengers wanted to hear nigger jokes. They'd say 'Come over here and let me rub your head.' I'm glad I never heard a passenger ask me to do that. I'd have been fired."

Dutch, riding the rails much longer than James, remembered the best and worst tippers. "We called the best tippers suckers, like the fish. Those were journalists, drunks, mobsters, and some names you might recognize: Humphrey Bogart and Eleanor Roosevelt."

"Who were the worst?

"Baseball players, especially Babe Ruth, musicians, stuck-up boarding school kids, and soldiers, sorry to say, but they never had much money. Then there was old man Rockefeller, handing out penny tips."

"What a skinflint," Mom said.

"We made up names for passengers and each other; a drunk was a hooch head; stuffed shirt, a suit and tie man, and a slick man, grease on his bottom. We called the conductor the Big-C. We called each other fluffers, short for pillow fluffers. I won't mention the nastier names."

Mom appreciated that.

"What I said about the soldiers is true. They would get drunk and get real mean. We transported lots of soldiers during World War II. I sometimes buffed a dozen sets of Army boots a night for no tips. They'd leave them outside their berths. The government considered our porter jobs so important in transporting the troops they never drafted most of us. Course I was in my mid-50s and too old by then. Passengers came down with all sorts of ailments, and more often than not, we would catch some bug and have to keep on working or be fired. We needed the money. We had elixirs for about anything. Did you know that bacon grease is great for hemorrhoids?"

"Dutch, Kurt didn't need to hear that," and then laughed. Looking at me, she said, "I'll tell you later."

"Sorry, I get to carrying on not thinking about who is listening. Emma, I mentioned a couple of weeks ago about trying to avoid the lines through the south. Porters never strayed far from the train at the southern stops. In 1930, they lynched a porter in Georgia only a quarter mile from his Atlanta-bound train. We never stopped believing it could happen even in the '40s and '50s. Pullman even segregated his trains through the south. We couldn't stop at the Kentucky state line and rearrange the cars, so the cars were realigned out of the run's origin, often in Chicago. Pullman wanted Negro passengers, good for business. For the southern routes, they put the Negro car right behind the locomotive. Those were some nasty fumes. That car also functioned as the baggage car. We gave them less service. The company wanted us focusing on the white passengers. We called those the 'Jim Crow Cars.' Duke Ellington had to rent an entire sleeper car for gigs down South. No hotels would accept him and his band."

"Beginning in the late '30s, more Negros bought cars, especially porters and postal workers. Even though the Jim Crow laws predominantly affected the south, Negroes were banned from basic services throughout the country. A Negro named Victor Green began publishing *The Negro Motorist Green-Book*. Mostly a travel aid, it listed hotels, gas stations, and restaurants that would welcome Negro business. Just one example, in the '30s not a single hotel in Salt Lake City allowed Negro guests. I learned that from the porters traveling through there. I even heard some national parks advertised 'Cabins for Colored.'"

James added, "I used that book once in the late '40s. My wife and I took our grandchildren all the way to Los Angeles, followed Route 66. No way we could have made that trip without it. Still, when we set out my wife fried up some chickens, boiled eggs, and packed sandwiches and water. We even carried a portable toilet in the trunk for bathroom breaks. We never knew when one of the kids had to go. Somehow, Albuquerque sticks in my memory; only six hotels out of one hundred allowed Negros."

"I know Kyle and Kurt have heard me talk about my childhood friend, Esther. What I failed to mention was that I lost another playmate after Esther and I began playing together. Her parents stopped letting her come by. And they were regulars at Dad's church. I was too young to understand it all, but I remember feeling very hurt. I am glad I chose Esther. She did not have any friends. Even though I have some miles on this body and some bruises to show for it, I have led a pretty isolated life. Your stories speak of a world I knew little of. It pains me to hear you speak of it. I am beginning to wonder what my church friends feel about us, knowing we are your friends."

James wanted to know from Kyle what he'd been hearing since Dutch moved out here.

"Not much. I'm the only one my age in Adams Creek. I don't really talk with my paper route customers except when I collect subscriptions. No one has said anything or acted differently. I think they know we're friends. Kurt fills me in on what you talked about down the river. Like Mom just said, no way I can understand what you and Dutch went through. I think Dutch is very brave moving out here. I kind of like it, especially the bacon on Sunday mornings. And he tells me stories."

"We think we've had it pretty rough, never much money, and losing Karl. But we have this farm, and it keeps us fed. We will have to continue another time. I have mending to do by tomorrow. There's still a piece of rhubarb pie left. Any takers?"

"No thanks, one piece of pie is my limit. Appreciate the fine meal, Emma. Kurt rightfully bragged on your fried chicken."

"Try to get home before sundown, James. The roads are narrow and get pretty dark out here."

"I'll be fine, Emma. Thanks for supper."

"These must be unfamiliar roads for you."

"I've been on them enough by now, and Highway 24 is just a few miles south."

I don't think I blinked for the last hour, my head filled with new images and words. Later I needed Mom to explain some of what I heard, including hemorrhoids. Some of what I learn makes me not want to grow up.

Fifteen

The next week, the Clay County sheriff's car filled the spot by Ole Steely where James parked his Studebaker. I found the sheriff sitting next to Dutch talking quietly.

"Hi Kurt, meet Sheriff Ben Sellers. Ben's father worked the Pullmans as a conductor. We worked some of the same routes over the years."

"Hi Sheriff. One of your deputies stopped by the house a couple of times after Dad died."

"Hey Kurt, your mom doing okay?"

"I guess. She keeps pretty busy."

"How are you doing?"

"Fine." I wished folks would stop asking.

"Kurt, I'd like your help. If you hear any threatening talk about Dutch around the neighborhood, would you let your mom know? I told Dutch not to move out here; Pops warned me he wouldn't listen," and winked at Dutch. "Dutch was saying he found manure in his mailbox a few days ago. Any idea who might have done that?"

I zipped my lips, shaking my head no. "Kyle and I are the only boys around our age in the neighborhood. Must be an outsider."

"Have you or Dutch seen any freight hoppers lately?"

I recalled seeing a shabbily dressed man on the road from time to time. They usually headed south down the riverbank. Mom said one stopped by the house from time to time while Kyle and I were in school. She always gave them a sandwich. Dutch spoke of one passing by the fishing hole on occasion and sitting a spell to share railroad stories.

"They seem pretty harmless. There's a spot further down the riverbank where they've squatted from time to time. I fish there now and then. I wouldn't call it a hobo jungle, 'cause I've never seen more than one person at a time."

The Cannonball rumbled through at high speed. Other trains slowed at the crossing near Carroll's store. Hobos could jump off or on.

The sheriff got up, adjusting his holster. "I think I'll head down there and look around."

I didn't tell him about the neighbor's comment after Crispus Attucks won the state championship. It seemed unnecessary since they had moved.

"Dutch, I almost laughed out loud about that manure thing."

"What for?"

"Kyle and I have pulled that prank on farmers in the area, the ones with the longer driveways, especially around Halloween. No way we would have done that to you."

Dutch chuckled, "Well if that's as far as it goes, I'll be fine. At least it was dry, like a cow pie. Could've been worse, could have been pig poop."

"Dutch, you scared living out here?"

"I'm too old to scare easy. Just the same, I keep my shotgun loaded by the front door. It's been nearly thirty years since that lynching over in Mason City. My kind never thought such a thing could happen this far north. Things are better in the north, though most folks still look down on us. There are plenty of Negro folk in Twin Rivers for James to spend time with and feel comfortable. The Klan flexed its muscles there back in the '20s, and all over Indiana, but it never became a sundown town to my way of knowing."

"Lynching in Mason City?"

"That's a story for another time, maybe over supper. You may meet someone some day who knows that story all too well."

"Okay, then what's a sundown town?"

"Sundown towns tried to keep Negroes out, not just in the South, pretty much everywhere, including Indiana. Some posted signs at their town limits saying, 'Nigger don't let the sun go down on you here.' I have not heard tell about those signs in this neck of the woods, though my friend Lucas tells me that Oakwood, about an hour south of here, posted a sign like that as recently as twenty years ago. I bet you didn't know that 1940 presidential candidate Wendell Willkie was from Oakwood. If a Negro didn't get out of town by dusk, the police could lock you up, or whites would harass or rough you up.

"But, back to your question. I got tired of living in a big city. Twin Rivers is a village compared to Chicago, but it's still a city. I've been keeping my own company for so long I've gotten used to it. Suits me fine when folks keep their distance as long as they don't bother me. Living here is far better than what I put up with all those years as a porter, least so far. You, your mom, and Kyle make it easier. I'm grateful. We can save talk about the Klan for another time–maybe next time around the supper table.

"Kurt, don't tell your Mom but I think I'm still digesting that rhubarb pie."

"That pie makes my mouth pucker up. It could have been worse; she could have served gooseberry or mulberry. Next time she asks you over, I'll give you a heads up about dessert. You can always say no."

"Too bad your Mom doesn't know how to bake a sweet potato pie, my favorite. My mom baked one once a week. We had a saying, 'A day without sweet potato pie is like a day without sunshine.' She also cooked up the best chicken and dumplings, and biscuits. I can still taste them all, especially a hot biscuit dripping with honey. "Mm, mm, mm."

I had never eaten sweet potato pie, but between sweet potatoes and potatoes, they could have been another food group.

Dutch noticed I didn't seem too chipper. "Why you so down in the mouth today?"

"Aw, I have to go in town tomorrow and get a couple of shots. Needles give me the willies. I've hated them ever since they gave us those polio shots at school a few years back."

"I don't think I ever had a shot. Polio is something nasty, so be grateful for those shots."

"I'd rather eat lima beans and rhubarb pie."

Days later, Mom and I sat on the front porch snapping beans. I survived the shots. I marveled over how fast and nimble her hands worked. We spotted Dutch walking by without his fishing gear. He called out asking if I wanted to keep him company up to Carroll's store. Mom approved, "Go ahead. We've snapped enough beans to feed Adams Creek."

Tagging along, cars I didn't recognize slowed, stared, and drove on. Dutch said he noticed it all of the time. Cindy McBrady, atop Calico, approached from the other side. I said "hi," but she only gave me a side-glance as she rode by.

"Looks like your arm didn't fall off from those shots."

"I look away and think about tossing a touchdown pass. That helps."

Up at Carroll's, Dutch gave me a nickel for a pop from the big, red Coca Cola machine. I loved slipping the coin into the slot, listening to the machine talk, and abracadabra, the bottle magically appeared.

While I chugged my pop, Dutch chatted with Charlie Carroll. Since the railroad track lay within slingshot range, Charlie peppered Dutch with all manner of railroad questions, the names of the lines, where coming from and where headed, and the various kinds of freight being hauled. While they were chatting, I filched a candy bar. Walking home, I asked about Charlie.

"He's always treated me fine. Course he likes my business. Down south, I think shop owners thought they would lose white customers if they served Negroes. Many were racist to the core anyway and just used it as an excuse. Charlie's good folk, he doesn't seem worried about selling to me or what folks might think. I've never seen anyone walk out when I enter the store."

While fiddling with the candy bar in my pocket, Dutch asked, "What's that in your pocket?"

"Nothing."

"Don't lie to me, Kurt. I saw you take that candy, but I don't think Charlie did."

I took out the bar and fessed up. We stopped walking.

"We're going to turn around right now and take that candy back to Carroll's. And you are going to apologize to Mr. Carroll."

We did, and I did; hardest thing I had ever done.

Now back on the road, Dutch said, "Let's just keep this between you and me. No need for your mom to know."

I heaved a big sigh of relief.

Back home, Dutch asked to seine for more minnows. We teamed up. I waded in upstream and scared the bait downstream into the net he kept stored in our back porch.

After Dutch left, I told Mom about Cindy not even saying hi. Mom said she didn't know the McBrady's well, not churchgoers, although they seemed friendly enough and always bought strawberries from us. "She and her husband divorced a while back. I suspect Cindy's mom told her not to speak with Dutch. She may feel like the neighbor lady who used the ugly word after Crispus Attucks won. You never know what lies in people's hearts or how they were brought up. It's easy to get set in our ways and be afraid of anyone not like us, Negro or otherwise. But you have to be taught to hate. Kids learn by watching and listening to their parents. Now go dig me some potatoes and sweet potatoes. Remember how I taught you, use the spade fork and try not to stick any. Start about a foot back from the plant. You are churning the soil not digging a hole. Brush off the clumps of dirt, and rinse them off at the pump. Then fill up a bucket of water. I will wash and scrub them before I make mashed potatoes."

Sixteen

Sheriff Ben Sellers came from a long line of Sellers in northern Indiana. Sellers, originally Scots, migrated to America in the late 1700s, making their way to Indiana after the Civil War. His dad, Gus, spent his career as a conductor for the Pennsylvania Railroad. Ben did not find the railroad life appealing, though he did travel often at discounted rates. There, he enjoyed the service of the Pullman porters. His dad spoke well of them calling many friends.

His family lived near the Negro enclave in Twin Rivers. Not only did he have Negro classmates in grade school, junior high, and high school, they played together in a nearby park after school and on weekends.

He lettered in football, basketball, and baseball, his grades falling short of qualifying for the Honor Society. College never appealed.

Graduating from high school as World War II ended, he joined the Twin Rivers police force. Shortly after, he married his high school steady girl. He rose to sergeant in five years. Known for his fair and calm demeanor, he began attracting attention in the county law enforcement community. He solved one sticky case after three years on the job. The Review wrote it up. In 1957, following the unexpected death of the county sheriff, he applied for and received the appointment to sheriff by the county commissioners, the youngest sheriff ever for the county. World War II thinned the ranks of county and city law enforcement. During the interview he prided himself for saying he had never fired his weapon on duty. The position of county sheriff, not an elected office, served at the behest of the county commissioners. Reappointments were commonplace unless proven incompetence, dereliction of duty, or death. Now with three young children, Sellers hoped to keep this job for as long as possible. A devout Christian, his family attended the Twin Rivers' Main Street Methodist Church.

When it came to dealing with the Negro community, he sought his dad's advice since so many worked the railroad. Gus and Dutch had become friends over the years. Gus taught Dutch the job of conductor, and Dutch often performed it without additional pay. His dad respected Dutch's role in the porter union, himself a loyal member of the Brotherhood of Railroad Trainmen. Gus served on the organizing committee for the annual convention held in Twin Rivers in 1935. Gus asked Ben to "look after Dutch out there." He spoke of Dutch's independence and wanting to be left alone after so many years of servitude. When Sheriff Sellers learned of Dutch's fishing hole, he asked his dad to come out with him to meet Dutch. While there he sat and listened to the two reminisce about those years on the railroad, a life he knew little of since his dad rarely talked about it after returning from runs. It was then he knew he could trust Dutch and vowed to honor his dad's request.

When Karl Bauman died, there was another reason to check in on Adams Creek. Even though Emma Baumann was old enough to be his mother, he felt protective towards her, knowing her to be a bedrock of the community.

Seventeen

The Christmas of 1958, Mom used her meager Christmas bonus to buy me a used Lionel train set, the one with the Santa Fe name on the locomotive, a complete surprise. "A church member mentioned she had this set to sell. Her son was well into his teens and losing interest. I went by her house. Seemed to run fine. I suspect Kyle can help you keep it running if you need help."

I needed Kyle's help, he a chip off of Dad's block. Dad's fix-it genes passed me by. Turns out Kyle liked running it as much as me, at least for a few months.

Later that winter, several days of zero degrees and below froze the river solid. One morning, Mom fixed on something out the kitchen window.

"Whatcha you looking at, Mom?"

"Old Dutch is ice skating." Pulling a chair over so I could see better, there he was, gliding on the ice.

"Imagine that, he can't swim but ice skates. What's he doing?"

"Those look like figure eights."

I watched a few more minutes. I couldn't skate but had a good excuse; ice skates cost money. I fared better on rented roller skates, barely. The owner of the Twin Rivers Riverside Park rink joked he didn't have to buff the floor after I spent an evening skating. Kyle and I played ice hockey in our regular work shoes on the small pond near our creek. We used small limbs for hockey sticks and rocks for pucks. Mom cautioned about the river icing over, but we snuck out anyway, south of Ole Steely. Mom could only see north side from her kitchen vantage point.

Two weeks later, a picture and story about Dutch's skating showed up in the Review. Mom said, "I didn't call the paper." Dutch later said he wasn't sure he wanted his picture in the paper. I teased him, "Not many folks get to see themselves in the newspaper." He said Negroes usually don't get their picture in the paper unless they have committed a crime or been accused of committing one. "Rest assured there are Klan members or Klan sympathizers who read the Review. Now they know where I live. I made a mistake. What is the name of that deadly sin? Oh yes, pride." Nothing seemed to come of it, leastways any direct way Dutch could tell.

At a supper the previous fall, Dutch schooled us about the KKK, though mostly from what he knew about down South.

I didn't see Dutch much during the winter. Weather allowing and the river free of ice, he cast a line off Ole Steely. If frozen over and thick enough, he cut a hole in the ice and dropped a line north of Ole Steely. I steered clear because Mom would have spotted me through the window.

Mom offered him space for his fish in our back porch freezer. She froze more vegetables than we needed for the winter. When Dutch stopped by for some of his fish, Mom shared the vegetables. The first time he came for dinner after Christmas, I showed him my train set.

"I heard about these but never seen one."

He told me how they arranged the various cars.

Kyle and I frequented the sledding run on the steep hill on the other side of the river. Kyle taught me the run the previous winter. Kyle always cautioned, "Make sure the handles are well-oiled for those sharp turns. Otherwise, you'll smack headfirst into that big thorn tree."

During one of our snowball fights, Kyle missed and broke a back porch window. Mom took the repair cost out of his paper delivery earnings. Kyle earned his driver's permit. Mom, showing the patience of Job, began teaching him to drive. Kyle ground lots of gears during those first attempts.

Our A & P purchases now included meat since we stopped butchering each year. Mom searched the paper, waiting for the sales. Our meals included more hamburger, meatloaf, stews, pot roasts, pork and beans, hot dogs, and the monthly ration of liver and onions. Even without butchering a cow or steer each year, she still bought liver. It's as if Mom read somewhere that eating liver made us stouter and smarter. If she claimed I could toss a football further, she could fry it up every night. When I asked her about it, she said, "I grew up eating liver and onions once a month and saw no need to change." I dropped the subject. Maybe to make amends, she sprung for sirloin steak twice a year. I finally talked Mom out of baloney sandwiches. I later learned hot dogs and baloney belonged to the same food family I labeled "some sort of meat." Mom patiently collected S&H Green Stamps, using their catalogue like she used Montgomery Wards and Sears & Roebuck.

In writing about years gone by, it is tempting to stretch tales, bordering on lore, "It hailed the size of baseballs," or "The mosquitoes were so large they landed at the nearby Bunker Hill Air Force Base and walked over." The winter of 1959 brought the most dramatic storms in all my years in Adams Creek. In February, a massive snowstorm and freeze blanketed the area; sleet and hail pelted us. Sleet in freezing weather is nasty, turning roads into ice rinks. Farmers patrolled the roads with their tractors looking for cars stuck in a ditch. Kyle and I considered joining the patrol, but Our Little Tractor That Could couldn't. Family-sized cars and pickup trucks weighed too much. Truthfully, the hail measured no more than the size of peas or rabbit turds, not baseballs. During the thaw, the river overflowed lapping up against our front porch. With nowhere to empty, the creek backed up and flooded its banks. The river crested to a foot below the bridge. Mom worried, "I hope Ole Steely holds up the next couple of days." The bergs thumped into the center abutment, wakening us at night. Ole Steely held and the road remained passable. With no basement, cellar, or underground storm shelter, our home, barn, and henhouse survived the flood without damage. The hens freaked out, and egg production dropped.

The other big news the winter of 1959, the Twin Rivers Beavers basketball team fought its way to the state final four, the furthest reached since 1934 when Twin Rivers won its only state championship. A promising young sophomore, Danny Boyette, James' grandson, lit up the nets as the top scorer, hard to guard with his long-range jumper. They met their match in the semi-final game with none other than Crispus Attucks, the eventual state champions. Though the Beavers did not win out, they exceeded all expectations, barely eking out a five hundred record through the regular season. Kyle took me to the raucous celebration when the team returned to Twin Rivers. The coach and the starting-five spoke, including Danny. I saw James there, beaming.

The Army shipped Ken to Korea following basic training. The crossing provided both drama and rough seas. Ken wrote nearly once a week. Mom shared his letters.

From the crossing,

"We left Seattle on November 29th and headed northwest toward a place called Adak, a southern island of the Aleutians. The reason we are going to Adak is to let off some dependents

of a few servicemen. We also have quite a few dependents going to Yokohama, Japan. We have run into some of the roughest sea in this area in the last eight years according to the crew. Below zero temps and a sea that bounces the bow of the ship 100 feet into the air with every wave.

"I don't know if you heard the story or not, but we rescued 55 people from a shipwrecked mail boat. If we had been a half hour later, we would have never gotten to them. The ship had cracked in two and was slowly sinking. The crew had abandoned ship and loaded into lifeboats at 6:45 PM. One half the ship sank at 7:00 PM and the other at 7:15. I was one of ten volunteers to help pull them out of the lifeboat by rope. We are now taking the survivors to Kodiak."

I looked up the Aleutians on the atlas.

The next letter read,

"We've been seven days at sea now, and I can't say I'm growing fond of the trip. Right now, the deck is very rough to stay on so they keep us off. The sea has gotten pretty rough the last three hours, which makes it rather hard to digest supper. If you want to know what we do with our time, we spend most of it standing in the chow line. After breakfast, we get into the one for dinner; after dinner we form the supper line. After supper, we get a rest from standing. This is not too much of an exaggeration either. With 1,000 troops and only one mess hall, it isn't easy."

A month later, I opened a letter on a day Mom worked late at the grain elevator.

"We are based only twenty-five miles from the DMZ. About all you can say about Korea is that it's backward and almost hardly civilized. I am enclosing an article out of the Stars & Stripes that best describes it. The people are still very poor. Everywhere we go, the Koreans stand around and watch us eat with hungry expressions on their faces. They are still recovering from the Korean War. There are those who do very well and make their money off the Army. To be plain about

the whole thing, most of the young girls between the ages of 15 & 30 are prostitutes. That is how they make their money off of the Army. They will come out to you in the field while you are sleeping or be in your sleeping bag when you get back from a field exercise. Then there are the thieves who will steal you blind. For this reason, all villages and towns are off limits except for Seoul. From what I have seen so far, I would say that 80% of the Korean people outside of Seoul still live in straw huts."

Mom chided me about opening the mail. Upon reading the letter, she expected my question about prostitutes and why a person could do such a thing. After an earlier letter, she explained to me why the Army still sent troops to South Korea, something about keeping the Chinese Communists in check. I learned about the Demilitarized Zone.

In a letter from his basic training base in California, and before he shipped out to Korea, he wrote this after reading Mom's news about Dutch,

"It sounds like life in Adam's Creek just got more interesting. There are several Negroes in my training company. They seem nice enough, but I would not say we were friends. President Truman integrated the Army back in the late '40s. There were also a few in my high school graduating class. I suspect that Dutch will need friends like you, Kyle and Kurt, so keep a watchful eye. Adams Creek folks are pretty set in their ways."

Despite the wicked winter, spring came early in 1959, producing blossoms, flower spurts, and the promise of bountiful gardens, fruits, and crops. With its onset came the drudgery of churning the soil and uncovering freshly grown rocks. April sprouted mushroom season. In Indiana, mushrooms meant morels, harder to find than a needle in a haystack, like striking gold. Time and again, Mom sent me out only to return empty-handed. I began to think myself cursed. They hid when they saw me coming. I fared better with nightcrawlers.

If one never lived through the four seasons in the northern climes, explaining the birth of spring is difficult; the easing of the chill, shedding of coats and sweaters, chirping birds, the thawing of the garden and flower patches, its soil ready for plowing and tilling, the lure of the outdoors, crop seeding, and for baseball fanatics, the crack of the bat. The crack of the bat meant another losing season for the Cubs. Folks hunkered down and battened down the hatches for winter. In the spring, much like the flowers, they blossomed with fresh personalities.

Later in the spring, while Kyle and I attended school, a car clipped Dutch on his way to Carroll's. Dutch did not turn as the car approached. The impact tossed him into the ditch, badly bruising his right leg and hip, but no broken bones. Knocked head first into the ditch, Dutch did not get a look at the car as it sped off. He heard a male voice shout "nigger." Dutch limped to our door. Since Mom had the day off, Kyle drove the car to school. Mom called James. Mom joined the trip to the Twin Rivers Memorial Hospital emergency room. The doctor felt no fractures, so he didn't order expensive x-rays. He prescribed some pain pills and sent Dutch on his way. James paid the fees.

Sheriff Sellers stopped by after supper. He wanted to ask about the neighborhood, much like he probed me down the riverbank last summer. Neither Mom nor I could offer any clues.

"When I walk with Dutch up and back from Carroll's, cars pass all the time, slowing and staring. No one said anything. This has to be someone from outside who drives through now and then, yet knows about Dutch. The only teenage driver in the area is Kyle. Cindy McBrady still rides around on Calico."

Mom recalled, "Dutch worried some about the article in the Review, but he had said he hadn't noticed anything different. I agree with Kurt, I don't think anyone in our neighborhood would take the risk of Dutch recognizing the car or the person. I've never heard such talk at church, but that could be because they know Dutch helps out now and then and comes to supper. I always tell Kurt to listen for cars approaching from behind, our roads being so narrow. Maybe Dutch lost some of his hearing. Dutch later told us James called the paper about his ice skating."

The sheriff confirmed Dutch's hearing loss, "He said as much when I talked with him. I suspect the car slowed some to make sure he could hit Dutch, wanting to scare him but not kill him. That's probably why no bones broke; he's lucky for that as old as he is. I made another pitch for him to move into Twin Rivers. He said no, of course."

Dutch came to supper two weeks later, limping and walking with a cane he whittled from a small limb.

"Dutch, we would miss you, but shouldn't you seriously consider moving into Twin Rivers? Your safety matters more to us."

"What makes you think it would be any safer in town? I like James and his family, but I've grown rather partial to you, Kyle, and Kurt. Nope, I'm staying."

Mom said, "Dutch, you are more stubborn than a Missouri mule."

For the first time, I thought about Dutch being killed here in Adams Creek. I could not imagine what he might do to deserve such a fate. Dutch was one of the nicest persons I'd ever met and certainly the most interesting. I hated snakes, blackbirds, rhubarb, and gooseberry pie and such. Hating another person, I could not imagine. Dutch was not a Negro. Dutch was a person and a friend.

Eighteen

One of the uglier incidents in Indiana history, if not the ugliest, scarred Mason City in 1930. A mob numbering in the thousands stormed the county jail and lynched two young Negroes. The two young men, accused of rape and murder, looked to be guilty of those crimes. They came upon a parked couple sparking just outside Mason City. They robbed and shot the man. He died the next day. A third Negro, Lucas Mayfield,* only sixteen, ran off before the shooting. The police came for him in the middle of the night and jailed him too. Word spread rapidly of a white woman raped and a white man killed, its message spread by radio and phone. The rape rumor incited the listeners more than the shooting. The message exhorted folks to converge on Mason City. People drove in or traveled by train from around northern Indiana to join the mob.

Estimates of crowd size varied from as high as fifteen thousand to the reported five thousand by the Twin Rivers Review. Thirty thousand called Mason City, home, nearly two thousand of them Negroes. The actual lynchers totaled a much smaller number. Many in the mob goaded the lynchers and cursed the Negroes, while others remained passive or curious.

The write-up in the Review read in part,

"The crowd gave the rioters its moral support, partly by cheers, mostly by passive inaction, which the sheriff and deputies feared to shoot. The mob attacked the jail at three points, the main door, through the garage, and from the roof.

"The sheriff and deputies fought the rioters at the main entrance, cracking heads with clubs, and hurling half a dozen tear gas bombs, but rifles and riot guns remained on the racks untouched. They were swept aside.

"The mob brought out the two Negroes. They hanged one at the end of a rope fastened to bars of a window on the second floor of the jail. They cut his body down and took it to the courthouse yard, where they hanged the second youth.

"The man who knotted the ropes around the Negroes' necks later walked into a restaurant with his wife and spent half an hour eating." **

After hanging the two Negroes, the mob returned for Mayfield. Already beaten by the police, the lynchers placed a noose around his neck where the two others already hung. A mysterious female voice in the crowd rang out claiming Lucas's innocence of any raping or killing. This calmed the frenzied crowd. They returned Lucas to the jail.

The sheriff sneaked Mayfield out of town to another jail for the night. He never filed charges against any of the lynchers. A judge sentenced Lucas to two to twenty-one years as an accessory before the fact. At his trial, the accusing woman admitted never being raped. Mayfield served four years in the Indiana State Reformatory before being paroled.

The Ku Klux Klan gained a foothold, plus political power in Indiana following World War I. Considered the most influential state Klan organization in the nation, if not the largest, membership rose rapidly to 250,000, which was nearly thirty percent of Indiana's white males. In Kendall, they held a rally with over 10,000 in attendance. Driven by nativism, the Indiana Klan's mission focused more on anti-

Catholicism, and to lesser degrees, anti-Jewish, anti-Negro, and anti-immigrant. They controlled many county and city governments like Indianapolis where they successfully lobbied for the construction of a Negro-only high school, called Crispus Attucks. Convicted of rape and murder in 1925, the Indiana Grand Dragon, once he realized he would not be pardoned, gave the press his rolodex file of Klan members in positions of power, then totaling over half the state General Assembly, the governor, and the mayor of Indianapolis. Following the Grand Dragon's conviction, and the outing of the governor for taking bribes, known membership dropped dramatically and closed the 1920's at around 4,000.

The Klan's involvement in Mason City remained in question since its known membership had plummeted so fast in the late 1920s. The key word "known." Clearly former "known" Klan members joined the mob in Mason City. How many actively participated in the lynchings will never be known. The legal system saw to that.

Newspaper stories in the lynching aftermath quoted authorities vowing to identify and charge the mob leaders. A grand jury convened weeks later. Despite many eyewitnesses, photographs, and newspaper reports, the lynchers got off scot-free.

A photo of the two young men hanging from the courthouse tree became an icon in the history of race relations in the United States. It inspired a poem titled "Bitter Fruit," later renamed "Strange Fruit" when set to music. Billie Holiday recorded and popularized it in the late 1930s. "Strange Fruit" served as a rallying anthem in the early days of the civil rights movement.

"Southern trees bear strange fruit
Blood on the leaves and blood at the root
Black bodies swinging in the southern breeze
Strange fruit hanging from the poplar trees."

Lucas Mayfield believed the voice of an angel saved him. He fathered five children and became a civil rights activist and a devout Christian. He taught people to forgive but not forget. Settling in Addison, near Indianapolis, he founded three NAACP chapters in Indiana and served as Indiana State Director of Civil Liberties for most of the 1950s where he investigated civil rights violations. After threats against him and his family, including a burning cross on his front yard, he left Indiana, moving to Wisconsin. Years later, after a visit to Israel, he founded the Black Holocaust Museum in Milwaukee.

* In real life, Lucas Mayfield is James Cameron. He published his story in the 1980s titled, *A Time of Terror – A Survivor's Story*. See Notes and Acknowledgements.
** This quotation is based on an actual front-page story in the Logansport Pharos-Tribune, published the day after the lynchings.

Nineteen

Arriving home the last school day in June of 1959, I celebrated no more nightly homework over the next two months. Mom mentioned Dutch stopped by to seine. Mom invited him to dinner the following Wednesday. Dutch appreciated the invite but said he expected a visitor, not James. Mom invited him, too. Dutch sure seemed popular for someone wanting to be left alone.

The day of the invite, I noticed a different car parked next to the bridge. Chores kept me from heading down the riverbank.

When Dutch arrived, he introduced Lucas Mayfield. Lucas looked to be closer to Mom's age. Sitting down to eat, Dutch began bragging on Mom's cooking. Mom blushed. Then began the supper of all suppers to remember.

"Emma, you remember the first night I came over for supper last summer?"

"Yes, you brought a mess of catfish and told us about your union."

"Remember when you said you didn't realize James and I were such bigshots? I told you about while serving in my position on the union's governing board I ran into a lot more important folks than James and me, especially at our annual conventions. Lucas here is one of them. Lucas started three NAACP chapters in Indiana, and he heads up the office of Indiana's Civil Liberties. Lucas came to our conventions and Pullman Porter union officials attended the NAACP national conventions. We became friends. He lives down near Naptown in Addison."

"Naptown?"

"Sorry, Indianapolis."

"Actually, I looked up to Dutch and what the Brotherhood accomplished after the long fight with the Pullman Company. How those porters managed to stay connected and united for twelve years is quite an accomplishment. I don't feel anything I have done can top that."

Dutch gave Lucas a look.

"Lucas, do you have a family?"

"Yes, ma'am."

"Please, I'm Emma."

"Thank you, Emma. My wife and I are blessed with five god-fearing children."

I knew what he meant about the god-fearing part. Maybe Lucas was a Southern Baptist. "Are you a Southern Baptist?"

"No son, I'm not. That is a white folks church. My family attends an all-Negro church. We have a lot in common with the Baptists. We believe in baptism by immersion."

"You mean dunking?"

Lucas smiled, "I guess so."

"When we're finished with supper, I'd like Lucas to tell you a story. You okay to talk about it, Lucas? I think these folks need to know. The boys don't have homework."

"Sure, I'm okay. It's been nearly thirty years, so I speak to it more easily now."

After a supper of small talk, Mom suggested saving dessert for later. Dutch and Lucas had piqued our curiosity.

Dutch began. "Emma, you might recall an incident in 1930 over in Mason City."

"You mean the lynching?" Mom glanced at me. "Yes, it was terrible. I had just turned twenty. My Dad read about it in the Chicago paper and remarked on it. He was horrified."

"It has been so long you can't have remembered the names of any of those involved. The mob lynched two Negroes. They brought out a third, a teenager, barely sixteen. Before they strung him up, a voice spoke up telling the lynchers he had nothing to do with any killing or raping. They returned him to his cell. Lucas was that teenager."

Our jaws dropped, gaping at Lucas. Western movies at the State Theatre in town portrayed the only inkling I had of hangings, so-called frontier justice. I did not know the difference, but lynching seemed an uglier word. Frontiers no longer existed, certainly not in Indiana in 1930.

Now I understood why Dutch gave Lucas a look.

"I was younger than Kyle. My family was poor, living in an old converted barn, just me, Mom, and two sisters. My step-dad and I were not close. He was rarely around. I hoped to enter high school in the fall. I had never gotten into any kind of trouble, but I hung out with some troublemakers from time to time, and in Mason City, there was little room for foolishness from Negro boys. It was our plight, make one mistake, go to jail, life over. Mom, a saint, washed and ironed clothes, cooked, scrubbed floors and other chores for white families. She held our family together.

"That day a bunch of us were just hanging out until after dark, but there was a full moon. Two fellows, Jimmy Ship and Tommy Smith asked me to tag along with them. Tommy had mischief on his mind and wanted to hold up somebody. I was sitting between them in the front seat. We drove out to a road just outside of town known for couples' sparking. To this day, I don't know why I didn't get out of there right then, but I felt kind of trapped sitting between them. We came upon a parked car. Tommy handed me the gun. I walked up to the car, opened the door and said, 'Stick 'em up.' I don't know why I did that, just young and dumb or wanting to be accepted by the older fellas. The couple got out. I recognized the man. I had shined his shoes lots of times. When I saw that he recognized me, it was like a bucket of ice water. I forced the gun back into Tommy's hands and lit out from there as fast as I could. After running several blocks, I heard shots. When I got home' Mom knew something wasn't right, my shirt dripped in sweat. I told her I had been playing football in a nearby vacant lot. Moms know. She knew I was lying."

Mom nodded knowingly.

"Several hours later, the police banged on the door, and took me to jail. The man died the next day and the word in the jailhouse was that the woman was raped. I knew Jimmy and Tommy would tell the police I held the gun. Remember, I was only sixteen."

I glanced at Mom and Kurt. The air had been sucked out of the room.

"I learned the police had charged me with just about everything in the entire penal code: first degree murder, assault, robbery, and rape. They put me in the all-Negro jail wing on the second floor of the jailhouse.

"Later they took me to a separate room. The sheriff and a bunch of policemen came in. I told the sheriff everything I knew. He didn't believe me. Someone hit me and knocked me out of my chair. Several police began kicking and beating on me. I nearly lost consciousness, tasting blood and feeling loose teeth. Finally, the sheriff stopped it. He handed me a paper to sign. He wouldn't let me read it. I signed it. That was a mistake, but I couldn't take any more beating.

"The next day began peacefully enough though I ached all over. I looked out over a street below and folks seemed to go about their business.

"After breakfast, we noticed a crowd growing outside. A fellow prisoner told me that I should be okay since mobs only take the law into their own hands down in the South. But then another man said that the headquarters for the Indiana Ku Klux Klan was only an hour away. That didn't set well.

"After lunch I got word that I had a visitor. Expecting my Mom, I rushed through the door. It wasn't my Mom but a white man wearing a bandana, like you'd see a bank robber wear. He asked me a bunch of questions, like my name, and left.

"Word got back to us that the Klan was planning a lynching and folks were coming in from all over northern Indiana.

"Now I was really scared, almost in a daze. I got down on my knees and prayed hard.

"Rocks began breaking the second-floor windows with glass flying everywhere. I looked out a window and saw a mob for as far as I could see. I heard voices call out, 'Turn those niggers over to us. Give us those black animals.' I actually recognized several neighbors and folks whose shoes I had shined. There were women and children everywhere. I kept thinking the policemen would soon break up the crowd and send them home. Finally, the sheriff did go out and tell the mob to go home.

"A big man showed up with a sledgehammer and began banging on the jail door. No one stopped him. Several fire trucks arrived to try to hose the mob down, but they were soon overcome by the crowd. After nearly an hour of pounding, the door gave way. The mob poured in, and the police stood by. The mob stayed on the first floor. I was on the second. They shouted out for Jimmy and Tommy, but no one gave them up. They already knew who they were, just like the man in the bandana who questioned me earlier. Soon, they had Jimmy. First, they beat him, and then they dragged him outside, putting a rope around his neck. The mob threw sticks and stones at him. They hung him from the window bars on the second floor. He hung there for about thirty minutes, the crowd cheering. Then they began chanting for Tommy Smith. The mob leaders came back inside and went to the wing where Tommy was. Again, the police stood by doing nothing. Tommy tried hiding under a bunk, but they dragged him out into the street, beating on him. One person rammed a crowbar into his chest several times. He must have been dead before they hung him from a tree in the courthouse square. Then, they took Jimmy down and hung him in the same tree. The cheering seemed to never stop.

"After about fifteen minutes of celebration the mob leaders headed back to the jail.

"I heard them coming up the stairs. They had ropes, clubs, knives, shotguns and rifles. One had a submachine gun. The man carrying the machine gun entered my cell. Several other men wearing Ku Klux Klan hoods came in, as did the sheriff. Another boy and I lied about who we were, and the sheriff supported their story telling the mob leaders I wasn't there. They paced around for a bit and then went back downstairs and outside. One leader said that Mayfield wasn't in there. No one believed him and the crowd began chanting, 'Mayfield. Mayfield. Mayfleld.' I thought my heart had stopped beating.

"The leaders huddled together and then returned back to the jail. The crowd cheered. They returned to my cell and asked all of the Negroes to line up. 'We know Lucas Mayfield is in here, now where is he?' An old Negro said, 'He ain't here.'

"Outside the chant continued.

"One mob leader slugged a prisoner. They threatened to hang every Negro prisoner unless they pointed me out. Finally, one of the Negroes turned toward me and pointed. They grabbed me and pulled me down the stairs and outside, shouting 'We got Mayfield.' The crowd pushed close for a chance to hit me, even little boys and girls. The chant, 'Nigger, Nigger, Nigger' rang out.

"Many of the police cleared a path through the massive crowd so they could drag me to the tree. Somebody yelled, 'Get the rope.' I cried out, 'I didn't rape no one.' I mumbled another prayer asking for the Lord's mercy.

"They tossed the rope over the limb and draped the noose around my neck. Then, the voice of an angel could be heard over the din, 'Put this boy back in jail, he did not rape or kill anyone.'

"The mob became silent. Then, the hands that had committed murder and beaten me gently and slowly lifted the noose from my neck. The mob began to slowly pull back. A path back to the courthouse cleared, and I began limping back. I looked at the faces, their gazes dropping to avoid my eyes.

"No one ever admitted hearing that voice or knew who said it. That's why I believe it was the voice of an angel.

"The sheriff met me at the courthouse steps saying they were going to get me out of there. I spent the night in a neighboring town's courthouse, returning in the morning. I saw the boys still hanging in the tree. I nearly vomited. The next day, I was driven down to the state reformatory in Plainfield. I finally felt safer."

Lucas then paused, and took a deep breath. Dutch patted him on the shoulder, saying he had heard this before when they both were attending a convention. "It doesn't go down any easier."

Tears flowed from Mom's eyes. Her glance toward me seemed worrisome. Kyle and I sat stunned, speechless.

Lucas began his story before dessert. Dessert now seemed like a good idea.

"Let's have some peach pie. Then, I want to hear what happened next. Please lord, let it get better from here."

"It does Emma. I'll jump around a bit between the time of the lynchings and my trial."

"Who wants ice cream?" Mom rarely bought ice cream. After the treat, we cleared the table except for Lucas's dish. Lucas began again.

"My mom visited several times. But to be sure, even though I was still sixteen and scared, nothing happened in prison that even comes close to that night of hell in Mason City.

"A few weeks after my time at Plainfield, they transferred me to a county jail in Addison. There, I met an interesting sheriff named Bernard Knight. Rumors filled much of my mind. One had the Klan planning a break-in to lynch me like they did the others. I went to Sheriff Knight pleading for my safety. He assured me 'Every prisoner of mine will have their day in court as long as I am sheriff.'

"In a later meeting he actually befriended me saying 'I've been thinking about you lately. I want you to treat me like a father, and I'll treat you like a son.'

"I did not know what to make of this. He made me what they called a turnkey trustee. He let me go to the store for the rest of the prisoners whenever they wanted candy, tobacco or cigarettes, this even though the State of Indiana had thrown the book at me. Maybe he had become convinced I was innocent.

"For his kindness towards me, the sheriff often got called 'nigger lover.'

"Sheriff Knight was not like most white folk and certainly not like other sheriffs, especially the one in Mason City. Each day he spent at the jail, he could be heard all over the jailhouse singing his favorite church song, 'The Old Rugged Cross.'"

Lucas broke into song, knowing the lyrics by heart.

"On a hill far away stood an old rugged Cross,
The emblem of suffering and shame;
And I love that old Cross where the dearest and best
For a world of lost sinners was slain.
So I'll cherish the old rugged Cross,
Till my trophies at last I lay down;
I will cling to the old rugged Cross,
And exchange it some day for a crown."

We sang this often in church. Mom joined in halfway through.

"It took nearly a year after the hangings for my trial. Remember they initially charged me with auto theft, rape, and murder. My Negro defense attorneys successfully filed for postponements. Each time the trial was put back, they dropped one of the charges. The remaining charge, accessory before the fact to first-degree murder, still carried the possibility of life imprisonment or the chair in Indiana.

"The trial brought back a lot of that fear, being on trial for my life, or at least I figured I was. My mom sat at the defense table with me.

"After the opening statements, the prosecution produced witnesses I had never seen before. One of the arresting officers claimed Tommy Smith told him I was the ringleader. Now remember, they both were older. The officer claimed we were going to terrorize the whole State of Indiana with robberies, murders, and rapes. Under cross-examination, the officer called the lynching's poetic justice.

"The sheriff and several officers testified, all denying I had been beaten and denying they had strung my bloody white shirt up the police station's flagpole. Then my attorneys produced a picture that showed it.

"Mr. and Mrs. Deeter testified, parents of the man Jimmy and Tommy killed. I felt badly for them.

"The most important witness, the woman they claimed we raped her, took the stand. She identified Tommy and Jimmy as the two who shot her boyfriend. She did not identify me. Most importantly, she testified she was not raped and there was never any attempt to rape her.

"After her testimony the judge got really upset at the prosecution for introducing my signed confession. The judge threw it out. My attorneys asked for a mistrial. The judge said no.

"I took the witness stand for four hours telling my story for the first time without being scared out of my mind. After me, there were some character witnesses including my mom and the pastor of our church in Mason City.

"The prosecution's summary to the jury sounded nothing like the testimony now on record. They went on for two hours. But I guess pretty much anything can be said in summation arguments at the end of a case. One of them even broke down in tears claiming he had never seen a crime so shocking, and I did it, ignoring the testimony of the woman. I wanted to scream at them.

"The trial lasted five days, a lifetime.

"Nearly three hours after adjourning to haggle over the case, the jury reached a verdict. They found me guilty of the final charge, accessory before the fact.

"The judge asked me if I had anything to say. 'No' I said. He then sentenced me to no less than two but not more than twenty-one years. My attorneys thought it would only be two years. They were thrilled. My attorneys asked for time served. The judge said no.

"After eighteen months, my attorneys petitioned the governor for parole. He turned it down. After two years, I appeared before a parole board. Then it took over two years to be paroled. But it took a new governor and a new parole board. I later learned that one member of the old board was a newspaper editor in Mason City–and a known Klan member. The new board granted me a five-year parole, meaning I could not slip up during those five years or I'd have to serve the rest of my sentence. I resolved right then that they would never see me again."

Lucas took a deep breath and looked down at his melted ice cream.

Mom dabbed her eyes, "So there you were at twenty years old and been through hell on earth the previous four years."

"That sounds about right. I don't have nightmares anymore, but I do worry that some racist wants to kill the third nigger from those days thinking they were doing justice."

"Dutch and I have talked about how you folks will still use that ugly term amongst yourselves, so I understand you using it. Kyle and Kurt know better, least I hope so. Will you make it up this way again?"

"Could be. I may drive up to see Dutch and James one more time before we move. I missed James this time. He is in Chicago visiting his daughters and grandchildren."

"You're moving?"

"Not right away, but yes, ma'am."

"What for?"

"I've had this job some ten years now. I investigate civil rights violations. As you might guess, that rubs white folks the wrong way. I'm tiring of the threats to my family and me. Last year, they fired up a cross in my front yard. I may move to Canada. I hear it's better up there."

"I can't even imagine."

"You know Mason City is known for something else besides the lynchings. I tried hard to forget about that place, but when actor James Dean died recently, I read he was born in Mason City one year after the lynchings. Ain't that something?"

As everyone got up to leave, I slipped out to the front porch to take a leak. Lucas joined me. He chuckled, saying Dutch told him about our outhouse.

"I've lived through some pretty tough times, but I've always had indoor plumbing."

I told him how much I appreciated using the restrooms at school.

"I have no idea what I want to be when I grow up. Right now, I like playing football and reading. But those lawyers who took your side, that seemed like a mighty fine job to have one day."

"I don't know whether I would have served more time or not, but I will always be indebted to them."

Through the open kitchen window, we overheard Mom talking with Dutch.

"Before I say this, I want you to know how important you have become to Kurt, especially since he lost his dad. He really looks up to you, and you are teaching him so much. I am grateful. But you, James, and now Lucas, are filling his head with some pretty frightening images and things he cannot understand. It frets me some."

"Emma, I hear you, but Kurt's a bright boy. You're doing a fine job raising him without your husband. He asks good questions. He is like a sponge. Plus, he has you to explain if I'm not around. I suspect he and Kyle now know more Negro history than anyone in Twin Rivers, even some Negroes."

"Just be mindful."

"I will."

I looked at Lucas, who said, "That mob spit some pretty nasty words at me. I tried leaving them out of my story. I'm at peace with the Lord now, so I find it hard to use those words anymore."

"I've probably already heard them."

"Not these, son."

"I promised Mom that as long as I was living at home, she wouldn't have to wash my mouth out with soap."

"You know, I threatened my children with the same punishment."

"What you told us tonight, I don't remember breathing. I felt scared right along with you. I hope you don't mind me saying this, but after tonight and what I've heard from Dutch and James about the porters, I couldn't help thinking about how lucky I am to have been born white."

"I don't mind at all. You're being honest. There have been times, not just in Mason City, I have wished I had been born white."

"Every *Readers Digest* issue has a section called 'My Most Unforgettable Character.' I'm only eleven, but I doubt I will ever meet another like you."

"I read the *Reader's Digest* every month."

Dutch walked out, and off they drove. I felt privileged to know them.

Back inside, Mom asked how I felt about what I heard during supper. She did not know I had overheard Dutch and her talking.

"Mom, I don't know how to answer. Since I've met Dutch, I've heard things I would never hear now or later in my life. I feel like I am in a one-of-a-kind history class. I like that. Lucas told me outside, he held back the worst words he heard in Mason City, if it makes you feel any better. As long as I live, I don't think I could ever understand the hatred that could cause a lynching. How can folks hate like that? I feel safe around Dutch, and James, and, of course, you and Kyle. I have you to explain stuff I don't understand. I'm okay. What I can't understand is Lucas saying lots of children joined the mob and said hateful things, even trying to hurt him. Explain that to me."

"Kurt, I can't. Like I've said, kids watch and mimic their parents. If you saw me treat Dutch like you heard that lady said a few years ago or if I told you to stay away, wouldn't you behave differently around him?"

"I guess so."

"The parents are the responsible ones. I am so grateful for having a friend like Esther at a young age and having parents who welcomed her family. It helped make me the way I am, and now I hope I am guiding you the way you are and will be the rest of your life. Kurt, you will run into bad folks, wherever you go, white or Negro. But at least now I hope you will keep an open mind and not judge anyone by their color until you know more about who they are and what's in their heart."

Twenty

In late June, a new family moved into the house directly across the river. Mom said she noticed a boy about my age. No one near my age lived within bicycle range.

June in northern Indiana meant strawberry season. I picked them toting a six-quart crate. Dad crafted the crates several years earlier. My transistor radio occupied one of the quarts. Chicago's WGN signal reached into northern Indiana during the daytime unless a thunderstorm blew through causing static. Jack Quinlan called the play-by-play, and Lou Boudreau provided the commentary. The Cubs occupied last place, again; two men on with two men out, Ernie Banks at bat. Pausing to wipe the sweat off I spotted him walking up our driveway. He looked about my size.

"Hi."

"Hi, what are you doing?"

"What's it look like I'm doing?" My mood fouled by another bad Cubs' game.

"Want some help?"

"Suit yourself. What's your name?"

"Jim, Jim Jenkins. Everyone calls me Jimmy. What's yours?"

"Kurt, Kurt Baumann. Where you from?"

"Fort Wayne, maybe a couple of hours from here."

"I know; I was born there. Aw, gosh darn it!"

"What happened?"

"Banks struck out."

"Banks is a Cub, isn't he? You a Cubs fan?"

"Yup, don't know why, they always come in last. He's a Negro you know."

"Didn't know that."

"I like football and basketball more, but there's nothing else on in the summer."

"In Fort Wayne, we listened to the Tigers' broadcast out of Detroit. I like basketball best. You watch the Cubs on television?"

"Don't have one."

"You don't have a television?"

Dad often talked about getting one. On Saturday trips to town, we stopped at Sears to look at TVs. "Have you watched the Rose Parade?"

"Of course, everybody does."

"Me too, but we go to town. Mom and Dad pretend interest in buying a TV. Meanwhile, Kyle and I watched the Rose Parade for an hour. Maybe I can come over and watch TV sometime?"

"I guess so, but I need to ask Mom and Dad."

"Why did you move out here?"

"Dad and Mom quit their teaching jobs in Fort Wayne and found jobs here. He and Mom wanted to live in the country. Fort Wayne's real big. Both of them grew up in the country and missed it."

"So you're a city slicker?"

"Maybe, but now I must be a hick like you."

I let the 'hick' comment pass since I called him a city slicker.

"What grade you in next year?"

"Sixth."

"Me too. We can do stuff together. No one close to our age around here except a girl, and she's a freshman next year."

"What's to do around here?"

"After my chores, I spend time at the river with my friend, Dutch, skip stones, shoot hoops, hunt birds with my BB gun or sling-shot, float the river, and kill snakes."

"Snakes?"

"We have water snakes, and there's water everywhere. They like to sunbathe on the rocks by the culvert over there. There are garden snakes; we call them garters. They sliver around in the grass next to the garden and creek. Water snakes and garter snakes aren't poisonous, but I kill them anyway. They freak me out. Watch where you walk and don't go barefoot unless wading in the creek."

"Who's Dutch?"

"He's a Negro and a retired Pullman Porter. When you meet him, I'll let him tell you about that. He moved in over a year ago and fishes down the riverbank south of Ole Steely." The way Jimmy reacted to my telling him about Dutch being a Negro, Dutch could have been purple, and it wouldn't have mattered.

"Ole Steely?"

"The bridge."

"Why did you name the bridge?"

"I guess because we've gotten pretty attached to it, sort of like how we name most of our cows and steers."

"What's floating the river?"

"We inflate an inner-tube like the ones used with tractor tires, walk up to the bend in the river past the end of the paved road, and float down to the bridge. Since my dad died a while back, we don't use the tractor as much, but we keep the old tubes patched up. Maybe Kyle will patch up one for you and you can float with us the next time. You know how to shoot marbles?"

"No"

"I'll teach you. We don't play for money. You got a sled?"

"Not yet."

"Way more fun than floating. We go sledding in those hills south of you on the other side of the river. You been to the carousel yet?"

"No."

"Twin Rivers has this really neat merry-go-round in the park by the Eel River. The goal is to win a free ride by grabbing the brass ring each time it comes around. I've snared my share, but I jam my finger a lot.

"Then sometimes Kyle and I get our kicks messing with folks."

"Messing with folks?"

"There's an old coot behind your house with a watermelon patch. We sneak in at night and filch a watermelon. We put manure in mailboxes, especially around Halloween, and especially the homes with the long lanes so they can't see us. Up the river, couples park and make-out. We sneak up and scare them. Sometimes a fellow gives chase, but we know the paths too well. We stretch a string across Ole Steely and hide on the railings under it. Once a car stopped and tried to find us. Stuff like that." I had Jimmy's attention.

"Ever been caught stealing the watermelon?"

"Nope. Mom doesn't know, least I hope not. Okay change that, of course she doesn't know. If she did, there would be hell to pay. Kyle calls stealing watermelon, filching, since watermelons aren't worth much. What's a few missing watermelons? Old man Moss can't see beyond his snout, but he's got the ears of an elephant. Each night at dusk he rocks on his front porch. The melon patch sits around back. We never eat them but take them up to Ole Steely and smash them on the rocks below just to watch the splatter. We give each one a splatter score. Besides, old man Moss can get kinda nasty. Kyle says it takes forever collecting his newspaper subscription, haggling all the time."

I told Jimmy about the 4-H Club and the county fair. "This year I entered the Forestry and Entomology competitions." Coming from a city, Jimmy knew little of the 4-H Clubs, and especially Entomology. I made it sound like a big deal, but truthfully, I could barely pronounce it.

Kyle and I attended monthly 4-H Club meetings, though as Kyle aged, he less so. The 4-H's stand for head, heart, hands, and health. Membership did not include dunking or uniforms, like in the Boy Scouts, so it suited me fine. At each year's Clay County Fair, Kyle and I competed in projects like gardening, woodworking, forestry, and entomology. We always took home blue ribbons. 4-H Club members might later join the Future Farmers of America, another step on the path to becoming a farmer. In the 1950s, farms passed on generationally. Few sons entered college. Those who did studied agriculture, majoring in, among other emphases, animal husbandry. What the heck is that? I once asked Mom to explain it. She knew what it meant she just couldn't explain why they called it that. I had zero interest in farming. I detested overalls, the farmers' uniform. They were Dad's favorite work clothes. Overalls had lots of pockets. Dad stuffed them with all manner of things so he wouldn't have to keep dashing to his workbench. Ken, Kyle, and I never wore them. I often went shirtless in the summer, anything to avoid the "farmers' tan."

Jimmy helped with my chores the next several days while Kyle vacationed at church camp. During strawberry season, we sold quarts roadside. Mom let me keep the money to buy clothes, a new transistor, and batteries. Jimmy wondered how else I made money, so I told him about catching worms for Dutch. He didn't think two quarters amounted to much. City slicker.

I never talked him into competing in the cow pie toss. "I don't care if it's dry and hard, it's still picking up cow manure." City slicker.

Jimmy sometimes joined my visits with Dutch. Jimmy took to him like old friends although he thought the uniform odd. Dutch filled him in. Jimmy said several Negroes attended his grade school in Fort Wayne. They ran circles around him on the basketball court. I told Jimmy about meeting Lucas Mayfield. He eyes widened. He knew nothing about the lynchings in Mason City and wanted to meet Lucas if the chance arose.

"Have you told your folks about Dutch?"

"Sure, they're fine. They had Negroes in their classrooms in Fort Wayne."

A small marsh bordered the tip of our property where cattails grew. One night, Jimmy and I carried a bundle to Ole Steely. I wanted to show him a game Kyle taught me. I dipped a cattail in a bucket of gasoline, lit it, and hurled it as far as I could down river. This reminded me of the flaming arrows in westerns. I tried it once with a bow but couldn't make it work. Jimmy and I took turns. I bested him, but he kept getting better. He beat me at arm farts, even louder than Kyle's. I bested him in hand farts, with larger hands. After each contest, we would launch into,

> *"Beans, beans the musical fruit*
> *The more you eat, the more you toot.*
> *The more you toot, the better you feel,*
> *So eat more beans with every meal."*

We became inseparable. He liked helping with my chores. I liked it too. I finished faster. I pestered him about coming over and watching TV shows like *The Rifleman, Gunsmoke, and Dragnet.* Mom admonished, "Mind your manners."

We made up our own rendition to the silly songs:

> *"Splish, splash, I was takin' a bath*

Long about Saturday night, yeah
A rub dub, just relaxin' in the tub
Thinkin' everythin' was alright
Well, I stepped out of the tub
I put my feet on the floor
I wrapped the towel around me and I
Opened the door.
And there I saw
A one-eyed, one-horned, flyin' purple people eater.
One-eyed, one-horned flyin' purple eater.
And it sang,
'Ooh, eeh, ooh, ah, ah, ting, tang, walla, walla, bing, bang
Ooh, eeh ooh ah, ah, ting, tang, walla, walla, bing, bang.'
And so I asked,
'Does your chewing gum lose its flavor
On the bedpost overnight?
If you pull it out like rubber,
Will it snap right back and bite?'"

I never told Jimmy about our Saturday night bath routine. I noticed their indoor plumbing the first time I visited his house.

One day, I challenged Jimmy to a race across Ole Steely. He trounced me, and afterwards called me lardass. I gave him a friendly shove. My fantasy about being the star quarterback for the Twin Rivers Beavers looked less and less likely. My gene reality painted a non-athletic future. We wrestled a bunch, all in fun. Whoever hit the ground first lost. It was pretty even-steven after several bouts.

Clearing rocks sped up with Jimmy's help. One day, an arrowhead surfaced as they did over the years. "Mom says the Eel River Tribe used to live in this part of Indiana. Says they were related to but smaller than the Miami Tribe. She also said an important battle called 'The Battle of Old Town' took place near here." Jimmy knew nothing of the Indian history in northern Indiana.

I told Jimmy as much as I could remember from what Mom passed on a couple of years ago after I uncovered my first arrowhead. "Mom says that Indiana means 'Land of the Indians.' Do you know any Indians?"

"Nope."

"Me neither. So it must mean 'Once upon a time Indians lived here but don't no more.' She says the tribes around here and in northern Indiana, besides the Eel River tribe, and the Miami, were the Potawatomi–try saying that fast five times–and the Shawnee. The Shawnee came from your old neck-of-the-woods, Fort Wayne. Their chief was Tecumseh. He and General Harrison got in a fight west of here near the Tippecanoe River. Tecumseh lost. Years later, the government forced the last of the Potawatomi Indians out west. She said lots of Indians died, mostly children. Says they called it The Trail of Death. The march began a bit north of here and passed through Twin Rivers."

"Why did they force them to do that?"

"Mom says the Indians had signed a treaty and then refused to leave. White folks wanted the Indians' land."

"If they signed a treaty and got money for it, why didn't they leave?"

"Mom says the Indians never took money. They did not use money to live on."

"So then we just took it from them?"

"Seems like that."

"Don't seem right."

"No shit, Sherlock." I looked around to make sure Mom wasn't near.

"Harrison, didn't he become president? I had to memorize the presidents last year in school."

"Same here, but yup, then he died a few weeks later."

Then just to show off, Jimmy said Potawatomi fast five times.

I said, "Okay, try saying whip-poor-will fast five times." Jimmy made it to three, and then stumbled.

I kept an arrowhead collection on my dresser. I let Jimmy keep this one, sealing our friendship.

I told Jimmy reading helped me pass the time, especially western biographies.

"I don't read much, but one of my favorites is, 'Under the Bleachers' by See More Butts."

I countered with, "Not as good as, 'Yellow River' by I Pee Freely. Or, 'Antlers in the Treetop' by Who Goosed the Moose?" I never did find those classics in the Twin Rivers Library.

One evening after supper around dusk I walked across Ole Steely to Jimmy's house. He saw me coming and came to meet me.

"You want to have some fun tonight?"

"It depends. What did you have in mind?"

"Let's take a watermelon from old man Moss's patch."

"You sure he won't catch us?"

"He hasn't yet. I told you he can barely see, but he hears well. About now, he's rocking on his front porch puffing on his pipe. I double-dog dare ya."

We waited until almost dark. The Moss place sat only about fifty yards from Jimmy's place. No fence separated the properties. A small barn bordered Jimmy's place and the Moss place. We waited behind it until the right time. Then we crept onto the Moss property and the watermelon patch. Jimmy stepped on a twig, snapping it. We froze.

"Who's back there? I heard you." He ambled around the side of his house yelling, "Git outta here!"

We got out of there, fast, heading for Ole Steely. Then we heard the shotgun, "BLAM."

Moss did not know where we were, so he probably aimed in the air just to scare us; at least I hoped so.

Jimmy and I arrived back across the river, and at our place, breathless.

Then Jimmy said, "Let's not do that again," laughing.

"He bought a shotgun. He may be half blind, but that's pretty scary. All he has to do is aim in a sound's direction like the twig you stepped on."

After we waited an hour, Jimmy started back home. "See ya later alligator."

"After a while crocodile." I went inside. Mom never said anything, so she must not have heard the blast.

Of all my projects with 4-H, entomology tested me more than any subject in school. The project requisites: catching and mounting thirty different insects on pins, identifying and labeling each one, family, genus and species, and enclosing them in a glass-covered case. I spent hours at the Twin Rivers Library. Each bug must appear as if asleep, fully intact, and wings and legs unbroken, kind of like Grandpa in the casket. I trapped most using a large mason jar without touching them. I placed a small rag soaked in ether and let the specimen lay in the jar until dead. I pierced it with a pin and mounted it in the corrugated display bottom. Dragonflies, followed by butterflies, drove me batty, even faster than bats. I bet they could give those B-47s over at Bunker Hill Air Force Base a run for their money. I spent hours by our swampy area with my net, straining to bag a dragonfly. Jimmy helped by standing at one end of the swamp and waving his arms, sending them back my way. I couldn't ask Jimmy to do more. The 4-H way meant do-it-yourself. I netted fluttering butterflies more easily.

Forestry proved less a test, requiring cutting wood from eight trees indigenous to Indiana, shaping into blocks, sanding them to a glass-like finish, labeling, and explaining the various uses. The rules allowed visiting a local lumberyard to cut smaller pieces of wood I could begin to craft. There was no need to take a chainsaw to a tree.

Jimmy had never been to a county fair. While the midway couldn't compare in size with the Indiana State Fair and its ginormous Ferris wheel, we took it all in, stuffing ourselves with cotton candy, snow cones, and corndogs. Never get on a whirling midway ride after downing two corndogs and cotton candy. My vomit just missed Jimmy. The carnies snookered us into several attempts to win a stuffed animal. "Step right up and win a prize. Everyone wins. Three chances for twenty-five cents." We stunk. Kyle claimed those booths rigged. What would I do with a stuffed animal anyhow? Kyle never admitted it, but we spotted him trying, hoping to win something for his girlfriend. Jimmy liked hanging around all of the animals, a first for him; cattle, pigs, and sheep, all to be judged in ways only judges knew. Exhibitors pinned the awarded ribbons, blue, red, and yellow, to each stall, pen, or cage. Jimmy tried to figure out how one won a blue ribbon versus a second or third prize. I lived on a farm, and I couldn't tell. At the end of the fair, they auctioned off the grand champion cattle and pigs for steaks and pork chops, soon to appear in a local supermarket. I told Jimmy my slaughterhouse story. He cringed.

One afternoon while touring the pig exhibits, Jimmy howled, "Look at the wiener on that hog!" Following his eyes, I said, "That's no wiener. That looks like a fully-grown snake." We both felt embarrassed staring but couldn't help ourselves. Some girls on the other side of the pen giggled. Then a woman saw what they were giggling at and shooed them away. Jimmy wondered if the wiener size earned the hog its blue ribbon.

I shared my story about the veterinarian and the glove and the insemination device. "The whole arm?" Jimmy asked.

"Yup, the whole arm."

"I think there are some things about farm animals I'd just as soon not know about or watch."

City slicker.

I scored a blue ribbon with my forestry entry and grand champion with entomology. The judge congratulated me on my perfect dragonfly. The Review printed my picture the next day along with other grand champion winners. Mom brought Dutch one day to see my exhibits. Kyle told me he walked around with them so that folks wouldn't think it odd to see an elderly Negro with our middle-aged Mom. The next summer, I planned on entering the gardening and forestry competitions.

The week after the fair, I traveled to Lake Tippecanoe for my first week of church camp. Jimmy couldn't join me because his family attended a Methodist Church in Twin Rivers.

The week after camp, I asked Jimmy if he wanted to float the river. Kurt had patched up an extra tire tube. Kyle, now entering his senior year, steered clear of us soon-to-be sixth graders. I suspect Mom volunteered him to drive us up the river. The river flowed slowly that day and nearly clear. Kyle dropped us off at the rope swing. Each summer, someone tied a rope and tire to a large limb overhanging the river, the depth around four feet. Jimmy and I took turns, seeing who could swing out the furthest. Jimmy won. Half an hour later, we floated our way down the river.

"Hey Kurt, what's this light-brown foamy stuff all over the surface?"

"I try not to think about it. Don't drink it."

The rapids next to our house north of Ole Steely barely challenged us. Still, Jimmy overturned twice. I knew the smoother route closer to the shore next to our farm. I figured Jimmy should get a proper baptism and float down the middle and over the rapids.

One week later, we asked Kyle to take us up river again. He grumbled but said okay. Once there, I thought I would ask Kyle for another big favor, not that I had any IOUs due.

"Kyle, are you doing anything the next couple of hours?"

"Nothing. Why?"

"The river's pretty tame today. I'd like to show Jimmy the river all the way to Davis Bridge. Could you meet us there?"

Surprisingly he said yes, probably because of Jimmy. Kyle, like me, fancied sharing our river with folks.

Shortly after Dad died, Kyle floated with me down there, about four miles. Ken, home from college for the weekend, came to pick us up. Folks drove out from town all of the time and put boats into the water at Ole Steely and floated all the way back to Twin Rivers, fishing along the way.

"You lead the way and watch out for protruding branches. Some are just below the surface. If they puncture your tube, you're stuck. There are no outlets I know of between Ole Steely and Davis Bridge. You'll have to walk out."

"Don't tell Mom."

I told Jimmy the plan. "Okay, but my folks can't find out either."

"Dokey okey."

We passed on the rope swing since Kyle would be waiting longer. Coming to the rapids near our house, I told Jimmy to follow me through. He never overturned. We passed under Ole Steely, still sitting defiant after so many years of trees and bergs bashing against it. Once under Ole Steely, we both loudly yelled "Hello," just to hear the echo. We passed Dutch at the fishing hole. He grinned and proudly showed off a nice sized bass. We drifted by the spot where hobos camped now and then, and from there, less familiar waters. We spotted two more fishermen casting from the banks. I had no idea where they entered the riverbank.

162

Several large rocks broke the shallow surface along the way but proved easy to navigate. We interrupted the turtles lollygagging on the rocks. They dove underwater; all in all, a pretty uneventful float. Kyle met us and drove us back home. Mom never had a clue, tending her flower garden. She loses a sense of time tending her flowers.

Jimmy joined my sixth-grade class in the fall. We rode the bus together. Indiana administered lots of small schools, many smaller than Milan, the state champs a few years back. Except for Twin Rivers, the high schools in our county schooled less than a seventy-five students. The parents in our township voted to send their children into Twin Rivers. It meant catching a bus early in the morning, sometimes in the dark, for the nearly hour ride into town, picking up kids scattered all over our township. Charlie Carroll drove the school bus. In the winter, if a threatening snowstorm approached, school officials let the bussed kids leave early, getting us home before the roads closed. Bussed kids loved snowstorms. Years later, I read about the ruckus caused by racial busing in the big cities. I thought, "What's the big deal?"

One October morning, Cindy McBrady plopped down in the seat in front of us and swung her legs up on the seat so no one could sit next to her. She made me feel funny inside.

"Can I ask you something?"

"Sure."

"I see you walking to the store with that Negro, and I know you spend time with him down the river bank. Do you like Negroes?"

"The ones I've met seem fine. Dutch treats me fine and teaches me all sorts of things. I probably know more about the history of Negroes and trains and the Pullman Porters than I will ever learn in school."

"My mom calls him a spook, says to never go near him. I won't tell you what else she calls him."

"Dutch wouldn't hurt a flea." Jimmy nodded in agreement. "Besides, he likes it out here away from too many folks. Likes being alone and left alone."

"Did I once see him go into your house around suppertime?"

"He's been to supper lots. That's when we hear all of his stories of the railroad. He's been all over these here United States."

"My mom thinks you're crazy having a spook in your house."

"He's not a spook. He is a person, and his name is Dutch."

With that she sat upright facing the front of the bus. Jimmy and I snuck a sideways look at each other. I liked Cindy less. Now, nearly two years since Dutch moved in, what trouble had he brought on anyone?

Jimmy and I talked sports all of the time. Mom directed, "Just one sport."I chose football and earned starting quarterback for the flag football team. Jimmy planned on trying out for the basketball squad. I loved Jim Brown, all-everything, even if he didn't play quarterback like Chip Hilton. Our team competed well but still placed third in an eight-school conference. Mom, Kyle, and Dutch made it to one game. I tossed two touchdown passes. We won.

Twenty-one

The first big snowstorm of the season blew though in early November. The freezing temperatures kept the ground blanketed, making the weekend perfect for sledding, no slush. On the Friday bus ride home, I reminded Jimmy about our favorite sledding area, steep with trees to steer around. Kyle named the run "Road to Hell." Jimmy's folks bought him a new sled. Ken passed his on to me. It ran well if I kept the runner blades and handle oiled. We agreed to meet at the hilltop the next morning.

The next day, I struck out for the hill pulling my sled behind me. Jimmy beat me there.

"Kurt, this looks pretty steep."

"Not yellow, are you?"

"I'm not yellow. I've just never done this before."

"As long as you can steer around the trees, you'll be fine. Leave your sled here, and I'll show you the trail." It wasn't a long trail, just steep. The real challenge was navigating around two large trees, a thorny one the widest menace. We half-walked, half-slid to the bottom.

"Think you can handle it? If you feel you're going too fast, drag your feet."

"I'm game."

Back on top, I picked up Jimmy's new sled. Noticing the stiff handle, I twisted it a few times to loosen it. "Your Dad should have oiled this."

"Dad and Mom went someplace before I got up."

"I'll go first. You can watch me on the way down. Road to Hell, here I come." I pushed off lying face down, my head and shoulders extended over the front and hands on the steering handle. Picking up speed approaching the first tree, I curved sharply right then twisted the handle sharply left, clearing the wide thorny tree. Reaching the bottom, I dragged my feet, slowing to a stop. Standing up, I yelled, "Your turn." I could barely see Jimmy through the trees, but I saw him wave.

"Here I come."

I had ear muffins on, but I heard the crunch and loud moan.

The page one story of the Review's Sunday paper read,

"ADAMS CREEK BOY DIES IN SLEDDING ACCIDENT"

"Jimmy Jenkins of Adams Creek died yesterday in a freak sledding accident about a quarter mile south of the Adams Creek Bridge. The coroner listed cause of death as a broken neck and blunt head trauma. Jenkins' sled failed to function properly, and he missed a sharp turn and crashed headlong into a large tree.

"Waiting at the bottom of the hill, Jimmy's friend and neighbor, Kurt Baumann, did not see the crash but heard it. Baumann had successfully navigated the run, named by locals as the 'Road to Hell,' and known to be risky, but was familiar with it having lived in the area for nearly ten years. Jenkins was new to the area as was his brand-new sled.

"Jenkins' parents, both schoolteachers in the Twin Rivers School System, had only moved to Adams Creek from Fort Wayne last summer.

"Both Jenkins and Baumann attended the sixth grade in Twin Rivers.

"Sheriff Sellers called the accident a tragedy and if he had known about the run, would have closed it off saying, 'It's quite a steep decline and requires skillful navigation around two large trees. It's not for novices.'"

"Emma Baumann, Kurt's mother, declined to let this reporter speak with her son, but later, Kurt's older brother Kyle told us he had introduced Kurt to the run two years prior, and he knew it well. If he had known the plans of the two boys, he would have gone with them, and 'maybe this wouldn't have happened.'

"The 'Road to Hell' is now officially closed."

Mom let me talk to the sheriff, saying I had to. Like my grand folks and Dad, they laid Jimmy in an open casket. Not too many attended, Jimmy's family not long in the area. I didn't want to go, but Mom made me. I sat in the back. I couldn't bear to look at Jimmy's face.

Driving home from the viewing, I asked if I could skip the funeral the next day. They canceled class.

"Of course not, Jimmy was your best friend. You have to pay your respects. It's the right thing to do. Why don't you want to go, Kurt?"

Silent for few moments, I said, "They're going to put him in the cold ground and cover him up with dirt and a cold stone like Dad and all my grandparents."

"You remember what they teach you in church about heaven? I am sure that is where Jimmy is."

"Ah Mom, are you saying his body isn't in that casket? It's in heaven? Then why do they put caskets in the ground and have cemeteries?"

"His body is in the casket, but his spirit is with the Lord in heaven. Most folks feel some comfort in visiting a gravesite. When I visit your dad's grave, I feel like I am with him, still talking to him."

That didn't make any sense to me. If a spirit wasn't a body, what was it?

I kept to myself the next few weeks, sitting alone on the bus. The empty seat belonged to Jimmy. Teachers stopped calling on me. When I walked into a classroom, kids stopped talking. I didn't know what felt worse, losing my best friend or feeling guilty about it. I called him yellow. One day I walked back up the hill. They posted a sign forbidding sledding. The Jenkins Family moved back to Fort Wayne. Mom never asked if I wanted to see the pastor.

Twenty-two

In January, I spotted Dutch fishing off Ole Steely, no winter storms or freezes since November. I joined him. After a spell, he said, "Sure sorry about your friend Jimmy. Nice lad. Bet you miss him a lot."

"I only knew him a few months, but we became best friends. Kyle is joining the Navy as soon as he graduates. Now you're the only friend I will have around here." Not that I considered Kyle a friend, but after Dad died, and as he got older, he began treating me more like a younger brother who needed an older brother.

"I appreciate that. I've kind of taken a shine to you myself. I never told you, but I lost my best friend when we still lived in Alabama. He drowned in a river, couldn't swim. That should have been enough for me to learn to swim. But once we moved north, I forgot about it and took a liking to ice skating instead. For some reason, ice doesn't faze me."

"I still feel guilty about calling him yellow."

"You didn't make him do it. Had I learned to swim I could have dived in and saved my friend. We all have our crosses to bear. My pappy once said trials and tribulations build character."

I didn't know what crosses to bear meant, but it sounded like something I didn't want to do.

"You saying this reminds me of Lucus Mayfield's story of the sheriff and 'The Old Rugged Cross.' We sang it in church last Sunday."

"Funny thing about that song. It and 'Onward Christian Soldiers' are two songs the Klan always sings at their cross-burning rallies."

"We sing that one too. Klan members are Christian?"

"They claim so."

"Why would burning a cross be a Christian thing to do?"

"You got me. And why are lynchings a Christian thing to do?"

Hymns comforted me, though I didn't understand lots of the words. Maybe they might make more sense after the preacher dunked me.

"You told us about the Klan a while back. Did they ever come after you or threaten you?"

"Never in any direct way as to notice. The Klan wouldn't have put the manure in my mailbox. That's small potatoes for them. More likely a youngster from outside Adams Creek did that. The thing about the Klan, they stay hidden behind those white head covers like the one Lucas mentioned that time in the jail. At their rallies, they wear a white sheet over most of their body. Sometimes the sheet has a cross on the front. The only people who cover their faces are the Klan and bank robbers. They want their identities hidden."

"At Halloween, Mom puts a brown paper shack over my head and cuts holes for my eyes and mouth. But I only do it to get candy and treats. Folks figure out who I am pretty easily. That's when Kyle and I used to put manure in mailboxes."

It bugged me hearing the Klan thought themselves Christian. I wanted no part of their Christianity or their God.

I hadn't been alone with Dutch since the bus conversation with Cindy McBrady.

"Have you been called a spook?"

Dutch chuckled. "Well, at least it's not as bad as coon, nigger, or nigger George."

"I thought spooks were ghosts and ghosts are white, aren't they?"

"Most of the time. This word began showing up in the late '30s connected to Negroes. It probably relates to spooking someone at night and since our skin is dark, we can spook folks easier. Negroes get spooked just like anyone else. Many think of Negroes as superstitious and therefore are easily spooked."

"Are you superstitious?"

"No, but it's not uncommon among Negroes, especially those who grew up in the Caribbean. They practice voodoo there, also in parts of the south, like down New Orleans way."

"Voodoo?"

"Don't know much about it, kind of a blend of religion and magic."

"Does the voodoo religion dunk when baptizing?"

"Don't think so. Funny story about that spook term, during World War II, the all-Negro Tuskegee Institute down in Alabama trained a corps of Negro pilots called the Tuskegee Airman. The pilots called themselves the Spookwaffe, making fun of the Luftwaffe, the German Air Force. The inside joke was that the Spookwaffe could sneak up on the Germans easier because the pilots were dark. The Spookwaffe shot down a lot of German planes during World War II, but it had nothing to do with their color. They were great pilots."

I never asked Cindy what other names she had for Dutch. I am sure one of them was Nigger.

Back home, I found the Caribbean on our atlas.

Near the end of sixth grade, the school system treated the six graders to a graduation train trip to the Museum of Science and Industry in Chicago. Sitting in a Pullman window seat, the sights of Chicago awed me, stretching as far as the eye could see and beyond, buildings piercing the sky. Masses of people everywhere. The porters busied themselves in other cars. I wished Jimmy could have seen this. I now knew what one of those destinations at the Twin Rivers Bus Depot looked like.

Twenty-three

Kyle did become more of a big brother than a fellow prankster or tormenter. I think Dad's darkness, rearing its ugly head now and then, and his beating on Mom, put Kyle on edge. Kyle took more of Dad's anger, moodiness, and impatience. And little brothers can be annoying. Mom ruled the roost. Her presence kept him in line otherwise he might have cuffed me around like Dad.

When Jimmy died, Kyle left me alone for a couple of weeks. One night just after lights out, he said, "Kurt, sure sorry about your friend Jimmy. I never lost a friend like that. He was a good guy. Must be hard."

"I miss him. Being out here on the farm and so far from town, I have friends at school but only see them at school or play football with them, nothing like Jimmy, living just across the river. I keep thinking I could have done something, and it's my fault."

"No, it's not. But it will take some time. I didn't worry about you going up that hill. I had shown you the run. You knew it. If I had known Jimmy was joining you, I would have come with you. I wouldn't have let him go down with a stiff sled."

"I was so excited to show him our run I didn't think, like wanting him to make that long river float. By the way, I never thanked you for helping us that day, not telling Mom, and picking us up."

"No problem, happy Jimmy got to do that."

"Nite."

"Nite."

Once he began driving, he stayed around less and less, spending time with classmates in town and dating. He kept the paper route but not because he wanted to. He and Mom felt I should be at least twelve to take over. Some customers, like grumpy old man Moss, needed extra attention, especially when collection time arrived. Mom relied on him less with just the chickens, garden, orchard, and berry patch to tend. He carried his weight helping prepare the garden each spring, and stocking the woodpile. Mom and I managed the rest. Every year, the four seasons eroded the roots of a riverside tree. Dad always instructed, "Knock to down and cut it up for firewood. Otherwise, the river will take it and cause trouble downstream." Kyle liked wrestling with the chain saw.

Although Jimmy was my best friend, Kyle thought Jimmy okay for a city slicker. He used to gripe at me, half-heartedly, "I never had a friend help me with my chores." He balked when Mom asked to take me along or teach me something, but less so with Dad gone. Kyle, like Dad, knew how to fend for himself. Either those genes passed onto him or he paid more attention when Dad worked the farm. I perfected daydreaming.

We never talked about Dad, but we shared a common bond of abuse and the late-night beatings in the kitchen. No words needed to be spoken. We knew Mom knew, but didn't blame her. We felt worse for Mom.

"Kurt, I'm outta here in a few months. It will be you and Mom. I know Dutch stops by now and then seeing if he can be of help. I don't think folks around here understand how Dutch became part of our family. Be aware. If you and Mom can handle a project, handle it. I know you're not real handy. Between the two of you, I'd bet you could manage most jobs. If you get stuck, ask Dutch. Make sure you are here whenever he comes for dinner. I trust Dutch. I worry more about what people think."

"Oh hells' bells Kyle, Dutch is older than dirt."

"I know, I know, and people don't know Dutch like we do. Be mindful okay? If you hear something, jump back at it. If it's really ugly, let Mom and the sheriff know."

"Okay."

"As long as I am stateside, when I get to the naval training center or wherever I'm assigned afterward, I will call and give Mom and you my phone number and address. Write it on the blackboard in the kitchen. If I'm at sea, it will be more complicated, but there will always be a way for you to reach me. Ken will do the same thing once he gets back from Korea. If anything happens to Mom or something you think we should know, call us. Tell the party line people it's an emergency and you need the line. Don't worry about the long-distance charges, and don't worry about people listening in. Promise me this."

"I promise."

"I know you have this dream about being quarterback for the Beavers. Sorry to say you may be like me and slow to grow. Ken was the same way. You're still only twelve, so a growth spurt could come at any time. If it doesn't, don't get too down on yourself. Nothing you can do about it. It's in your genes."

I knew about genes. Kyle began his growth spurt his junior year.

On another night after lights out, Kyle surprised me with this, "How you doing with girls? I know you like Cindy McBrady."

"Not as much after a conversation on the bus last fall. Her mother calls Dutch a spook."

"So I heard."

"Geez Kyle, I'm only twelve. I feel funny around Cindy, but I don't think on it much. She's three years older, and taller. Cindy rides a horse; I ride a bike."

"When I visit home on leaves, I will be interested in how you will change."

I had no idea what he was talking about.

"If Dad were still alive, maybe he would talk to you about sex, but I doubt it. Dad never said diddly to me."

Later the next day, Kyle added more advice. "I told Mom it's time for her to ask favors from church members to come plow the gardens and berry patch each year. She will want to do it, and it's still too big a job for you, maybe in a couple of years. Don't let Mom use the chainsaw for firewood. I taught you how. There's always a tree down somewhere on our riverbank or south of Ole Steely. It's Mabel's property south of the road, but she will let you clear it. Hook up the wagon and go cut it up and put it in the barn. If you really get stuck, call Ken when he gets back from Korea. He can get away for a day now and then. Okay, one final thing. I know you don't like guns. You will soon be the man of the house. Practice shooting. Keep the rifle nearby. You and Mom don't scare easy. If you need to use the rifle, you're the best one to use it. Promise me you will practice. We're pretty safe out here, but who knows. Things have gotten a little stranger with Dutch around. It's just you and Mom. If a critter takes out after the chickens, you need to set the traps and keep an eye out, okay?"

"Okay." Traps scared me. Once they are set either in the barn or near the chicken coop it's too easy to forget where they are and step in one. They snared a stray cat just often as a critter.

Kyle seemed done with his advice, but I had been wondering about something else. "Kyle, did you ever want to kill Dad?"

"Sure, several times. I told Mom. Scared her to death."

I did not tell Kyle I felt the same. "What kept you from doing it?"

"Thinking about something, especially killing, and doing it are two different things. I get angry like anyone else. But I never thought I was like Dad. I took it out on you now and then, but not in a way that would really hurt you. Dad made me boil. I think I probably wanted to scare him into stopping, but really could never have pulled the trigger. I don't know. Anyway, I'm glad I didn't. I'd probably be in jail."

I never thought about the jail part.

"I always meant to ask what made you want to join the Navy? Dad served in the Army Air Corps, and Ken joined the Army. The Atlantic's a long ways away, the Pacific even farther. The Navy owns you for four years."

"I don't have a good answer. When I first thought about it, Dad was beating on us, and Mom. I wanted to get as far away from here as possible. After Dad died, I had second thoughts, but decided it still made sense for me take some time, and get away. Our world is pretty small here in Adams Creek. Going right into college made no sense for me. I had no clear course of study or a career in mind. Besides, my grades, while better, weren't good enough for any scholarships. Mom didn't have the money. I had no interest in what Dad did, stuck in the states the whole time. They don't call it the Army Air Corps anymore. It's the United States Air Force. I remember being in awe of those planes over at Bunker Hill Air Base when Dad would take us to those open base days. I don't know, maybe it's because I didn't want any part of what Dad did. Ken seemed pretty focused out of high school. You and Ken are better students. I will miss Mom, and even you. Hell, I'll probably kick myself later, but right now the Navy looks like a whole new world. I just hope I have sea legs, hard to know growing up in these parts. Floating the river is a far cry from the ocean."

Twenty-four

The 1960 summer to remember began with Beau Braddock moving into the vacant Jenkins' house. One day in mid-June, a 1956 Chevy pulled into our driveway. Kyle left for the Naval training base north of Chicago the week prior. Mom left in the morning for her elevator job. Out stepped Beau, flat-top haircut, smoking a cig, wearing jeans and a white t-shirt with a cigarette pack rolled up in a sleeve, like James Dean in the movie *Rebel Without a Cause.* I stopped pushing our blade mower.

He towered over me a good six inches and must have outweighed me by fifty pounds. Something about him said, "Be careful." I would need to bend over backwards to stay in his good graces. He seemed tense, itchy; his eyes darted around, rarely fixing on mine. Except for the hair, he acted like a hood. Kyle warned me hoods usually carried knives. I missed my brother.

After exchanging names, I asked, "Where you from?"

"Birmingham, Alabama. My old man and I just moved here. He's a truck driver and is on the road a lot."

"And your mom?"

"She left when I was ten for another man. Haven't seen her since. My aunt, uncle, and cousin live in Twin Rivers.

They've been up here for ten years or so. They kept bugging Dad to move up here. This place sure seems dead."

His accent sounded like one of the Southern Baptist preachers during summer Revival Weeks. I couldn't imagine why a wife would leave her husband for another man. Then I remembered Dad beating on Mom.

"Well, you got a car so you can go into town anytime you want. Kendall is bigger, farther south. Is that a V-8 in there?"

"Yup, what's it to ya?"

"Just wondering, it sounded like it."

"You know about cars?"

"Not much. The family who owned the house you moved into had one like it."

"My dad told me what happened after he drove up to Fort Wayne to complete the sale. Too bad you lost your friend."

It didn't sound like he meant it.

"What grade will you be in?"

"Junior," he said, taking a drag.

"My brother, Kyle, just graduated and enlisted in the Navy. He left a week ago, so now it's just Mom and me. My oldest brother Ken just returned from Korea. He graduated from Indiana Tech before joining the Army. He lives in Harrison."

"I have an older brother in the Marines. What do you do for fun around here?"

"If I had a car like you, my list of fun would be a lot different. I bet you would find how I pass the time pretty boring. I have my chores like mowing the lawn and weeding the garden. I fish, shoot hoops, keep the blackbirds out of our orchard, attend church, and spend time with my friend Dutch down the riverbank."

"Is he that nigger I saw walking across the bridge the other day?"

"Dutch is a Negro."

"He's a nigger. Down South, we kept his kind in place in their part of town. That nigger King is looking to get himself killed one day with all of the stuff he is stirring up."

I decided not to say any more about Dutch.

"You play any sports?" He looked large enough for football.

"Nah, I'd rather shoot pool or cruise around in my car. When my dad is on a run, I head down to Kendall or Harrison, though with Indiana Tech there, it's kind of a stuck-up town. I like Kendall better.

"Any girls around here?"

"Just Cindy McBrady. She will be a sophomore this year. Rides around on her horse Calico a lot. There are lots of girls in Twin Rivers."

"Twin Rivers High is half the size of my old school in Birmingham. I'll check out the chick crop this fall. This Cindy person, is she cute? Is she stacked? Is she fast?"

"Stacked?"

"Man, are you stupid? Does she have a sexy body, is she fast?"

"I think she's cute." I hadn't thought much about the rest of her. No one ever called me stupid. I also didn't know what fast meant but decided not to ask.

"See you around." He got in his car, backed out and once on the road, peeled out, leaving rubber.

Beau Braddock oozed trouble. Besides Kyle, I missed Jimmy. I thought about calling the sheriff but decided against it.

Twenty-five

After Kyle left for the Navy, I inherited his paper route, about thirty-five customers spread over a seven-mile circuit. I inherited his bicycle although once he learned to drive, he used the car on the route on days when Mom didn't need it for work. Each weekday after school, I folded the papers, stuffed them into a bag draped over my shoulder, and headed out, rain, shine, sleet or snow. I delivered the Sunday paper before church. The route netted around $7.50 a week.

Kyle trained me several weeks for the turnover, introducing me to all his customers, though most families I already knew, many from church.

I often timed my last stop at Cindy's house to shoot hoops with her brother, three years my junior. He looked up to me, something new for me. I'd catch a glimpse of Cindy brushing down or feeding Calico. The first time she gave me a ride, she told me about taking Calico on the weekends to the various horse shows around northern Indiana. I could see the McBrady house from my bedroom window. Now and then, I noticed their pickup leaving the house and pulling a horse trailer. Calico was no Silver. I don't think I ever saw her gallop.

Dutch remained a Sunday-only customer, his two-room shack an oasis in the dead of winter, smoke spiraling from the chimney. Thick bacon sizzled and crackled in an iron skillet, its savory smell mixed with the earthiness of brewed coffee, both stronger than the odors of an old man's cluttered shack. Dutch's food groups must have been fish, bacon, and coffee. Dutch insisted I sit a spell. I always did, although never long. His stop sat halfway through my route, and I needed to get home to wash up and change clothes for church. Dutch's bacon made my Sunday mornings.

On an early stop, Dutch took down something tacked to the wall and handed it to me. "You know what this is?"

The document looked really old, some of the writing hard to read.

"That is my grandpa's slavery bill-of-sale. The slave owners kept these as proof of ownership. When slavery ended, my grandpa's owner gave it to him. It became worthless. My pappy said the owner took a liking to grandpa, him being a house slave. I keep it as a reminder of where I came from and to never forget."

One summer Sunday in late June, Dutch let me know he planned on visiting his sister in Alabama for two to three weeks in late July. He would either bus down or she would drive up. "I hope she can get away and come fetch me. Don't much like taking the bus down South." He would remind me a week prior so I wouldn't stop those Sundays.

In the spring of 1960, a mangy dog showed up one day and stayed. I couldn't make out his breed, a blend of some sort. I tried shooing him off. He kept returning, tagging along. No dog to call my own, unlike Ken and Kyle, I gave in and adopted him. I threw him into the river, against his will. He needed a bath. I named him Tippy, inspired by my recent camp experience at Lake Tippecanoe. Mom laid down the law, "Tippy is your responsibility." But she always made sure Tippy feasted on any leftovers headed for the compost. Our family never bought dog food. Once outdoors, he never left my side. When I inherited the paper route, Tippy kept me company, often pausing to sniff and leave a mark. Late one June afternoon at the end of my route, I gained speed coming down the hill across the river and sped across Ole Steely. Tippy trailed about fifty yards back. A car passed me. I heard a crunch and a piercing wail. The car hit Tippy and flipped him over the railing and into the river. I leapt from my bike and raced down the riverbank. Wading waist-deep into the slow-flowing waters, I grabbed Tippy and brought him ashore. I carried him home and laid him on our back porch, covering him with a blanket. I wondered what caused him to run in front of the car. The driver felt badly. "Your dog just suddenly crossed over in front of my car." Something probably distracted Tippy, like a fluttering Monarch butterfly. He died the next day.

Mom told me to dig a grave for Tippy near the creek and bury him. She said make it deep enough or some animal will sniff it out and dig it up. I thought about heaven, still conflicted about whether it existed or not. I thought if it did, I hoped there might be a dog heaven and Tippy would be there. Later I felt guilty about not leaving a marker.

Two weeks later another dog showed up, akin to a golden retriever but with sandier hair. I named him Sandy. I still wasn't sure about God, but maybe I showed up on his radar and he sent Sandy. I never let Sandy join me on my paper route. Each day, I shut him in the barn until I returned. When I let him out, he leapt on me, almost knocking me over.

Ken returned from Korea the summer of 1960, his Army commitment fulfilled. A month prior to his return, he sent a funny attachment to one of his last letters, created by another Korean veteran and meant to be shared with fellow GIs returning home soon. It read in part,

"Dear Civilized People: Very soon now, the undersigned will be once again in your midst, veteranized, immunized, Orientalized, and demobilized, to take his place again as a

human being with freedom and justice for all, engaged in life, liberty, and the somewhat delayed pursuit of stateside happiness.

"In making your joyous preparations to welcome him back into organized society, you must make the following allowances for the crude environment that has been his miserable lot for some time. In a word, he might be a little 'Rice-Paddy Happy,' suffering from the 'Korean Crud,' or a little 'R & R' wear, but no sweat!

"Be especially understanding when he is in the company of women, particularly young and attractive specimens. After many months touring the Orient, he believes he has been cheating the women back home by staying away for so long, and will probably try to make up for lost time."

Ken signed the letter, Ken (Kim Yung Boon) Baumann.

He only stayed home a week, no doubt due to not enough "young and attractive specimens" in the area. It was the first time just Ken and I lived at home after Dad died. He still spent time in Twin Rivers with old high school friends, but less than before since several had left for new horizons. Old girlfriends either moved away or they and Ken had drifted apart. He asked about Jimmy and Tippy. I found it hard to talk. I still wondered if he knew about Dad beating on Mom, but never asked.

He needed a job the rest of the summer to save money for a master's program at Indiana Tech. Dutch and James proved right about how little the Army paid soldiers. He found a good-paying job near the campus, one he could continue part-time while a student. Mom felt relieved.

In early July, I returned to the Lake Tippecanoe church camp, still without pajamas. Now the only one besides Mom at home, I began wondering how I might be of more use. I felt guilty having fun at church camp while Mom held down the home front. Mom didn't seem fazed by it. It helped knowing Dutch would check in to see if she needed anything even after remembering Kyle's cautions.

I tried hard to avoid any contact with Beau. He often sped by in his car. A few weeks after he moved in, Cindy rode into our driveway on Calico. She never rode into our driveway. I stopped weeding the green beans and walked up to greet her.

"Kurt, have you met Beau?"

"Yes."

"Do you know anything about him?"

"Not much other than he moved up from the south. His dad drives big rigs and is gone a lot. He will be a junior next year."

"He creeps me out. When I am out on the road exercising Calico, he comes up to me in his car and says stuff I have never heard before–sexual stuff."

I had not felt kindly towards Cindy since last fall's bus conversation. I had no advice to give her, not because of what she said, but because Beau scared me too, and I couldn't help her.

"All I can say is if I hear anything, I will let you know. He asked about you when he first came by after they moved in."

"What did he say?"

No way would I repeat all he said. "He wanted to know if there were any girls around. I mentioned your name. I probably should not have said that. Sorry. He said some other stuff I won't repeat."

"Like what?"

"He asked if you were cute and stacked."

"And what did you say?"

"I said I didn't know what stacked meant but I said I thought you were cute." Once I spoke, I wanted the words back.

"Why Kurt Baumann I never knew you thought I was cute, you charmer you," she grinned.

About then, I wanted to crawl under a rock. "I gotta go finish my chores."

"Okay, let me know if you find anything else out." She turned Calico and headed out the driveway. My body felt funny.

A week later, I sat with Dutch at the fishing spot. We probably had not exchanged ten words in thirty minutes.

Low and behold, Beau Braddock showed up.

"Hey Kurt, hey nigger, catch anything?"

I glanced at Dutch. He stared straight ahead, and then said, "A couple of suckers. They remind me of you, hard to digest."

Beau had no clue about suckers but knew Dutch had put him down.

"Look nigger, watch out around here. In the south, we knew how to deal with uppity niggers. You are lucky you live out here, but my Dad knows some folks, so watch your step."

Beau found a large stone and threw it in the river next to Dutch's line.

"What the sam hill are you doing? Man you have got to be dumber than a bucket of rocks."

Before 'rocks' escaped my mouth, I wanted it back. Beau lit into me before I could even raise my arms and protect my face. He pinned me to the ground and flailed away with several knuckle sandwiches, his face reddened. I had never seen eyes like that, something not human. I swear he might have killed me. Over his shoulder I saw Dutch pick up a stubby limb and whack Beau across the head. He fell over, stunned. I got on my hands and knees and crawled away. After a moment, Beau regained his focus, looked at Dutch still hovering with the limb, got up, and dashed back up the path.

Dutch asked if I was okay. Then he said it looked like I would have two good shiners the next day. My lips tasted bloody, but the teeth felt intact.

"Thanks Dutch. If you had not been here, I'm not sure what might have happened. At least he didn't pull a knife."

"I thought I noticed one in his back pocket. Knives don't scare me, but he might have used it on you. You need to be careful what you say around him and try to stay away from him altogether."

Returning home, I told Mom what happened. She got very upset and wanted to walk across the bridge to talk to Beau's dad. Looking out the kitchen window, she noticed his pickup truck missing. She packed some ice in a towel and pressed it to my eyes.

"Kurt, that boy is trouble. Try to stay away."

"I've been trying to avoid him. But he showed up at the fishing hole."

A few days later, I wanted to skip some stones. Someone filched my stash.

After my encounter with Beau, I rode my newspaper route more cautiously, always turning my head anytime a car approached from my rear, the narrow roads barely passable when two cars approached in opposite directions. Twice I spotted Beau's oncoming car and moved as far to the road's edge as possible without ditching my bike. Each time, Beau swerved near me, flipping me the bird as he drove away.

The summer put me on edge. Jimmy had died in the fall, Kyle joined the Navy in June, Tippy died, Beau shook up the neighborhood, and Ken lived and worked thirty miles away in Harrison. Only Mom and Dutch remained. I saw Dutch once a week. The next time James came out, Dutch and I shared our encounter with Beau. James suggested I try to stay away from Beau unless with someone else. "Less likely he might do something, though it didn't matter when Dutch was here, since he doesn't consider Dutch human."

I didn't know who he meant about someone else. Not any else's around, now with Jimmy gone.

"When Mom goes to her job at the grain elevator, I'm alone."

"Do you have a gun?"

"I have Kyle's rifle. We keep it on the back porch. I don't shoot it much. Mom hides the bullets."

"Smart lady. I suggest if you get scared you head for the woods up river from your property or head down the river. You know your way around here and Beau would not. Or get inside and lock the doors."

"Our house doesn't have any locks."

Heading into the woods north or south of our farm sounded like a good plan. I wondered how fast Beau could run since I knew my way in the woods along the riverbank.

"I could shimmy up a tree. Beau doesn't look like a guy who would bother climbing a tree."

Dutch said, "You know, I don't think I ever climbed a tree. Not about to start now."

A couple of nights later after supper, I retreated to my favorite spot on our creek's bridge. I thought some on Jesus's Beatitude, "Blessed are they who mourn for they shall be comforted." I wasn't feeling comforted. Mom came out, sat down, and put her arm around me.

"What do you think about out here all alone?"

"I'm not alone. The frogs, fireflies, crickets, and whip-poor-wills keep me company. Sometimes I think about all the places where this creek water will go. It would be neat to follow it."

"I think all three of you boys will end up chasing dreams in places I will only see in magazines. You all have a restless spirit. That's your dad in you. None of you are farmers. But

Adams Creek fits me like a pair of well-worn shoes. I'll bet you still think of Jimmy."

"Sure, but not as much. Is that wrong?"

"Of course not. Just like when I lost your dad, I had to get on with taking care of this farm and you boys. I wish you felt more comfortable with our pastor. You've had a rough year. I'm happy you got away to church camp. Did you find anyone there you could talk with?"

"No, it's hard to spill your guts to someone you have known for only a few days. Actually, I like talking things out with you and Dutch, James too. I miss Kyle. He became more of a big brother after Dad died. Ken didn't stay long enough for me to feel any closer. Beau scares me, and you have work at the elevator three days a week. I wish I could've stayed at church camp all summer."

"I wish I could have afforded it for you, at least another week. Even if I could, camp doesn't work that way. Only one week each summer is reserved for kids around your age. When I was your age, I only had to deal with a broken leg and catching that awful flu that killed so many people like your dad's mother. Nothing like what you have gone through lately. I never lost a best friend or even a pet dog. Yes, I lost Esther, but it's not the same as losing a friend like Jimmy."

Mom mentioning the flu reminded me I had contracted every disease making the rounds; chicken pox, mumps, and measles.

"Being out here tonight helps, sorting things out. Speaking of Beau, James wondered if we had a gun. I told him about Kyle's rifle and you hiding the bullets. I never told you this, but I don't like guns. I think the day Dad took me along to the slaughterhouse will never leave me. I can still see as if it happened yesterday. I've seen Kyle shoot birds. I've actually hit a few. Seeing a steer shot between the eyes is not the same."

"I don't like guns either, never shot one. I feel badly about asking your dad to take you that day. Growing up on a farm, your Dad and I saw a slaughterhouse as a regular part of farm life. My family butchered a lot of hogs, but I never saw it done. I don't think your dad kept a shotgun and rifle because he felt unsafe. I think he thought we might need it for a rabid dog, a fox, raccoon, or muskrat threatening our chickens or something larger scaring our cows. Ken and Kyle liked to hunt rabbits. Your dad wasn't much of a hunter. You know we see deer now and then in the pasture across the road near the tree line. Karl could never bring himself to shoot a deer even though we could have used the meat."

I liked hearing Dad couldn't shoot a deer, part of the good Dad. I couldn't imagine eating a deer. Who could eat Bambi?

"I talk to Jesus sometimes. He is someone I would like to be more like. He seems easier to talk with than God, and the church has paintings of him."

"It pleases me to hear that. I like talking with Jesus, too. I know what you mean."

"Thanks Mom. I'm doing okay, but could you ask God to ease up? Dutch said trials and tribulations build character. I've had enough character-building to last a while."

She laughed, kissed me on the forehead, and said, "I'll put in a special request."

"Mom, I've been meaning to ask you, did you and Dad wish one of us was a girl? And did you plan on Ken, Kyle, and me each being six years apart?"

She smiled, "I think now is as a good time as any to tell you this. Two years after Kyle was born, I became pregnant again, hoping for a girl. I carried the baby almost to full term and then lost it. To this day, I am not sure what went wrong. Bringing Ken, Kyle, and you into our lives went pretty smoothly. It devastated Karl and me. The baby was a girl. We had picked out a girl's name, Emily."

"I'm so sorry, Mom. It would have been neato to have an older sister."

"I don't think much on it anymore, nearly fifteen years ago. But I'm not sure Karl ever got over it. It reminded him of losing his mother and a baby brother to that horrible Flu Plague. As for your second question, no we did not try to stretch out having you Kyle, and Ken. We tried, like with Emily, but sometimes the good Lord has other plans."

Hearing that Mom would have named a girl Emily, I had another question. "How come all three of our names begin with a K? I'm not complaining. I like my name."

Mom smiled, "That's your Dad's doing. If a boy, he proposed the name. If girl, I would. Course, we both had to support the choices. Your Dad was proud of his German heritage and the name Karl with a K and would never change it like some German immigrants did. So when it came to boys' names, he began with the Ks."

"So we are kind of like the KKK."

"Kurt Baumann, what an awful thought."

"Sorry, Mom, you know I like to mess with words. I'll bet if I told that to Dutch, even he would chuckle."

"You know, I believe he would, and probably say 'I trust your meaning.'"

"What other names besides Emily did you think of?"

"I liked the name Esther, mostly because of my childhood friend, and partly, while not a favorite book of mine, because Esther is one of the books of the Old Testament."

Mom came out for another reason that night.

"Kurt, I waited too long to say this. I guess I waited for you to be older hoping you would understand what I have to say. I had this talk with Kyle just after your dad died. I knew he took after you and Kyle. You never deserved it. I felt bad about giving you a swat now and then. I let you and Kyle down. I should have protected you. My father and mother swatted me from time to time but not like your dad did to you and Kyle. I knew he carried a demon. I figured it out after our marriage. He was so good in so many other ways that I stayed with him. I thought I could help. I think it began when he lost his mother at age nine. He had to grow up faster than a boy should. Maybe that led to his smoking. A lot of young men smoked in those days. Now you have to grow up too fast.

"I know you know your father was a very intelligent man. Maybe too much for his own good. He struggled with authority, feeling smarter than his bosses. I think he felt like a failure. It hurt his pride being a janitor in Twin Rivers. Always remember this: there's nothing wrong with doing any job, even janitor, if it pays the bills and supports your family. He did that, but it gnawed on him. I tried to talk him into finding a counselor at the Twin Rivers State Hospital. He refused. Money might have been the biggest reason, but I think his pride, too. Your Dad believed in God but didn't feel comfortable in church, so he had no relationship with our pastor. You know the feeling. Is any of this making any sense?"

"Sure Mom, I guess. I wondered what you were thinking during those times. Kyle and I noticed you were always overly nice to us for a couple of days after he took after us. I admired Dad. I never told you this before, but I don't think my feelings for him included love, leastways as I understand love. Dad never hugged us, and I can't recall ever feeling like hugging him."

"I'm so sorry to hear this. I understand. Kyle told me the same. Can you forgive me?"

"Good grief Mom. Why should we have to forgive you when Dad was beatin' on you? You have to have known Kyle and I heard it all. I get it that kids need disciplined and maybe even swatted now and then, but kicked and punched and pinching the flesh of our arms? But I cannot imagine how Dad could hit you. Did he also pinch your arm?"

"Yes."

"How could you still love him after that?"

"I don't think I have an answer that you would understand. As a Christian, I made a vow. And besides, when I thought on it, I did not know where to go. I guess one of my brothers or my sister would have taken me in, but I felt I would be a burden. So I never brought it up. Then I thought about you and Kyle and decided to tough it out, hoping it was a phase he was going through, hoping it would pass. It did, but not in a way I wanted. Losing him was hard. Looking back, I'm sure it was that breakdown he had in Fort Wayne before you were born."

"I said earlier that my feelings for him did not include love. That's only the half of it. I actually hated him. I never told you this, but I thought about killing him after one of those kitchen beatings."

Mom gasped. "Kyle said the same but he was older. I never feared you might have had similar thoughts."

"I feel funny using that word. It's the first time I've felt that way about another person, and I felt it about my father. It was because of how he treated you. I wanted it to stop. I felt helpless. Beau scares me something awful, but I don't hate him."

"I want you to know that your father loved you and was proud of you, at least one side of his personality."

"If you say so. I'm sorry he never felt that way about Kyle."

"So am I. Or at least he never showed it in a way that Kyle felt it. I think your dad was afraid Kyle might never go to college. And you know how much your dad wanted that for Ken, Kyle, and you. So he was harder on him."

"What does throwing a pitchfork at one of your sons have to do with college?"

"I cannot explain or try to justify some of what your dad did. I was horrified when I heard of it and told your dad so in no uncertain terms."

I gave her a hug. As she got up to go back inside, I said, "Don't forget my prayer request." She smiled, nodded, and walked back to the house. I heard her softly crying.

I thought some on wanting to kill Dad more than once. Was my anger any different than his? No, I did not like guns, yet a gun would have been my only option. Mom hid the bullets, so it seemed an idle threat. I remember Kyle saying, "There is a big difference about having a thought like that and actually doing it." He's right. Still, feeling hatred chewed on me. At that moment, I resolved to never own a gun once on my own.

I entered two exhibits in the county fair; forestry and gardening, grateful neither tested me like entomology. For forestry, I collected, mounted, labeled, and described fifteen indigenous Indiana leaves. For gardening, I selected five vegetables to display in perfect ripe condition: carrots, potatoes, radishes, tomatoes, and sweet corn. I won grand champion in gardening, earning another photo in the paper. The honor almost made up for all those years harvesting rocks. Almost.

Between the fair and church camp, my summer had some ups to balance the downs. But my summer to remember had only begun.

Twenty-six

The third week of July, on a Wednesday morning, Mom and I picked blueberries near the bend in the river. I loved blueberries, my next favorite pie after peach. Picking berries a few hundred yards from the road kept us too occupied and detached to notice any activities on Ole Steely or the road. The previous Sunday, Dutch reminded me to skip the following few Sundays. He would be in Alabama. "If you don't see me sooner, when you see smoke coming out of my chimney, you will know I'm back." He didn't say which day his sister would come for him. I had not noticed him fishing earlier in the week, so I figured he must be long gone. The wind blew easterly, rustling the leaves. The Wabash Cannonball whistled through. No unusual sound teased our ears.

I listened to Mom tell how much she loved picking blueberries as a young girl. "I could never keep blueberry stains off my clothes, I was so clumsy. I think your grandma would have happily chopped down the bushes." She told this story, hoping I'd be careful. Few stains are harder to remove than blueberry. You might as well burn the clothing. Each time we picked blueberries together, I drove Mom batty singing,

> *"I found my thrill*
> *On Blueberry Hill*
> *On Blueberry Hill*
> *When I found you."*

Dutch told me about Fats Domino once being a passenger on one of his runs.

Mom insisted blueberries didn't grow on hills. No hills broke the plains of her childhood homes in eastern Illinois. So I improvised,

> *"I met my match*
> *In a Blueberry Patch*
> *In a Blueberry Patch*
> *When I found you."*

Mom groaned, "Kurt Baumann, you've found your calling, making up silly songs."

Returning to the house thirty minutes later, we spotted Calico tied up next to Ole Steely. This seemed odd, Cindy dismounting from Calico near Ole Steely, especially after being told by her mom to stay away from Dutch. I doubted Dutch fished down the riverbank that day, so she must have gone down for another reason. She usually rode up to Ole Steely and turned back westward. I never saw her cross. Maybe she tried, but Ole Steely spooked Calico. I mentioned this to Mom, now washing the blueberries. "Maybe she decided she would go see Dutch anyway. She's of that age."

"I'm pretty sure Dutch is on his way to Alabama. What do you mean, 'of that age?'"

"Age thirteen to fifteen can be rebellious years for parents. She might be of a mind to do the opposite of what her mother tells her."

"Were Ken and Kyle that way?"

"Kyle more than Ken, but not so much. Even with Kyle, I think it had more to do with your dad than anything else. I can't say firsthand about girls, but other mothers have confided in me about younger teenage girls being a handful.

Now that it's you and me, I don't expect sass from you. You're the man of the house now."

"Of course, and I'm just about perfect," I said, grinning.

"We'll see." She mussed my hair.

"Were you a handful to grandma?"

"Of course not, I was just about perfect. Now go see what Cindy is up to, you being the unofficial sheriff of the riverbank. Maybe she took a liking to fishing."

"If I'm going to be the unofficial sheriff of the riverbank, I want a badge and a horse."

"Even if I could afford one, no horse comes on this property, except maybe Calico."

Leaving the house, I approached Ole Steely. Calico knew me and did not react. I patted her face. She whinnied. "Hey girl, what's Cindy up to?" Curious, I started down the familiar path. Coming upon the fishing hole I froze. Cindy lay on the ground face up, not moving. Her jeans were lowered down to her knees, her blouse partly unbuttoned. I did not know if she was dead or just unconscious, but I sure as heck wasn't going to try and find out. I hightailed it back up the path, slipping several times.

At the house, gasping for air, I screamed for Mom to come quick.

She wiped her hands and followed me down the path.

At the fishing hole, Mom covered her mouth and cried out, "Oh Lord! Oh Lord God!" She didn't touch Cindy, but waited to see if her chest was rising or not. It wasn't.

We stumbled back up the path. She called the sheriff, gasping, "Sheriff, come quick! Cindy McBrady is lying by the riverbank south of the bridge. I don't think she was breathing!" Later, she told me she heard several clicks during the call.

The sheriff arrived ten minutes later, siren piercing the village air. Mom repeated what we had seen. We walked back down the path. The sheriff asked us to keep behind him several paces. "Are you sure she is dead?"

"No, but I watched for few seconds to see if her chest moved. It didn't."

Once there, he took in the scene asking if any of us had touched Cindy or anything else.

"No," we both exclaimed.

He checked Cindy's pulse and walked around the fishing hole perimeter, looking at the ground. "Not seeing any clear fresh footprints. Looks to me like someone tried to fuzz them over. I see footprints that look the size of Kurt's, also yours, Emma. That's about it."

Then I noticed, "Sheriff, her cowgirl hat is missing." The three of us scanned the area but found no sight of it.

We followed the sheriff back up the path to his car. We did not hear what he called in, but within ten minutes several more cars arrived in chorus of screaming sirens. Neighbors began arriving by foot or car, standing back from the sheriff's cars. Feeling in the way, Mom and I walked back to our front yard. I looked back at the scene, and for a brief moment thought that Ole Steely knew what happened.

Deputies followed the sheriff down the riverbank. One stayed at Ole Steely to keep the road open and the crowd under control. As cars slowly drove by, he waved them through. Many parked and joined the growing throng. Now and then a deputy returned to his car and said something into his car radio. One jumped in his car and drove west towards Carroll's. Minutes later, an ambulance arrived. Mom and I walked back to the throng. They carried Cindy's body up the path on a stretcher and placed her on the ground near the ambulance. We heard the wail of Mrs. McBrady getting out of a deputy's car. The sheriff put his arm around her and asked her to identify the body. She did and then threw herself over the draped body, sobbing uncontrollably.

She composed herself and stared at the sheriff, shouting, "You know who did this. That old nigger did this! Cindy told me he scared her, and I told her never to go down the riverbank! You find him and you string him up!"

Then she looked at Mom and me. "And you, you nigger lovers made him feel welcome here, having him over for supper and who knows what else!" The neighbors and passersby stared at us.

The sheriff put his arm around her and escorted her back to a car telling the deputy to take her home. "I'll be by later."

I looked at mom, her face ashen, hands shaking. What did Mrs. McBrady mean by "Who knows what else?"

After the ambulance and the car with Mrs. McBrady left, the sheriff asked a deputy to walk Calico back to the McBrady place. He asked to speak with us.

He wanted us to repeat exactly what we remembered. Mom said she needed a little time to herself. The sheriff chatted with a deputy and then returned. We told all we remembered. He asked if we knew of Dutch's whereabouts.

Fighting back the tears, I said, "Sheriff, Mrs. McBrady has lost her gourd, gone plum crazy. No way Dutch could have killed Cindy even if he were around. I know Dutch; he's my friend. He wouldn't hurt a flea. Last Sunday, Dutch told me his sister would be driving up to take him down to Alabama for a few weeks. I'd bet he is long gone."

"Do you know how to reach his sister?"

"No, Dutch doesn't even own a phone."

I asked if he knew Beau Braddock.

"Yes, why do you ask?"

I told him about my encounters with Beau since he moved in, the first conversation, then the fight, and what Cindy said earlier. I had not seen Beau for a few days. The sheriff made some notes. "When is the last time you saw James?"

"A couple of weeks ago."

"Anything else you remember about Cindy from bus rides or school in Twin Rivers?"

"Not much. Cindy attended middle school, a freshman last year. I just finished sixth grade at a different school. I did see her real friendly once with a boy at her school this past year when the school bus stopped for the trip home, but just once. He looked older, older than middle school age. He didn't seem Cindy's type or at least how I think of her. He slicked his hair back, kind of like a greaser."

"Kurt, how do you know greasers?"

"Aw Mom, I don't. Kyle pointed one out now and then so I would know who to stay away from."

"I'll ask Mrs. McBrady when I see her. I am going to head over to Beau's place, then Dutch's place, then into town to see James. Beau should know how to reach his dad if I need to talk with him. I'll be back. We blocked off the river path, so don't go back down there for a while."

The crowd at the bridge milled around for an hour or so, chatting and looking our way.

Thirty minutes after the sheriff left, a reporter arrived asking to talk with us. Mom refused, saying we need to speak with the sheriff first.

Mom contacted both Ken and Kyle. Ken asked if Mom wanted him to drive up. She said no, "We'll be okay, just pretty shook up. I'll keep you posted."

The front-page headline the next day read,

"GIRL FOUND DEAD IN ADAMS CREEK."

"Cindy McBrady of Adams Creek was found dead yesterday, her partially clad body discovered at an Eel River

fishing hole just south of the Adams Creek Bridge. Her death was ruled a homicide.

"The coroner said McBrady died from strangulation, and though there appeared to be an attempt of sexual assault, there is not evidence of such, nor blood anywhere.

"Sheriff Ben Sellers is leading the investigation but so far has little to go on. The fishing spot is known to be a favorite of Dutch Clemons, a retired Pullman porter who lives in Adams Creek. Initial investigation indicates Clemons was visiting his sister in Alabama at the time of the murder. A neighbor boy is also being investigated as to his whereabouts. The sheriff said neighbor Kurt Baumann, twelve, discovered the body after noticing McBrady's horse tied up near the bridge. Sellers said McBrady was not known to leave her horse and venture down the riverbank. McBrady lived with her mother and younger brother a quarter mile west of the river. She frequently rode her horse over the roads in Adams Creek west of the river. Her father lives in Illinois. Mrs. McBrady, emotionally distraught, was brought down to the bridge to identify the body.

"The sheriff's department is interviewing neighbors, teachers, and classmates. If anyone has any information, please contact the Sheriff's Department.

"Emma Baumann, Kurt's mother, and the second person to discover the body, declined an interview with this reporter and declined her son being interviewed as well.

"McBrady was slated to enter Twin Rivers High School as a sophomore this fall."

The story upset Mom both because of the implication Dutch might be involved and the 'neighbor boy,' thinking people might think it meant me.

"Mom, I think this is something Beau could have done. The look in his eyes when he tore into me that day scared the bejesus out of me. I hope to never see a look like that again. If he was trying force Cindy into sex and she said no, it could have set him off. He carries a demon. I'd bet worse than Dad's. And he's much stronger than Cindy."

"Let's see what Sheriff Sellers learns when he talks with him, but I would hope no one around here did this awful thing." Mom sat down and read the story again, hands shaking.

Sheriff Sellers returned the next day and sat down at our kitchen table. He asked us to once again go over everything we remembered.

He went by Dutch's place and talked with Widow Kreider. She showed him a note from Dutch saying his sister had driven up and taken him down to Selma, Alabama for a few weeks. The note asked her to collect his mail. "She thinks the note could have been put in her box either the day before or the day of the murder. She doesn't get much mail anymore and sometimes forgets to fetch it. She also told me Dutch paid his rent in advance. Since I had not met widow Kreider before, I asked her if she knew Dutch was a Negro. She said 'Oh yes;' her eyesight wasn't that bad. Dutch seemed like a fine person from the first time she met him and was always very respectful. 'He's been a good renter, pays like clockwork.' She's even had him in for coffee and cake a few times, amazed by his stories. A couple of neighbors asked about him in a way showing they disapproved. She told them to mind their own business. She said, 'It's the Christian and neighborly thing to do.' Dutch even brought her a bass on occasion. I also talked with everyone who lives between the river and Dutch's place. No one recalls seeing him on Wednesday. Could be he's come and gone from the river so often no one gives a notice. Also asked the same about Beau. Again, no one could recall, though they did remark on his lead foot."

The sheriff visited James, and he validated the story saying he had not seen Dutch in a week, but he had mentioned about his sister coming to pick him up. "James only knows Dutch's sister as Bessie and has no phone number or address for her in Selma. He does not even recall Bessie's married name, the one that might be in a phone book. That seemed odd to me thinking surely Dutch would tell his best friend how to reach him. Then I remembered how private Dutch is. Looks like I can't speak with Dutch until he returns. I will check his house every day, but in case you see him first, call me. I also checked out Beau's whereabouts. His alibi seems solid. His cousin verifies he and Beau were hanging out together in Twin Rivers around the time this would have happened. Beau's uncle and aunt were working, so they had nothing of use to add. Beau's dad isn't due back until tomorrow. I don't know how to reach him, nor does his sister, but we've contacted the company he works for. Maybe he can shorten his run. So far, I've got nothing. Maybe it was one of those hobos who pass through from time to time. Kurt, just being honest, but I thought about you."

Mom gasped.

"Relax Emma, I have to consider all possibilities. I worked through it quickly. Cindy is taller than Kurt and probably even weighs more. She could have fought him off. Besides, there is no evidence of any conflict between Kurt and Cindy. Her mom verified that once she calmed down a bit. Only a few minutes passed between when Kurt went down the bank and the time he rushed back up here, according to you. Not enough time to surprise Cindy and commit this crime. Kurt would have had to hit her from behind with a rock or a chunk of wood. Cindy had no head abrasions.

"I told Mrs. McBrady what Kurt said about a greaser-looking guy at the school bus stop. She said she had seen Cindy with him once at a basketball game last winter and told her to stay away from him. She said Cindy could be rebellious. Anyway, she said the boy's family moved away last spring. She did not know where. I asked her if she knew Beau. She said she didn't, though Cindy said he bothered her on the road a couple of times." The sheriff then asked us to not talk with the press about this. "I've told you more than I've told them, but you are extremely critical to my investigation. I tell you things, hoping it might trigger something."

I looked at Sheriff Sellers differently from then on, not imagining anyone ever considering me capable of murder.

God must have been busy and didn't hear Mom's prayer request.

Ken ignored Mom's response and drove up that night. He was at work when Mom called. The place felt safer with him around. Mom seemed less tense, even if only for a night. He said he needed to get back for work the next day.

A week later, Kyle came home from naval training camp for a few days before shipping out to his first assignment at the naval base in Norfolk, Virginia. Mom kept all of the newspaper articles. I felt safer even though he hung out much of the week with friends in town. He went over to Beau's house and told him to stay off our property or he would have to deal with him the next time he came home. He said Beau laughed at him. "Good thing he didn't call me a nigger lover." Kyle grew a lot late in high school both in height and weight. Beau would have been overmatched especially now with Kyle in peak shape from Navy basic training.

Ken drove up for a long weekend before Kyle shipped out again. Mom enjoyed having her three boys under one roof, if only for a few days. Both Ken and Kyle spent more time in town than at home. They talked about going over to talk with Beau. Mom suggested they should not. "If either of you were going to be around, it might matter. Making a threat and then leaving wouldn't help much. I think it best we just go about our business and stay clear of Beau."

The more I thought on it, the more it chewed on me. If the sheriff had nothing but the hobo theory, it still made no sense why Cindy would have gone down the path to talk with Dutch? Dutch is now seventy. Cindy is fifteen. Why would a teenage girl want to talk with a seventy-year-old Negro? Surely not because of the nice things I said about him on the bus last fall. Maybe she had gone down there before when I never noticed, just to spend time by the river, like when I was at camp or at the fair. It might be possible. I liked going down there alone and often did before and after Dutch showed up. If she did and a hobo came upon her while there, could that be it? Dutch told the sheriff hobos were pretty harmless. I still think it more likely Beau came upon her, if in fact she liked going down there or just did it for the first time. But the sheriff said Beau had an alibi.

I knew nothing of Beau's family in Twin Rivers. Based on Beau, I'd be suspicious of any alibi they provided. Yet how could the Sheriff prove the alibi false?

I thought about Dutch down in Alabama. If James did not know how to reach him, how could he know about Cindy's murder? Maybe that's just as well.

Twenty-seven

On a mid-August morning, Dutch knocked on our door. He asked his sister to drop him off at James' place. "James kept all of the newspaper clippings, knowing I would want to read up. James drove me out. I wanted to talk with you before I talked with the sheriff. Hard for me to think about that girl being killed at my favorite fishing hole. I'm still shaken from it all, even after studying the papers. I am relieved I wasn't around." His decision to hold his address or phone number from James seemed farsighted. "Best things had a few days to calm down. I'll give the Sheriff Bessie's phone number. No doubt he will want to contact the authorities in Selma to speak to her after he rings her up."

Mom started to pick up the phone to call Sheriff Sellers, but Dutch asked her to wait a bit. He wanted to hear our story first. We repeated everything we did and could remember and what Sheriff Sellers said to us including the hysterics of Mrs. McBrady. Dutch asked about Beau and whether we had seen him or his car that day.

"Sounds even more like I'm lucky I wasn't here and lucky there is not a Mr. McBrady or at least one who lives close by." Dutch knew Mrs. McBrady lived alone with her two children. Turns out Cindy's younger brother spent that fateful week visiting his father in Illinois.

"Dutch, we were so worried about you. Your sister coming up to pick you up was almost ordained. God was looking out for you."

"Well, that could be since it worked out for the best. Feel free to call Sheriff Sellers now. I'll wait for him at the house." Dutch walked back home.

We remained in the dark for a couple days, not knowing how the sheriff's questioning ended up. Dutch had not returned, nor the sheriff. The paper updates told us less than we already knew. We picked more blueberries, and this time Mom baked the pie.

Dutch came back the next day and told us what he knew. Sheriff interviewed him, called Bessie in Selma, and asked the police in Selma to follow up on his questions. The sheriff did not have to share any information with Dutch, but since he had a history with his father, he told Dutch his story checked out. The sheriff asked Dutch about any more threats against him. Dutch said no but then again, he didn't have a phone and maybe folks didn't know where he lived. "But there was that article and picture about me ice skating over a year ago in the paper, and of course the hit-and-run driver."

The next time the sheriff stopped by, I mentioned that maybe Cindy liked going down to the fishing hole just like me and had done so when I wasn't home. I never recalled seeing Calico tied up by Ole Steely. A hobo could have surprised her that day. The sheriff pondered this a bit. Then added, "Oh, by the way, Cindy's cowgirl hat was found snagged on a low-hanging tree limb close to Twin Rivers. Nothing of any interest on it. I dropped it off at the O'Bradys."

One week after Dutch returned, the paper floated the idea the murderer might have been a hobo passing through. Sheriff Sellers did not push the theory nor deny it. He had nothing else.

School would start soon. I visited Dutch a couple more times. He seemed relieved no one bothered him, leastways so far. We learned Mrs. McBrady continued haranguing the sheriff over the phone every day.

"I keep thinking someone will show up at my door with a gun or a noose. Those times should be behind us, but I can't help having those thoughts. Who did this befuddles me. The hobos I met the past few years didn't seem the sort to do such a thing. Could have been a freight hopper I've never met. The sheriff said he checked out the family of the boy you saw Cindy with once at the school bus stop. They moved two hundred miles away. Seems too far for an old boyfriend to drive that far and get caught up in something like this. The sheriff has no leads."

"He scared me saying he thought about me."

"Just doing his job, Kurt. He worked it through pretty quickly. Take no offense. In any crime, pretty much everyone is a suspect from the get-go. I feel fortunate that my sister came up to pick me up the day before this happened. Maybe your mom was right, God looked out for me."

"Dutch I thought you didn't believe in God."

"I never said such. I just said there is no proof. Being a Negro and believing in God is tough when I think on how badly we have been treated. Gave me pause. Did God not notice? A part of me wanted to believe. Maybe he got around to looking out for me. No way you could ever understand it. Had I been here that day, who knows what might have happened? I will say Sheriff Sellers seems the sort who would be more like Lucas Mayfield's sheriff friend down Addison way. I like to think he would have protected me. But sheriffs, even good ones, are not safe when folks get riled up. A crowd forms and then becomes a mob. All it takes are a few rabble-rousers."

"Did you wonder about Beau?"

"Yes I did. I asked the sheriff about him. He says Beau's alibi checked out. He was with his cousin in Twin Rivers around that time. Like I said, I cannot figure out why Cindy would have even come down to this fishing spot in the first place. Makes no sense."

Twenty-eight

A week later, on the first day of the fall school semester, Beau went missing. Mom and I spent the two days prior to school's start at Aunt Mildred's house in Monroeville. I usually begged off these visits, my cousins being girls. Now with Kyle in the Navy, Mom wouldn't leave me alone overnight.

When I got off the bus, the sheriff's car was back in our driveway. He and Mom sat at the kitchen table.

"Kurt, Beau's gone missing. He did not show up for school today. His dad said when he came home last night from a run, he found Beau gone. Anything you can tell us?"

As much as Beau scared the bejesus out of me and I went out of my way to avoid him, I shuddered at the sheriff's news. First Cindy, and now Beau.

"Sheriff, I think the last time I saw Beau might have been a few days ago when he sped by. He always sped by. I noticed his car in front of his house across the river the day we left for my aunt's house. I have not been face-to-face with him since he lit into me on the riverbank. I tried avoiding him, though he scared me a couple of times on my paper route."

"What happened?"

"I don't think he wanted to hit me like whoever hit Dutch. He wanted to force me into the ditch."

A front-page story the next day reported Beau missing. Sheriff Sellers, like Cindy's murder, had no clues. He did speculate about bad elements in Kendall where Beau was known to visit with his dad out on a long haul.

Maybe Beau missed Alabama and ran away. But his car sat in their driveway.

Dutch stopped by on his way to Carroll's wondering about Beau's disappearance.

"I tried steering clear of Beau after he beat on me awhile back. He never came in our driveway after that first time. I still have never met his dad. They don't subscribe to the paper."

Dutch said he only noticed whether Beau's car or his dad's pickup sat in their driveway or not. "A couple of times when he passed me, I saw someone in the front seat who looked to be older. Had that greaser look. I'd get off the road if I saw him coming. My new hearing aids help. I learned my lesson. He would swerve close to scare me and shout out names. Someone messed with the fishing hole; both the log and fishing pole holders disappeared. I'm sure Beau tossed them into the river. I told the sheriff this."

Mom said, "I did finally meet the boy's father a couple of weeks ago when I saw his pickup in the driveway. He looked tired from another long haul. Beau had not told him anything about what happened with Kurt. I told him what Kurt told me and apologized for Kurt's taunt. He said Beau had a short fuse, said his mother had one, too. He moved up here to be close to his sister and Beau's cousin. He said it was probably a mistake to get him a car but decided to do so when they moved out here. He might not have bought it if they had moved into Twin Rivers. The price here was so cheap after the Jenkins family left, too good to pass up. I had an odd feeling about him, the way he carried himself and the way he looked at me, though not much eye contact. I had no reason not to believe him. Dutch, he never said anything about you. I told all of this to the sheriff."

"Mom, you never told me this."

"Sorry Kurt, it didn't seem important. I had the sense Beau's dad would talk with him. Only this mattered."

The sheriff ordered dredging of the Eel River between Ole Steely and all the way to Twin Rivers, plus the stone quarry east of town.

Several days passed. On Saturday, Sheriff Sellers returned to tell us Beau's body had been found by a cornfield close to Kendall. He had nothing else to add but thought we would want to know.

The lead story the next day read,

"BEAU BRADDOCK'S BODY FOUND NEAR KENDALL"

"Beau Braddock of Adams Creek was found dead yesterday near Kendall. Braddock, the second Adams Creek teenager to be murdered in less than a month, was found between a row of trees and a cornfield beside a dirt road about four miles off Highway 35, six miles southeast of Waverly. He had been dead for several days. The coroner listed the cause of death as strangulation, though a noose hung around his neck and his mouth and throat were stuffed with dirt. The coroner confirmed hanging was not the cause of death.

"Both Sheriff Sellers and the Harrison County Sheriff are investigating, since it is not known where Braddock was killed. Braddock and his father lived across the Eel River less than a few hundred yards from scene of Cindy McBrady's murder a few weeks ago. Braddock was interviewed as to his whereabouts the day of that murder, and his alibi proved solid.

"This time, the Baumanns, Emma and Kurt, neighbors from across the river, spoke with this reporter. Kurt Baumann had an earlier run-in with Braddock on the riverbank with Braddock bloodying Baumann and blackening both eyes. Dutch Clemons, the retired Pullman Porter interviewed in the earlier case, rescued Baumann from the much stronger and older Braddock, Baumann saying, 'He could have killed me.' Baumann said he saw Braddock speed by now and then, but he had not been around him since the incident on the riverbank. 'I didn't like him from the first day I met him, shortly after they moved in.'

"Baumann, readers may recall, lost his best friend, Jimmy Jenkins, to a sledding accident this past fall. The Jenkins family moved away shortly after.

"Braddock's father, a long-hauler and away most of time, moved here from Alabama early this summer and bought the Jenkins' place. Braddock's aunt, uncle, and cousin live in Twin Rivers.

"Sheriff Sellers is not saying whether he thinks there is any connection between the two murders, but it seems unlikely. Braddock was known to visit Kendall when his father was out of town on a run.

"Braddock was slated to enter the junior class this fall at Twin Rivers High School."

I had never met Beau's dad, but I felt badly. Based on the newspaper story someone strangled Beau, but stuffing dirt in his mouth seemed something awful.

I pleaded to God, "Please make this stop."

Two people had been killed, all in a short time. I liked one, not the other. For the first time, I wished I liked our pastor. Fortunately I had Mom and Dutch.

Dutch came by the house again, this time for supper. He first checked with me about dessert. "I'm not sure what it is, but it's not gooseberry or rhubarb."

"I really disliked the boy, but what a terrible thing. I am still not convinced he had nothing to do with Cindy's death. The sheriff seems pretty sure of his alibi. When it comes to family, I think alibis come too easily. It's hard to rat on kin."

Mom wondered why Dutch felt that way.

"Just something in my gut. The hobos I met over the years were not violent types. They begged, they might filch something from time to time, but never violent. No doubt there are bad elements, but I never met any. They were just scratching out an existence, no family to speak of, wanderlust in their bones. Hard to imagine any of the ones I've met killing another, especially a girl. Again, why she would have gone down there in the first place? I guess it is possible she decided I was okay to be around because she trusted you folks and moseyed down. Kurt's theory makes more sense. She liked the fishing hole. It's possible she came down the path previously, and once seeing me there, turned around. But the likelihood that a hobo would come down that path at just that time doesn't add up. Surely someone would have recalled seeing one on the road. I am out of other possibilities."

"You would know hobos better, having spent time with them. Whenever one came to the door for something to eat, they were always grateful and respectful," Mom commented. "But without any evidence to support Beau doing it, what options does the sheriff have? Did you think the noose around his neck meant anything?"

"I gave it some thought. Naturally makes me think of lynchings. Maybe the killer or killers thought it might throw off the authorities. I do know there are a lot more Negroes in Kendall than Twin Rivers. Probably bad elements there, Negroes and whites. James said such, and the killer or killers wanted the law to look at the Negroes. We will see what comes from that."

"I hope they find who killed Cindy and Beau. It would sure settle things down around here."

"So do I. I don't need all this attention. I just want to fish and go about my business."

Mom served up chicken and dumplings and sweet potato pie. I liked my first sweet potato pie. Dutch wore a smile a mile wide.

A week later, the Review headline read, *"Serial Killer in Adams Creek?"* The article speculated about both homicides and whether related or the random work of a serial killer. Sheriff Sellers stopped by again, clearly not happy with the article. "I have interviewed everyone in this neighborhood, and there is not a single suspicious person around here; no one with a record, no one with a history of saying crazy things or acting out of line. I would wager no one from around here put manure in Dutch's mailbox or ran him down. Neither Cindy nor Beau was killed with a gun, so I can't even try to match a bullet. If either one had been hit from behind with something like a large stone, an older person or a person with a smaller size could have surprised them, then strangled them. Cindy and Beau had no head contusions. I can't make hide nor hair out of the idea someone would target this place, like a former resident with some kind of vendetta. I asked around. No leads. I asked the paper not to run the article."

The newspaper story rattled Mom. She made changes. She put double-bolt locks on the front and back doors. She first had to replace the back door, it being so weathered. For a month, she slept in Kyle's bed. We stashed a baseball bat under each bed. I reflected on the promise I made to myself just a few weeks ago on the creek bridge. Our single-shot, bolt-action rifle remained cradled on the back-porch wall, but now with the bullets nearby. With Mom's approval, I took it down and practiced several days in a row. Mom still refused to fire it.

Fear colored the air.

Both murders remained unsolved. The newspaper articles ceased. The sheriff stopped by now and then, checking up on Dutch and us. Dutch reported no new targeting incidents. Days became weeks, and weeks, months. I settled into my new school, now in the seventh grade.

Twenty-nine

Years later, I reflected on Adams Creek where nothing happened except the four seasons, deep freezes, thunderstorms, and the occasional minor accident. In my Adams Creek years, not a single tornado ripped through, our home or out buildings never at risk other than the 1959 flood, though the threat often lurked on the horizon. I remembered, more than once, home alone, standing in the middle of a field, scanning the horizon in case a funnel touched down. With a visual warning, I could take cover under Ole Steely or in a ditch.

In a very short span, less than a year, three people died–two murdered–and my dog. Other than auto accidents, I doubt three people died in Clay County over the same period. Remembering the God of retribution our pastor preached on, what sins might we have committed to upset God? After all, we led peaceful, and God-fearing lives. This drama and trauma knocked us into a daze, not like in a big metropolis or a land far, far away, but across the river, and down our riverbank. Was Beau the combustible toxin coming from Jim Crow country? If Beau killed Cindy, as I still suspected in my craw, what did this have to do with Dutch? He enlivened and educated our lives even as his presence unsettled the neighborhood. He did not light the fuse. Or did he? Now Beau had been murdered.

God and I remained at odds. I remembered Dutch wondering if God paid any attention to the plight of his people over all the years since abducted in Africa and brought to the "land of the free." Compared to Dutch's complaint, mine seemed as insignificant as a poison ivy rash. How could a loving God allow two perfectly innocent people, Cindy McBrady and Jimmy Jenkins to die, or even a bad seed like Beau? Other than the circumstances, I never fretted over Beau's death, harboring no emotion. Mom felt differently. If God doesn't meddle in people's lives, what does he do other than, like that lucky old sun, "roll around heaven all day?" If we try our best, stay out of trouble, shouldn't we be safer? I remained more comfortable with Jesus. Jesus I could visualize. Through the sixth grade, I hadn't progressed much on this faith thing and my confusion over God, but accepting Mom's religion. I could do a lot worse believing what she believed simply because she came pretty close to perfection, my Jesus on earth, even if she didn't step between Dad and Kyle and me. Kids take it on faith their parents know best, including religion. At some point, a light goes on inside us and we "get it." I still did not "get it." I liked my Baptist Youth Fellowship group led by Mrs. Williams. I loved church camp, pajama hijacking notwithstanding. I warmed, seeing Mom embraced by her fellow church members. They brightened her day. Dutch was right, modeling myself after Mom could be my guiding light. I could ask myself, "What would Mom do?"

Dad died too soon to model much other than the bad stuff: smoking, the anger, and the beatings, especially Mom. I benefitted from his gentler genes, my love of books, music, and my good grades. I try to remember this. I wonder how my life might have progressed differently if Dutch had not come along and adopted us, and we him, shortly after Dad died. When Jimmy died, Dutch was there. When Cindy died, he remained a steadying presence. Between Mom, Dutch, Kyle, and Ken more remotely, I felt my life filled with family helping me learn to live. I could write a master's thesis about Negro history, trains, and the Pullman Porters. I learned about theses from Ken's schooling.

Cindy McBrady's death continued to chew on me, her lifeless image on the bank chiseled into my memory forever. And those "what ifs." What if she had not gone down the riverbank? What if I had been near the house mowing the lawn or hoeing the garden with a vantage point of noticing all? And the biggest what if: Jimmy's sled was properly oiled, or him taking a pass on the sled run, not dying, and Beau never moving into the neighborhood. I call them the "but fors." One thing led to another, and another, and another. Now three people are dead, two remaining a mystery. Does God know? Mom counsels God knows all. Maybe someday he will let us in on who killed Cindy and Beau.

I entered the seventh grade. The intermediate larger school brought in kids from three other grade schools, some familiar because I competed against them in football. My new classmates knew of me, my name showing up in the paper surrounding the deaths of Jimmy, Cindy, and Beau and the photos from 4-H. This notoriety put me ill at ease. Their distancing didn't approach the aftermath of Jimmy's death when it seemed I carried a plague. I never faulted my classmates; they didn't know what to say. No seventh grader went out of their way to avoid me, but time needed to work its healing power before any sense of normality returned. After losing Jimmy and joining a much larger school, new acquaintances took, though slowly. Mom let me try out for football, now tackle football. Friendships came with my new teammates but none as close as Jimmy's.

Ken drove up every other month. His weekend job kept him from visiting more. He and Mom spoke on the phone at least twice a month. With Kyle gone and with many of his high school buddies moving away, we spent more time together. He still felt more like an uncle. He enjoyed my retelling of the exploits of Dutch and James, and even joined me on the riverbank a couple of times. I welcomed stories about Korea. One day, he asked me to walk with him up to Ole Steely. We both gazed at the flowing water. Then he said, "Kurt, Kyle told me about Dad and his beating on Mom. I pressured Mom about it, though it was not something she wanted to talk about. You need to know that Dad was not like that when I was growing up. I remember a good father. Sure, he swatted me from time to time when I deserved it. I now know more about his past than I did then. I remember that time in Fort Wayne. I was around seven or eight. I did some research in college. Dad had a nervous breakdown."

"What's that?"

"It's usually caused by a severe depression, or extreme anxiety."

"What's depression?"

"Well, think on how you felt when you lost Jimmy, and also Tippy. For a time, you were depressed weren't you?"

"I suppose, I just know I felt very sad, and lonely."

"But you kept going, getting up every day, and going to school. For Dad, maybe life started piling up, losing his mother at age nine, he and Mom struggling through The Depression, all of the odd jobs and job changes, battling every day just to eke out a living, and one day he didn't want to get out of bed. I did notice a change when he finally revived himself and found a new job. Then you were born, and we moved here. I did not see the beatings coming. I was already in college by then. I never knew until I returned from Korea. Mom and Kyle kept it from me."

I told Ken about my talk with Mom on the creek bridge a while back.

"She told me. Told me about both you and Kyle wanting to kill Dad. I guess I would have had to be here to understand that. I'd like to think I would have charged downstairs, stopped it, and told Dad to never hit Mom again."

"The first time it happened, I wanted Kyle to do something. Then he reminded me he was smaller than Dad. You know about the pitchfork?"

"Kyle told me. But what I wanted to talk with you about is Kyle talked about the three of us making a vow, and I agreed."

"What kind of vow?"

"We vowed that no matter what happens to us, especially bad stuff, and no matter how angry we might get, we will never ever hit our wives. And even more, we will not verbally abuse them, like calling them names or demeaning them in anyway. Everyone knows that children see their parents as role models. Well in this case, Dad modeled the exact opposite of how we see ourselves living our lives. We draw the line. It stops with Dad. Can you swear to this, no matter how frustrated or angry you might become? Remember, both you and Kyle felt like killing Dad."

"That's easy, of course. I think Kyle and I had thoughts of killing Dad to protect Mom. I told Mom I could not imagine how a husband could hit his wife or say what we heard him say to her."

"Nor can I. So, you doing okay after all that happened last summer?"

"I guess so, seems like a long time ago now. It's good to have Dutch and sometimes James to talk with. I still feel some guilt over Jimmy."

"Kyle was right. It's not your fault. You have to let that go."

Easier said than done.

We spotted a turtle squatting on a rock.

"You ever hit one?"

"Nope."

"Me neither. Yet somehow I could bag rabbits. Maybe I missed on purpose. Never seemed very sporting to shoot at something just sitting there. Well, we make an exception for blackbirds going after our cherries."

"Roger that."

"Pretty sure Mom didn't have a recipe for Turtle Soup. But a rabbit might be supper."

"Mom says the time you spent in the Army and Korea helped you think things through."

"It did. After getting my master's I plan on going after a PhD, but probably not at Indiana Tech. I am applying to the University of Wisconsin in Madison."

"What's a PhD?"

"It stands for Doctor of Philosophy."

"I didn't know you were majoring in philosophy. What kind of job is that?

"I'm not majoring in philosophy. I am majoring in Education Administration. My goal is to be a professor and teach future school administrators. You can get a PhD in lots of areas. I think centuries ago, the study of philosophy was a common degree. So they just kept the name for all sorts of courses of extended learning. It is the highest degree a person can get, unless you end up becoming a doctor."

"Will I have to call you doctor or professor?"

"No, I'll always be Ken to you and family, but my future students might, as might my colleagues."

"You must be pretty smart, like Dad."

"Mom says you're pretty smart yourself."

"So far, so good. I'm a bit worried about the sciences once I get into junior high and high school. Kyle griped a lot about Chemistry and Physics. I don't think that part of Dad got into my genes. Dutch learned me about genes."

"I struggled with those courses myself."

Ken put his arm around me as we walked back to the house.

Dutch remained a Sunday paper only customer. I still saw James a few times a year. His grandson, Danny, as a senior, led the Beavers back to the state finals in 1961, this time losing the semi-final game to conference rival Kendall. Danny held the all-time Beaver scoring record for a long time.

The spring after the 1961 season, I found James with Dutch again at the fishing spot.

I lamented to James, "I wish I had seen Danny play. I read all of the write-ups in the paper."

"I never missed a home game and even went to some away games. Boy, he shot the lights out. Don't know where he got it. His dad never played basketball. The Beavers had a great year except for Kendall. They whipped us pretty good three times, twice in conference play and then in the final four. Danny's a good boy. He is getting some college offers but from smaller schools, not the Big Ten. Would have been nice to see him play down the road with the Engineers or the Hoosiers."

"Speaking of the Hoosiers, where in tarnation did that name come from? Mom says she hasn't a clue. I'll bet my dad would have known."

James took a stab. "I heard lots of stories, and I don't rightly know which is true. I hanker for the one told by Hoosier James Whitcomb Riley." He chuckled, "I actually read some white literature. He claims that early settlers, following a bar fight, might find a severed ear on the floor and ask, 'Whose ear?' Over the years, this evolved into Hoosiers."

"James, that's a bunch of hooey."

Dutch, in James's defense, said, "I suspect in high school, you will read about how folks down Louisiana way became known as Cajuns. They originally were called Acadians. Hard to figure how that became Cajuns. My folks spoke of it."

I changed the subject back to basketball. "I shoot pretty well, but I'm just not quick enough for basketball, especially defense, or maybe even for quarterback. I did make the team. Tackle football sure beats on you, much more than flag competition in grade school. There's always something hurting, a sprained ankle or wrist, jammed finger or a bruise. To tell the truth, I don't like getting hit. Fortunately, a quarterback doesn't carry the ball often."

"I would have thought growing up on a farm might have toughened you up more."

"Me too. Maybe I'm not nasty enough. Must be part of my genes. You have to want to hit people to play tackle football. I think Mom hoped I would choose basketball, worrying about injuries. Maybe I should focus on my singing."

My voice began changing to tenor. Throughout high school, I sang in both the choir and a smaller ensemble, called Swing Choir. I soloed in church and the choir. I began getting invitations to sing at weddings and special events. Not surprising, I aced history though no course compared to those riverside or kitchen table supper classes. Though Dad, my math tutor, died years earlier, I did well in math, even algebra, and geometry. If my classmates ever harbored any higher airs toward me, they developed amnesia and one year elected this clodhopper a class officer.

A wrought iron fence surrounded Twin Rivers High School, a three-story weathered red brick structure filling a city block. Ivy climbed its walls. It could have doubled as the inspiration for the classic graduation song, "The Halls of Ivy." Our class sang it at our graduation ceremony.

"Oh, we love the halls of Ivy that surround us here today,
And we will not forget though we be far, far away.
To the hallowed halls if Ivy, every voice will bid farewell
And shimmer off in twilight like the old vesper bell.

One day a hush will fall;
The footsteps of us all
Will echo down the hall and disappear.
But as we sadly start our journeys far apart,
A part of every heart will linger here."

The summer after my sophomore year, the Review stopped using paperboys, changing to automobile mailbox delivery with much longer routes. To make up for the income loss, I hired out most days each summer at a dollar an hour, baling and stacking hay in barns, my forte. I saw Dutch less, though sometimes I stopped by after church.

My face began sprouting hair, Kyle's aftershave advice: Old Spice. Prior to this transition, the only odor I sprayed on, OFF, the musk of country folk.

The Chicago Cubs continued to stink. In 1962, the newly formed New York Mets won only one regular season series. Yup, against the Cubs.

I dated often, though like Dutch and his lady friends, none took. Good friends partnered with me at both the Junior and Senior Proms. I harbored no expectations to fall in love with a classmate, marry, and remain in the area. I left high school a sexual novice and a non-drinker unless you called my twice a year tablespoon of bourbon for sore throats drinking. I think the awful taste carried over from my early years and tainted any interest for alcohol through my teens.

Kyle returned from the Navy at the end of my sophomore year and took a factory job in Indianapolis. He drove up for a night every month or so if Mom and I couldn't figure out a task. He and I laughed over his comment about his interest in seeing how I would change now knowing what he meant. Ken, now married, entered a PhD program in education administration at the University of Wisconsin in Madison. We saw him a few times a year.

The Chip Hilton football fantasy never materialized through the rest of my secondary schooling. Those genes Dutch explained one day on the riverbank programmed a different genetic mapping. Well into my sophomore year, my height and weight framed a body too small for the quarterback competition. And there was that lack of speed thing. My conflicted brain probably hindered me. Except for writing, I did everything right-handed: left-brained or right-brained? I blame my first-grade teacher for sticking a pencil in my left hand. There must have been some sort of test. Maybe my head injury at age four scrambled my brain. Kyle may have been right. I warmed the bench through my sophomore year. I left the team after the season. Soon after, I began a growth spurt. I found no amusement in this, maybe God's humor, he being our creator as Mom reminded.

God and I reached a tentative pact. If he watched over Adams Creek more closely, I would consent to dunking. After an uneventful 1961 and 1962, my church dunked me in a neighboring church's baptismal, the water clearer than the Eel River or the family's communal tub water I washed in until Kyle left. The preacher still intoned, "In the name of the Father, Son, and Holy Ghost" before dunking me. I let it pass. I preferred my creek side chats with Jesus. Mom joked, "With just you and me, after Communion Sundays, I won't have to make Sunday dinners."

"Not funny, Mom."

Beau's father moved into Twin Rivers shortly after Beau's death.

Mrs. McBrady and her son moved away the summer of 1962.

As the years progressed, Dutch and I still lolled away days down the riverbank. He continued sharing remembrances of his Pullman years, and I continued peppering him with questions about places beyond my narrow experiences. He expounded even more on the labor fight to form a union. Late in the summer of 1963, following the famous March on Washington, where Martin Luther King delivered his "I Have a Dream" speech, Dutch gave me a short history lesson on A. Philip Randolph. Dutch credited Randolph with the launching of the Brotherhood union, the porters recruiting him to lead the movement in 1925. They needed a leader and a visionary from outside the company and free of Pullman's spies. Randolph's leadership and perseverance finally drove Pullman to the bargaining table. Randolph later turned his attention to civil rights; especially in the aftermath of Brown versus Board of Education, compliance resisted throughout the South. Randolph met and mentored Martin Luther King. It was Randolph's dream for a March on Washington. Dutch and James thought about going, but James fell ill so they scuttled the plan.

The passage of the Civil Rights Act of 1964 stirred Dutch to his core; he couldn't stop talking about it. "I feel like I rolled a lucky seven in a crap game."

In my junior year, we finally bought our first television, a used black and white. Except for history, my grades began dropping like a watermelon tossed off the bridge, from an A minus average to C Plus. I found it all watchable, *The Red Skelton Show* a favorite, its skits with Clem Kadiddlehopper and Freddie the Freeloader, and the iconic sign-off, "Goodnight and God Bless."

Early in my senior year, the Key Club chose me for membership. In Twin Rivers in the 1960s, Key Club, exclusively male, seemed more akin to a high school version of a college fraternity without the pledging process. Ken explained fraternities to me should I ever become curious when I entered college. Current Key Club members nominated candidates, who were then given a thumbs up or thumbs down. I felt honored. When I told Dutch, he congratulated me, being a clodhopper and all.

Key Club is a service organization first and foremost. This appealed to me. In Twin Rivers, the club also put on an annual revue called Key Club Kapers. What now is a painful memory, in 1965, my conscience failed me, and the learning from Dutch and James. Key Club added a minstrel show to its annual Kapers musical revue. As a known singer and soloist, the revue's directors asked me to solo. I did. Six other club members put on blackface and unflatteringly mimicked Negroes.

To this day, I do not know why I did not refuse to sing or even remain in the club. Did I sit on my conscience because, even though my classmates elected me a school officer, and the Key Club voted me in, I still felt the outsider? I loved singing and watching an audience's response. Was that it– the audience accolades? Mom, learning of this, refused to attend the show and reminded me of her admonition after she heard my story, at age eight, about the neighbor lady following Crispus Attacks winning the state basketball championship: I should never go along just to get along. A couple of weeks after the show, the American Legion in Twin Rivers invited Key Club to perform the revue. There in the front row sat three Negro veterans of World War II. Their expressions did not change during the entire minstrel. I saved all printed programs from school plays, concerts, and church listing my name as either an actor or a soloist. I kept the Key Club Kapers' program.

I could have kept this from Dutch, but decided to fess up a few days after American Legion show, while down the riverbank. The American Legion show did gnaw at me. In typical fashion, he spat, took off his hat, and scratched his head. Then he gave me a look that ripped out my guts, worse than Mom's looks, a look of sadness.

He remained silent for a few moments, even the river flow seemed to pause, and then said, "Of course you know how much this hurts to hear, and from you. You failed this first test, but there will be others going forward. You, and your conscience, need to have a little chat. You are still far from the man you will become. I know you know better, in your heart, and will do the right thing the next time and any time after that. We all go through life wanting do-overs. I have lost count of how many I times I wanted to rewind Father Time. Time can heal, but it does not forget. Now git on back up the path. I don't want to see your face for a bit. We will put this behind us and start fresh the next time we meet." For several days, I mulled it over and over while moping around. I did go along to get along.

I never earned an F my senior year, but I barely scraped through Chemistry. My GPA up until my senior year earned me a small academic scholarship to a church-based college in Indianapolis. Mom financed the balance of my tuition, room, and board with a loan secured by the farm. I worked part-tine as a janitor in my dorm to earn spending money. When I dropped out, this loan debt burdened mom. I paid her back during the first year of my three-year Army tenure.

Mom brought Dutch to my high school graduation ceremony. Ken drove home from Madison, and Kyle from his job in Indianapolis. Five Negroes matriculated in my graduation class. None of them became friends, acquaintances only.

Later that summer, the Voting Rights Act passed. Dutch beamed, "The good Lord can take me now."

Also later that summer, Medicare became the law of the land. Mom breathed a sigh of relief, knowing she would not be a burden to her boys.

When I left for college, Dutch gave me twenty dollars after insisting I sit a spell and have some bacon. We shook hands as I left, tears watering our eyes. I stopped by when home from school holidays and Christmas and Spring Break, again before leaving for basic training in Kentucky the summer of 1967, and finally in the summer of 1968 before shipping out to Germany.

"Dutch, you will love this story. I was stationed at the White Sands Missile Range outside of Las Cruces, New Mexico when my orders for Germany came through. That's not the entire story. The hospital operated just fifty beds and treated pretty routine medical cases. I never got used to the climate or the surroundings, very hot and desert-like. I hiked up the nearby mountains pretty far to even see lots of trees. I missed the Midwest. Boredom doesn't begin to describe my mood. After four months, I walked into the personnel office and volunteered for Viet Nam. Can you believe it?"

Dutch eyed me. "No I can't."

"Something weird came over me, though I wouldn't call it patriotism, something about being in the thick of it with my generation. It certainly wasn't wanderlust. Kyle would say it was falling off the swing when I was four. Two months later, the personnel officer called me into his office."

"Well Specialist Baumann, I have your orders for Viet Nam."

I gulped.

"Other orders arrived the same day. These orders are for the 97th General Hospital in Frankfurt, Germany. Which do you prefer?"

"Sir, I will accept the orders for Germany."

"How this happened made no sense. Thankfully, the folks at Army headquarters in DC were not on the same page. Maybe it was my German name, Baumann. I am grateful the officer gave me a choice."

Dutch smiled broadly. "Sometimes life deals us a royal flush, sort of like back in 1960 when my sister came to pick me up the day before Cindy was killed."

"Dutch, I need to ask you something. While growing up, I always referred to you and your race as Negroes. I remember when you told me about the NAACP, and when it was formed back in the early 1900s, and used the words, 'colored people.' And I remember asking you about this back around the time of the murders. Since I have been in the Army, I am hearing Negro soldiers wanting to be called black. I want to be respectful. Is black the term I should now be using?"

"If it is just you and me, it still don't matter much. I am Dutch, and you are Kurt. This it the way it should be with anyone once you get to know a person. Best you begin using black if you are speaking about my kind. Any race deserves to be called what they want to be called and not someone one else's label. You, meaning white folk, don't get to pick what to call me. That needs to stop. Lots of turmoil in the bigger cities these days. Lots of pent up anger and frustration. I don't condone violence. If I were a younger man, I suspect I'd be right there with my fellow blacks, but only for peaceful protest. I am more like Reverend King, rest his soul. I did what I could for my Porter brothers. I served my time. There is progress, what with the Civil Rights Act and the Voting Rights Act. But true acceptance and integration will take a long time I fear."

I was stationed at White Sands Missile Range when Reverend King was assassinated. Mom had written that Dutch had been by for supper shortly after and could not stop talking about it. "He was quite shook up about it."

"Dutch, I sure hope you're still alive, frying up bacon, and landing a bass when I get back."

"Me too. Listen up now. You get your head squared away over there in Germany. And when you come back, you get busy with finishing your college education. If I had a do-over, I would have gone on to college."

"Dutch, I figure things will most likely be different. Mom feels the same as you, even though she knows she can't help me much. I promised her I would. I just need a little time."

I gave Dutch a hug, catching him off-guard. I suspect a long time had passed since his last one. Mom taught me to hug. He appeared frailer. I wondered if I would ever see him again.

On my flight to Germany, I could not sleep. In my wakefulness I also wondered if I might never return to Adams Creek other than to pass through or visit Mom. Other 'come hither' images teased me, like the sunny Rose Bowl scenes each New Year's Day, or the iconic images of the Lincoln and Washington Monuments in our nation's capital. Siren songs? The appeal of 'the other' enticed me more than any feeling of no longer belonging.

Basic training in Kentucky, medic training in San Antonio, Texas, and my first posting in New Mexico did little to wet my wanderlust (I never considered Nam a travel destination). Those were military bases, but new horizons nonetheless. Surely Germany would prove venturesome even given the comfort and familiar language of a military base and hospital. Soldiers in the know informed me a GI could travel almost anywhere on a three-day pass. Peering over a map, the possibilities seemed endless. I saw new adventures and explorations in my future.

When you grow up in or spend enough time in environs like northern Indiana, you feel it in your bones. You know it from squishing its dirt between your toes, a refreshing summer dip in a river, smelling its soil, inhaling its air, exploring its back-roads, living its seasons, speaking its lingo, or becoming involved in a tavern fight. But even then, you may miss something, especially if missing an ear. A part of me would forever remain a Hoosier. You can leave it, but it never leaves you.

Dutch fished less, finding the walk taxing and the seining challenging, even baiting a hook, as Mom reported. He quit chewing tobacco. Mom and James looked in on him, bringing cooked meals. The Adams Creek Baptist Church ladies cooked for and looked after shut-ins, even non-members, even Dutch. Mom delivered those meals. Mom never wrote much about those visits, other than saying she had done so, but I imagined him frying up some bacon and asking her to sit a spell and chat the day; lots of living between those two and lots of rail miles on Dutch. Both James and Mom brought him supplies. Widow Kreider passed. Her will stated any new owner must allow Dutch to continue to rent, a request honored by the new owners.

Thirty

A year after Dutch's passing, I mustered out of the Army, my Estimated Time of Separation (dubbed ETS) calendar shrunk to one day. Standard banter between soldiers always included the question, "When's your ETS?" If less than six months, you wore the much-longed-for badge of being "short." Each morning of my final year, after a shower and shave, I ceremonially crossed off another day. Throughout my two-year posting, I fed my wanderlust. The three-day passes, plus leaves, found me discovering England, Belgium, France, Austria, Italy, and Spain. Not bad for a clodhopper from Indiana.

The last day of hospital ward duty, the nurses and fellow medics anesthetized me with a fifth of vodka mixed with orange juice, steering me clear of patients. Upon turning twenty-one, my ward and barracks' buddies recommended a Screwdriver for my alcohol baptism. The Army cured me of my alcohol abstinence. After sleeping off the Screwdriver buzz, I stayed up all night playing Solitaire. Turtles crossing the road outside my Adams Creek farm moved faster than time that night. The long-anticipated day began with an eight-hour flight from Frankfurt, Germany to Newark, New Jersey, and then on to Fort Dix for final mustering out. I scored a window seat wanting to peer down on a country I hoped to visit in the future under different circumstances. Clear skies favored me. Finding the music channel, I plugged in my earphones. The timing could not have been more serendipitous. Simon & Garfunkel's "Bridge Over Troubled Water" neared its end. As my silver Boeing 707 began its slow turn to the west and homeward bound, the lyrics fed my soul:

"Sail on, silver girl, sail on by.
Your time has come to shine.
All your dreams are on their way."

I thought about the day in the personnel office in New Mexico two years prior. I rolled a lucky seven. Yes, time stopped in the Army, though now three years older, and hopefully a bit wiser. I felt hopeful, my time at hand, and the days of marking time, past. Tick tock, tick tock, tick tock.

My conscience and I made peace over Jimmy's death. Military service gave me time to reflect and recharge my batteries.

While serving in Germany, Ken finished his PhD and became a professor at the University of Wisconsin. Kyle shifted his paradigm from a mediocre student and entered college with a mission. I matured from my early college malaise and question of "What am I doing here?" to "It's time to step up." I hankered for a do-over. Good Dad would have been pleased. Otherwise, I might have taunted myself with, "You must be dumber than a bucket of rocks."

My second day home, I walked across Ole Steely and halfway up the hill to the graveyard. Passing by Jimmy and Beau's old house, I noticed a car in the driveway and two young children frolicking in the yard. I found Dutch's tombstone in the farthest corner from the road, separate from the other tombstones and markings. The tombstone's size surprised me, larger than the others. The tombstone read: "Joshua 'Dutch' Clemons. Born 1890. Died 1969. Founder of the Brotherhood of Sleeping Car Porters. Loved sweet potato pie and landing a bass." At the base, I placed a bouquet of snap dragons in a Hills Brothers can.

A blue jay jabbered in a nearby tree branching out over the graveyard fencing. Another jay nested nearby. I invaded their territory. I asked the scolding jay, "Are you Dutch?" I smiled about fearing this cemetery as a youngster. Maybe cemetery fears fade when you know a person buried there.

Hearing movement behind me, I turned to see James, limping and looking like death's bed. James' wife passed before Dutch, shortly after I left for Germany. We chatted a bit, reminiscing. He shared with me the day he found Dutch on the bank slumped over as if nodding off.

"What a way to go, hoping for a bass." Following Dutch's wishes only a short obituary appeared in the paper, no services. Mom kept a clipping. James said, "At first, Dutch's marking was quite small. When the union heard about his death, it paid for this tombstone, one befitting his brotherhood service all those years. They wanted to bring his casket to Chicago, but he left instructions to be buried here. Something about this place got inside his bones. Never one to draw attention–his color did that–he did say he wanted to integrate this cemetery. He also said that if heaven existed, at least he wouldn't have to deal with prejudice anymore. Souls don't have color." James noted the irony of the Pullman Sleeping Car Company and Dutch dying in the same year.

James drove me back home but did not come in. Mom said James had stopped by. She told him where to find me. James left Mom a large sealed envelope, saying his doctor informed him he only had a few months left. When he passed, he wanted Mom to pass the envelope along to Sheriff Sellers.

Mom and I kept looking at the bulky envelope pondering its contents, tempted, but duty-bound by James' instructions.

Several days later, I visited Dad's grave. I noticed two robins, Dad's favorite bird, perched on a nearby fence. In 1957, Mom buried him in a church cemetery four miles away, not in nearby Mount Calvary. "I wanted him near a church."

When I returned from the cemetery, she wanted me to know more, now that I was older.

"It was a struggle for me, but I was bound and determined to give him a proper burial in a proper plot and with a proper headstone. Your dad did not have many friends, so not many attended the viewing. I think more came out of friendship for me than for mourning over your dad, especially my church family. It took me a year to pay off the debt with the funeral home. Ken helped some. I am forever indebted to them for extending me the credit."

Mom wished to be buried next to Dad. She asked Ken to handle the arrangements "when the good Lord calls me home." I went with her during a few visits while living at home. If nothing else, the Army years gifted me time to reflect on my father and what made him tick, but more about understanding than forgiveness. As Dutch said, "time never forgets." I could never forgive the beatings, and the sounds from our kitchen; you never forget those. Now all of his sons experienced fits of restlessness and uncertainty.

By now, I felt up to talking with Mom about Dad. She shared their early years including about fifty letters she saved from their courting days in the early 1930s. They exchanged hand-written letters twice a week. The Army Air Corps employed his radio skills on temporary assignments throughout the west. During those postings, he helped build, wire, and operate radio stations used exclusively for tracking the Army Air Corps postal service. His letters called them ships, not airplanes. He returned to the farm in northwestern Indiana six months before they married early in 1935. As a reserve, the Army Air Corps used him as needed over the Illinois state border at Chanute Field.

I pored through the letters, searching for clues. I found no signs of his demon. Other than what Ken said, I had no cognitive first-hand experience with the aftermath of his nervous breakdown. None of the letters struck me as love letters, though affection showed. He often began "Dear Sweetheart," but more often, "Dear Emma." The mundaneness of each day filled the pages. One such letter read,

"Last Thursday, we decided to cut oats instead of fishing and thus finished that evening. Then yesterday, one of the neighbors came over and wanted us to finish cutting for him. We had put the binder away, but if it doesn't rain today, his field will be finished by this evening with enough time left to get the binder put away again. It may not be worth our while to get the machinery out for such a short job since he had only thirty acres. But a fellow can't refuse when a neighbor's binder breaks down and he is left with some grain uncut. Our machine could handle another hundred or hundred fifty acres each year nicely.

"Dad is mowing the weeds around the oat fields, and the girls have just gotten back from picking blackberries from along the road. Did you get many tomatoes over at your brothers? We are having all that we can eat twice a day and about every other day, there is enough sweet corn for a mess. Sunday afternoon, my brother-in-law and my cousin went fishing. They stayed till about eight and came back with a three-pound walleye. We had a bass in the horse tank that weighed about a pound, so the two of them made a mess.

"My sister made some soap from that recipe last night, and this morning it still hadn't gotten hard. Right now, it's about the consistency of cake batter. Looks as though she will have to use it with a spoon or something. When she first

started, she was wondering how that colored lard could ever get white, but it turned out alright that way.

"You should get this letter Wednesday, so that won't allow enough time to get a reply and then write to you again. Thus, till I hear further plans, I'll expect to find you at the picnic Sunday."

Dad always signed off with, "Your sweetheart, Karl."

Dad was a man of the soil and remained one until his early death. His acquired skills, like setting up radio tracking stations and operating them, never elevated him to his sense of self-worth.

Thirty-one

James' obituary appeared in the Review two months later. Mom and I attended the viewing, the only white folks there besides Sheriff Sellers. I felt comfortable looking at James in the open casket. I finally met his grandson, Danny, now married with two young children. His grandpa spoke often of Dutch, our family, Adam's Creek, and the homicides. Mom told the sheriff about the envelope. He came by the next day.

Sitting at the kitchen table, he opened the large envelope finding two envelopes, one with his name on it, the other, mine. He opened his and scanned the lengthy letter as if looking for something. Suddenly, his eyes widened as he slowly shook his head. I detected a slight smile. "Beau Braddock killed Cindy McBrady. Dutch and James killed Beau. This here is a confession."

He handed the letter to Mom, standing near him; she read out loud, her hands shaking and voice quivering. I remained standing although my legs felt jiggly.

"I put this confession down in hopes it will put behind for all the terrible murder of Cindy McBrady. I do this with a peaceful heart though not without some remorse."

Mom took several deep breaths, and sat to steady herself.

"The day Beau killed Cindy, I had gone down the river another fifty yards to try my luck at another fishing hole. Actually, I was at the spot where a hobo occasionally camped while passing through or waiting for another train. The wind came easterly and not from up or down river. The grassy bank would have made it hard to trace a footprint. I was feeling pretty good, landing a nice sized bass. I heard the Wabash Cannonball whistling through, and then I distinctly heard a girl's voice, 'Stop it, Beau!' My new hearing aids had been serving me well. I had not heard Cindy's voice, so I didn't place it. To my dying day, I will feel badly about not racing back up the riverbank. Had I done so, could I have saved her? Did I pause because of my color and Negro history being filled with ignorance, hate, and lies? Maybe. But also, Beau could have had a knife or a gun. A knife wouldn't have scared me, but a gun would. Thinking back, surely Cindy McBrady would have fingered Beau and not me. I never met her, other than passing each other on the road to Carrolls on occasion. She always avoided eye contact, even when I'd tip my hat. Kurt always had nice things to say about her except for that one time on the bus. No matter, I hesitated. Then I noticed the familiar cowgirl hat float by. I knew then it had to be Cindy. I eased my way slowly back up the riverbank. Once at the spot, I saw Cindy's body. Her chest wasn't moving. I saw no blood. Her jeans were unzipped and down to her knees. Her underwear looked to be in place. Her blouse partially ripped open, her cowboy boots still on, and hat missing.*

" *I rushed back to get my gear, and my bass, and returned back to where Cindy lay. The path back up to the bridge was the only way I knew how to get out of there. I thought about crossing the river to the other side but the river flowed deep enough to scare me since I couldn't swim. I was already plenty scared. I grabbed a broken tree branch to fuzz up the footprints. I walked hurriedly back up the path to the bridge trying to stay on the grassy side to avoid leaving any footprints. Calico was tied to a fence post. Once at the road, I assumed my normal pace, heart still pounding. I saw neither hide nor hair of Beau, his car gone from his driveway. I remember noticing it there when I passed by on my way down the riverbank that day. I don't think anyone saw me, but I had no way of knowing. No car passed me, and no one worked in their front yard. Folks were at work or some place. Old man Moss wasn't rocking on his front porch. By then, I had been up and down that road so much with my fishing gear, I didn't stick out anymore, even being a Negro. I fought hard to keep my wits about me, repeating to myself, 'Stay calm, Dutch. Stay calm.'*

"As luck would have it, or God's grace, James was already scheduled to come fetch me and take me to town for my shopping. I needed some things for my trip to Alabama. He showed up shortly after I got home. I told him we needed to leave quickly. First, I took care of some duties. I packed my personal stuff, some clothes, and shut the place down. I left the monthly rent and a note in widow Kreider's mailbox saying 'I have gone to Alabama to visit my sister for two-three weeks.' I asked her to collect my mail. I remembered to bring my bass to give to James. On the way to town, I told James what happened. He nearly drove off the road. He even stopped for a spell just to catch his breath.*

"Collecting ourselves, we began mapping out a plan. As we entered Twin Rivers on a back road, we heard the sirens heading east on Highway 24. When we got to his house, he called Lucas Mayfield in Addison. Fortunately, he had not moved yet. James told his wife that if the sheriff came by, she was to say he had gone fishing on the Wabash a few miles east out Highway 24 and would be back soon. Grandson Danny was playing basketball at a city park. James told her he would fill her in when he got back in a couple of hours. Back in the car, James drove me to Addison, an hour's drive, carefully watching our speed and obeying all traffic laws. James* *dropped me off and headed back home hoping to arrive before the sheriff. I called my sister and told her about the change in plans. She had planned on driving up that coming Friday. I probably would have been safe in Addison with Lucas until Friday, but Lucas volunteered to drive me down to Alabama that Wednesday afternoon, thinking it best I get out of Indiana."*

I said, "I remember Dutch telling me his sister would be picking him up and to cancel his Sunday paper delivery until he returned. I don't recollect if he said which day."

"The sheriff came by James' house before he returned from Addison, but our story worked, James making sure he walked in with his fishing gear and my bass. He would claim no knowledge of when my sister was driving up and taking me back to Alabama for a few weeks."

Sheriff Sellers nodded his head.

"James could also claim he had no way of contacting me. He did not know my sister's married name, nor her phone number, or her address in Selma. He did not have to lie about it. He only knew her as Bessie. I thought it best to keep it that way. Bessie knew how to reach James if anything happened to me in Alabama. So Sheriff Sellers had no way of reaching me. The listing in the Selma phone book was in her husband's name. The sheriff did not know our connection to Lucas Mayfield, so he had no reason to track him down either. Certainly, James would not have told him. And if Emma passed on Lucas's name to the sheriff, Lucas could claim no knowledge and say he had not seen me since he visited me a year ago this past June. Lucas would have enough time to be back in Addison, driving straight down and back in less than twenty-four hours. He did that."

Mom stopped reading. "You know I never even thought about Lucas in this matter."

"My sister drove me back to James' house three weeks later. She knew that I would be giving her number to Sheriff

Sellers. We went over the dates to make sure we were on the same page. I had her saying she picked me up the day before the murder–would have been a Tuesday–and we drove straight through to Selma. I won't repeat here all that transpired the week I returned. All this is known. James now had Bessie's phone number because I called shortly after I arrived in Selma. Not recollecting right now whether that would have been Thursday or Friday. But at least when the sheriff first interviewed him, he could claim ignorance of how to reach me. Turns out, the sheriff never talked with James again while I was in Alabama, so he didn't have to lie then either. James and I talked on the phone several times. He said he was saving all of the papers. I believe our connection to Lucas remained unknown to Sheriff Sellers until the reading of this confession."

"You know, I thought about contacting the Selma police with a description of Dutch and sending them a picture of Dutch from that newspaper story. But Selma is a pretty big town. A police chief doesn't suddenly pull a whole bunch of police off regular duty to track down a person, even a Negro, unless there's a pretty clear reason to do so and not just tying up loose ends. If Dutch hadn't returned in a few weeks I might have done that, especially if no other lead materialized. Course by then, if Dutch had killed Cindy, he could have been anywhere."

"The next time I went down the bank to fish, the hole looked pretty much as before. When James joined me, we began talking. It seemed plain to us Beau would likely get off scot-free. We had read the papers and knew about his alibi. We talked about people we knew over the years, like Beau, who seemed to get off too easily, especially if a Negro was involved. All the stories we read about or were passed up and down the lines grind at your core over time. I spoke about the guilt I carried for not immediately dashing up the riverbank. Maybe I could atone for my inaction even if it meant taking

the law into our own hands. As we talked, we knew another person, maybe even Kurt, could die at Beau's hands, him being bad seed through and through. We looked at each other with a silent knowing. We knew what we were obliged to do.

"Lastly, we talked about getting caught. This gave James pause because of his wife, children, and grandchildren. I only had a sister. James warned we might be put to death but it would hinge on whether a jury or judge believed my story of what I heard on the riverbank. He said there was no chance I would walk, even if a jury believed my story. We knew justice would not bend our way. There would be a jury but no jury of our peers. He said the best we could get would be manslaughter. Even then, we would live out our lives in jail. We had reached seventy, a milestone not reached by a lot of Negro men. For our kind, we viewed our lives a success. If we got away with it, most likely we'd be gone within ten years anyway. We felt the risk worth it. We heaved a big sigh and then clinched our right fist downward in solidarity. We began thinking through a plan.

"But before acting on our plan, on a day when neither James nor Kurt came down the bank, Beau suddenly appeared, surprising me. He sat down on the bank saying nothing. After a spell I looked over at him and said calmly, 'You know, you're not going to get away with it.'

"Beau's face paled. Then he said 'Old nigger, I don't know what you are talking about.' And with that he got up and stomped back up the path.

"James and I thought long and hard about how to do this. Should we lure Beau to the fishing spot, kill him there and carry him back up to the bridge and put him in James' trunk? After my brief encounter with him, it did not seem likely he would venture down the path again. Carrying him that far could be difficult, even for two of us. Could we run him off the road and abduct him? Too risky another car would come by.

Even on country roads, there is traffic. We needed to corner him, since surely he could out run us.

"In my times back and forth to the river I noticed how often Beau's dad's car was gone. There appeared to be a pattern, being gone four to five days at a stretch. We looked for a time when he had left the previous day. The entrance to Beau's enclosed front porch faces west towards the river and away from view from the two houses about an acre behind the house, and like the Moss place, both faced east and towards the road to my place. So it seemed likely a person could enter the Braddock house unseen, especially at night. It worried us some that the Braddock entrance could be viewed from Emma's kitchen window, even activity at night. When I learned of the visit to Emma's sister-in-law, I knew the timing was right.

"We finalized our plan. We would kill Beau and dump his body in some remote field close to Kendall. We had heard there were bad elements down there. We would do it at night, stow the body in James' trunk, and then find a place to dump the body during daylight the next day. It might be too easy to get lost at night on some unfamiliar dirt road.

"Beau looked to be a handful, but James and I were pretty fair-sized so we thought if we got the jump on him, we could pull it off. The evening of our plan, we made sure Beau's car was in the driveway. James and I drove slowly up the driveway without headlights and parked just in front of the house. I had a large handkerchief soaked with ether. After we put on gloves, I knocked on the porch screen door. Beau opened the screen, looked at us and began to close it. We barged through and tackled him to the floor. I forced the cloth over his mouth. With both of us holding him down, he was out quickly. James sat on him while I choked the life out of him. We had decided to choke him, since he had choked Cindy. Although both James and I owned a shotgun, they are too loud and too messy.

"Once he stopped breathing, James took a turn for good measure. We looked around outside to see if anyone was around or at least as near as we could tell, then carried Beau's body to the trunk of James's car. We checked the porch with a flashlight to make sure nothing looked out of place or if we had dropped anything. There did not appear to be any evidence of a struggle. There remained the slight scent of ether, but that would be gone by the time Beau's dad returned or the body was discovered. Tire tracks would be hard to trace. The driveway was gravel. Just to be sure, James later replaced the tires down in Harrison. He said he needed new ones anyway.

"We drove out the driveway, turned the lights on, and slowly drove back to my place. We spent the night there; James slept in my chair.

"We headed out the next morning at normal speed. Again, we fretted about being pulled over for any old lame excuse. A couple of cars passed us before we reached Highway 24, but no one I recognized. We had no spot in mind but headed southeast once we reached Highway 35, again watching our speed. A few miles southeast of Watson, we left the highway, drove for a couple of miles, and found a dirt road. We followed that for a mile or so to a row of trees beside a cornfield. The corn reached above our heads. Checking to see if any cars were around, we carried Beau's body and put it between a tree line and the cornfield. We were not planning to bury him, figuring he wouldn't be found for several days. The weeds were high enough so that the body could not be seen from the road. Whoever owned or worked the cornfield would probably discover it. Just to make a point, we put a noose around his neck and stuffed his mouth with dirt. He was a foul-mouthed killer. I worried some later about the noose, thinking someone might make a connection to Negroes and to James and me. No one ever did to my knowledge."

Sheriff Sellers nodded his head. "That did confound me some after it became clear Beau had been strangled and not hung. If he had been hung, I might have shifted my thinking. I did think briefly about Dutch and James and them sending a message. I couldn't see them overcoming Beau. If Beau's head had been bashed in with say a large rock and then strangled, it might have shifted my thinking, one of them maybe coming up from behind down the riverbank. But what would be their motivation for killing Beau and taking such a chance, being Negroes? Besides, Beau had an alibi. They had seen it in the paper."

"James drove me home and went back to town saying he would make sure nothing of interest could be found in his trunk. We figured it would be a few days before someone found the body.

"When they found Beau's body the sheriff talked to me not as a suspect but just wondering if I had noted anything of interest around the Braddock place. I told him about Beau coming down to the fishing spot but of course didn't tell him what I said to Beau. I was certain the sheriff would never think we could do such a thing, being Negro, why take the risk, and being so old. It was good to have an attorney like James to tell me what to say or not to say.

"One thing still puzzles me to this day. Why did Cindy go down the bank with Beau? Kurt had told me about his conversation with her and how Beau made her uncomfortable. It doesn't make any sense. Since nearly a year has passed since that time, and the now putting this in writing, I have pondered another possibility. Maybe Cindy simply decided one day to go down the path, not knowing whether I would be there or not. And if I were, she would be less afraid because of how Kurt spoke about me. Beau could have seen her tie up Calico from his house across the river and then surprised her. I will give her the benefit of the doubt about being afraid of Beau based on her brief encounters and

what she told Kurt, and that she didn't feel some rebellious attraction to boys like Beau to spite her mom. We will never know.

"I remember Emma saying God had looked out for me when my sister took me back to Alabama the day prior to Cindy's murder. I knew better. But I must say James and I were very fortunate to have not been seen that evening in Adams Creek or driving away the next morning. If Mrs. Kreider did not notice or hear James's car, no one did."

Sheriff Sellers said, "Yes, Dutch's place is at the north edge of Adams Creek. Not many cars travel the road between him and the river. Folks would have gone to work by the time they drove out heading for Kendall."

"Being a lawyer, it was hardest for James. I knew I could not tell Sheriff Sellers what I knew about Cindy. Who would have believed me, especially after all of the bystanders heard Mrs. McBrady's rage? It would have been the word of a Negro versus the word of sixteen-year old white boy. Despite Beau's reputation, I could not risk that. Some might feel we are no better than those folks over in Mason City in 1930, thinking they were taking justice into their own hands. But those two boys were in custody and would have been prosecuted for their crimes, and yes, likely executed. Beau walked free. We felt better about ourselves when it was done. I will die peacefully with this secret.

"I want those who read this to know, especially Emma, Kyle, and Kurt, prior to this incident, I have never killed anyone, come close to killing anyone, or threatened to kill anyone. Yes, James and I both carried a bitterness from all the years of kowtowing and being treated like lesser human beings. After it was finished, we talked about this and whether this motivated us more than anything else, a chance to strike back. We were comfortable with our motives, to do justice where it would likely never happen.

Though we carried some anger, even hatred on occasion, James and I are no Bigger Thomas. I remember telling Kurt before he shipped out to Germany that I was more like Reverend King. I told him this after I knew what James and I had done. I guess some things are hard to figure. I hope you will understand.

"James and I agreed that the last one living would carry on this letter's caretaking and get it into Emma's hands once our time to go was at hand. We both agreed Emma was the person we could trust to carry out our instructions."

Both Dutch and James signed and dated the letter nearly a year after the summer of 1960.

Dutch added a more recent footnote, the handwriting harder to read.

"I'm sorry I never got to see Kurt again after he left for Germany. I loved the boy. Tell him I left something under the bridge. I just hope no large storm surge washed them away. The second envelope is for him."

Mom asked the sheriff if he had any inkling whatsoever that Dutch and James could have done this.

"No Emma, but am I mighty relieved to read this. This hung over me like a bad dream these past ten years. I'm lucky I kept my job. The county commissioners were none too pleased the cases remained unsolved. It now all makes sense. I was never sold about the hobo possibility, but what else did I have to go on? Hobos are pretty hard to track down. I never closed the case, thinking some witness would come forward. Well they finally did. I had no reason not to believe Dutch's story. It never seriously crossed my mind that James and Dutch would kill Beau, being Negroes and pretty old, like Dutch wrote. Even with Dutch's history kowtowing to whites all those years, he never seemed the type to carry a grudge or the kind to lash out if provoked.

"I think his whacking Beau over the head that time on the riverbank is the only time he hurt someone around here, leastways that I am aware of. Dad said Dutch was known on the railroad lines to be a well-mannered porter, towed the line, and made friends easily. His coldcocking Beau seemed like a natural reaction, more looking out for Kurt than some deep-seeded hatred. When talking with James at the time, he mentioned both he and Dutch turned seventy earlier that year. Like Dutch, I figured Beau being bad seed and all, he probably got in some trouble with some folks down in Kendall. Since Cindy appeared strong enough to put up a fight, we checked her fingernails for any skin. Nothing. Regardless, I recall looking at both Beau and Dutch's faces, even asked them to show me their arms. Didn't see any scratches, bruises, or bites, though Dutch might have had time to heal before I saw him. I remember Mrs. McBrady saying Cindy could be rebellious. Who knows how the divorce affected Cindy? Maybe she liked defying her mom and she was attracted to boys like that greaser Kurt saw, and to Beau, regardless of what she said to you, Kurt, earlier that summer. And maybe Dutch's theory is correct. Beau was watching her from across the river."

Mom said, "In all the years since that summer, Dutch never let on to any of this, and I never suspected. What a burden to carry with you for what, nearly ten years? I guess it helped getting it on paper within a year and hatching a plan for it to eventually come out. Maybe when this becomes known, it will put Mrs. McBrady at ease about her certainty Dutch was to blame. Least I hope so."

Mom handed me the second envelope. Inside I found five hundred dollars in tens and twenties, a note–this one also harder to read–and a tattered paper. "Do us proud Kurt, get your college degree, and no matter what, remember what we learned you." The gift came from both Dutch and James. The tattered paper was Dutch's grandpa's slavery bill-of-sale.

After the sheriff left, I walked down to Ole Steely to where I used to keep my stones. I found four Hills Brothers coffee tins filled with near perfect skipping stones. The river flowed slow and smooth. I used up one can, most tosses counting at least five skips. "That's for you, Dutch." Later, I followed the now overgrown path down to the fishing hole, avoiding the thistles, rolled a log next to the bank, found an errant small branch, and began whittling a slingshot.

The following day, the paper printed the entire confession letter.

Epilogue

Sheriff Sellers tracked down Beau's cousin now living in Ohio. He confessed to the alibi lie. Beau arrived at his house early that day in 1960 and threatened him if he didn't tell the sheriff Beau was with him since mid-morning. Like me, Beau scared him. The cousin also said Beau bragged about knowing the person who knocked Dutch into the ditch, but did not disclose the name. Sheriff Sellers did not file charges. Beau's dad moved back to Alabama where the sheriff tracked him down. He told the sheriff one of the reasons he accepted his sister's prodding to move to Twin Rivers was an assault and battery charge on Beau's record. At age fourteen, he beat up another boy, nearly killing him. As a minor, he avoided jail, claiming self-defense. The dad thought a fresh start in Twin Rivers might help. Sheriff Sellers tracked down Lucas Mayfield, now living in Milwaukee to tie up loose ends. The sheriff now knew Mayfield's horrific history.

Twin Rivers' black folks had a second reason to venture out to Adams Creek besides fishing. Mom later said she saw who she believed were Twin Rivers' white folks at the gravesite, in addition to Adams Creek residents. She always found the marking adorned with flowers in the warmer months. Neighbors and church folks treated Mom like a celebrity.

Twin Rivers' storied train culture drifted into obscurity, its only remnants a small museum where the Pennsylvania Railroad Depot once stood and an annual commemorative Iron Horse Festival.

They tore Ole Steely down, weakened by the years of battering tree trunks and bergs, its secrets never revealed. Like the Eel River, the stories Ole Steely could tell. For the Baumann boys, the memories lived on. They constructed a two-lane concrete mass with reinforced abutments. Even in the rural Midwest, a one-lane steel bridge had become a relic.

A year later, Twin Rivers tore down the halls of ivy.

Mom retired from the grain elevator and taking in knitting and laundry, but stayed on the farm, comfortable with her church community and neighbors, still fitting like well-worn shoes. She lived on Social Security, and with the aid of Medicare, battled arthritic hands, bean-snapping days over. She volunteered twice a week at a Twin Rivers' nursing home. They called her program, "Reading with Emma." She sold "The Little Tractor that Could," marveling at the sale price of $1,500, a thousand more than she and Dad paid in the early 1950s. She donated the cider press to the Clay County Historical Society, the orchard now with only one apple tree, but productive enough for several apple pies. She shuttered the henhouse, but continued cultivating a small garden patch, rhubarb, and her flowers. She only ventured into the back acres during blueberry season and to gather walnuts.

Ten years after retirement, Mom sold the farm for $135,000 and moved into an apartment in Twin Rivers. She felt she had struck it rich. She gave most of it away to her grandchildren and to the church. Mom and Dad paid $6,000 for the farm in 1950.

Kyle graduated from college and returned to the Peace Corps, first as a recruiter, then trainer, and finally in administration. When I see him twice a year, he calls me Kurtsy.

I kept my promise to Mom–and Dutch and James–returning to college shortly after mustering out, not in Indiana, but at the University of Wisconsin, influenced by Ken's recommendation, the out-of-state tuition more affordable with the GI Bill. I finally read *Native Son*, ruing the missed opportunity to talk about Bigger Thomas with Dutch and James. I read *Self Reliance.* Part of my undergrad curriculum included two advanced psychology courses chosen as electives hoping to understand Dad's demons and for my own demon monitoring. As of this telling, Ken, Kyle, and I have kept any boll weevils at bay, and kept our vow to each other. Upon reflection, we all have our boll weevils, and the best we can do is keep them from gnawing on us.

Graduating with a Bachelor of Arts in Political Science, I earned a law degree at the Duke University School of Law. After practicing defense law for five years, I joined the Department of Justice Civil Rights Division in Washington, DC. I hung the now-framed slavery bill-of-sale on my office wall, never to forget. Next to it, I hung the now-framed program from Key Club Kapers.

Along the way, I took up the piano, sitting in on weekends with a jazz quartet and riffing pretty well for a white guy. They even let me croon now and then. I leave the scat to others, not in my genes.

Mom prodded me to attend church regularly. I did not, comfortable with confronting life's trials and tribulations with my own reflections, processing life's lessons, or pondering what my three wise teachers would do: Mom, Dutch, and Jesus.

My wife and I named our daughter Emily, and our son, Dutch.

Author's Notes and Acknowledgements

Most of the towns and cities depicted are not fictitious but with fictitious Indiana names. Twin Rivers is Logansport, Kendall is Kokomo, Harrison is Lafayette, Mason City is Marion, Munson is Muncie, Addison is Anderson, Indiana Tech is Purdue, and so on. Clay County is Cass County. The township of my youth was Clay Township, the one that voted to send its children to Logansport. I kept the names of the larger cities and the rivers. The setting and the recalling of daily doings in the 1950s on the small farm in Adams Creek (Adamsboro) are from my childhood memories, and mostly true.

I did know a Dutch, as a boy, who lived in a shack across the river. He was a retired railroad worker, and Caucasian. He fished off the bridge and down the riverbank and ice-skated. He was a Sunday-only newspaper customer and did fry up the best bacon in my memory. My family named our only dog, a golden retriever, Dutch.

Except for the name Twin Rivers, the railroad anecdotes are factual, based on my research, as are the Indian, KKK, and Pullman corporate history and anecdotes.

Two non-fiction books were critical sources for this story, *Rising from the Rails* by Larry Tye, and *A Time of Terror – A Survivor's Story* by James Cameron, as noted in the narrative. There may be other first-hand accounts to lynchings by a survivor, but I am not aware of any. While one can find a lot of information about the Pullman Porters on the Internet as I did, if you have any interest in the history of the Pullman Porters, Larry Tye's book is the source. Some of its anecdotes are fictionalized in the narrative I highly recommend Tye's book.

James Cameron self-published after failing to find a publisher willing to take the risk. The Black Classic Press republished it in 1994, but is no longer the publisher of record. The book was re-released in 2016, and is available on the Amazon and Barnes and Noble web sites. Chapter nineteen is a very condensed recounting–with name changes–of the fateful night in 1930, and Cameron's trial and prison time. Cameron founded the American Black Holocaust Museum in Milwaukee. After closing during the 2008 Recession, plans are underway to reopen the museum in a new building: abhmuseum.org.

I also sourced several books and materials from the Cass County Historical Society in Logansport, Indiana, one mostly a pictorial history; *Where Two Rivers Meet.* I visited the A. Philip Randolph Pullman Porter Museum in Chicago. I spent time in The Depot, a small museum at the site of the Pennsylvania station in Logansport. I found one small paperback, an abbreviated version of the Porter Rule Book from 1893 put out by the University of Michigan Library. Captain Stubby was an icon in north-central Indiana. His real name was Tom Fouts. He published several short, paperback joke books. You can find those online. He wrote columns for the *Prairie Farmer* periodical.

I thank the following friends: Gary Campeau, Bingshen Chen, Ken Evans, Pam Galera, Cori Jones, Dave and Julie Kitchell, Carol Longo, Sandy Minc, Diane Adams Reed, and Craig Silver for reading and reacting to the manuscript. I send a second shout out to Pam Galera, who read it a second time, not as a grammar Nazi, but for content and continuity. I also thank my twenty-year book club from North Orange County, CA for empowering me to read over two hundred novels I doubt I would ever have read. This helped shape my writing.

Lastly, I thank Sinisa Poznanovic for the cover and back cover design, and Ashley Evans, my proofing pro. I found both freelancers at Upwork Inc., upwork.com.

Song Credits

Song	Writer	Year
Black and Blue	Fats Waller	1929
Blueberry Hill	Al Lewis	
	Vincent Rose	
	Larry Stock	1940
Bridge Over Troubled Water		
	Paul Simon	1969
Does Your Chewing Gum Lose Its Flavor		
	Multiple writers	1959
Frog Went a-Courtin'		
	Unknown	1548
Halls of Ivy	Henry Russell	
	Vick Knight Sr.	
I'm So Lonesome I Could Cry		
	Hank Williams	1949
In the Garden	C. Austin Miles	1912
It's Me Oh Lord	Abbey Lincoln	
Jump Jim Crow	Author Disputed	1828
Lucky Old Sun	Beasley Smith	
	Haven Gillespie	1949
Oklahoma	Richard Rodgers	
	Oscar Hammerstein II	1943
Old Rugged Cross	George Bernard	1912
Purple People Eater	Sheb Wooley	1958
Rock of Ages	Augustus Toplady	1763
Shall We Gather at the River		
	Robert Lowry	1864
Splish Splash	Bobby Darin	1958
Strange Fruit	Abel Meeropol	1937
Swing Low, Sweet Chariot		
	Wallace Willis	pre-1862
The Froggy He Am a Queer Bird		Unknown
This Ole House	Stuart Hamblen	1954
Wabash Cannonball	William Kindt	1904
Witch Doctor	Thomas Kerry	1958

Made in the USA
San Bernardino, CA
04 April 2019